Demons of
Bourbon Street

Books by Deanna Chase

The Jade Calhoun Novels
Haunted on Bourbon Street
Witches of Bourbon Street
Demons of Bourbon Street
Angels of Bourbon Street
Shadows of Bourbon Street (March 2014)

The Crescent City Fae Novels
Influential Magic
Irresistible Magic
Book Three in the Crescent City Fae series (June 2014)

The Destiny Novels
Defining Destiny (Dec 2013)

Demons of Bourbon Street

A Jade Calhoun Novel

Deanna Chase

Bayou Moon Publishing

Acknowledgments

Thank you as always to my team, Rhonda, Angie, Susan, Chauntelle, Lisa, and Cassie. Your help is appreciated more than you know. And to my amazing readers, I love you all. Thank you.

Chapter 1

My ex-boyfriend's childhood home loomed in front of me. Once upon a time, the sight of the old farmhouse filled my heart with joy, comfort, and even contentment. Three emotions that didn't come easy for me. Now guilt and fear dominated.

Peering through the heavy rain, I spotted a shadow at the window. The curtains opened, revealing a portly, middle-aged woman.

I twisted to glance at Kat in the back seat of the rental car. "Dan's mom is staring at us."

"Time to quit stalling then." She unbuckled her seatbelt and grabbed the door handle.

"Wait. Give me a second."

"We've been sitting here ten minutes."

"She's right, love." Kane reached across the seat, his broad shoulders filling the space between us. He squeezed my hand. "It's better to get this over with."

"I…just need a minute." I hadn't seen Dan's parents since we'd broken up almost two years ago. Mrs. Toller, who'd once thought of me as her daughter, blamed me for shredding her son's heart. I guess he conveniently left out the part about him cheating on me. Not that I planned on telling her. Seeing her again was like using my own heart for a pincushion. Tiny little stabs, one after another.

None of that mattered now. Dan was missing because he'd sacrificed himself to save my mother from a demon. But I was going to save him, and Mrs. T's friend was going to help.

Thunder boomed overhead in the Idaho sky.

The rain needed to stop. At least long enough for us to get onto the porch. The last thing I wanted to do was face Dan's mom looking like a drowned rat. My faltering confidence depended on stylish hair and a dry outfit.

The familiar spark in my chest responded the second I reached for it. "Ready, Kat?"

"I've been ready," she said with a heavy air of impatience.

Magic strained to burst from my fingertips. I pushed the passenger side door open and yelled, "Halt!"

Another rumble of thunder drowned out my voice. And just when I'd decided the spell hadn't been specific enough, the rain stopped and a sliver of sunshine peeked out from behind the clouds.

"Hurry, the break won't last," I called to Kat as I jogged toward the house.

She caught up with me on the steps of the porch just as the skies opened up again, pummeling the farm.

"Umbrellas would have been simpler." She pressed close to the house, trying to avoid the horizontal rain.

"I accidentally left them in Gwen's mudroom."

She smoothed her bright red curls and moved to the door. Before she knocked, it swung open.

"Katrina! I'm so glad you're here." Dan's mother crushed her into a hug, squeezing hard enough that my ribs ached in sympathy. She pressed her face into Kat's shoulder as her body shook with muffled sobs.

"Oh, Mrs. Toller. Don't cry. We're doing everything we can to find him," Kat soothed.

The older woman released Kat and sniffled.

"I'm so sorry, Mrs. T." I grabbed her hand and squeezed.

Her lips twisted into a grimace. She tugged out of my grasp and seemed to consciously erase all emotion from her face.

Too bad the disdain streaming off her prickled my skin and my heart. Sometimes being an empath sucked. Gone were the days when Mrs. T had been a stand-in mother. I'd lost her after I dumped Dan. But after all this time, I wasn't prepared for such a personal rejection. A dull ache blossomed in my chest.

"Jade." She gave me a short nod then turned back to Kat. "Come in. Izzy's waiting."

I cast a glance at the rental car, wishing I hadn't insisted Kane wait outside. A more sensible person would have stayed at Aunt Gwen's, but his overprotective nature prevented him from doing anything that reasonable. I waved, hoping he could see me through the heavy rain, and followed Kat into the house.

The sound of my boots echoed off the white wood floors as I moved into the spacious living room. Nothing had changed. A rustic pine wood-framed sofa, covered in deep plum cushions, and its matching loveseat framed a stark white area rug. A floor-to-ceiling bookcase lined one wall, and a mounted five-point elk hung center stage over the stone fireplace.

A wave of sadness rocked me. The last time I'd been in the house was the day Dan had proposed to me. The day I'd broken his heart.

The image of his shocked face as I revealed my empath ability swam in my mind's eye, quickly morphing to outrage when he realized I'd been spying on his emotions for years. Shame coiled through me.

I shook the memory off. This wasn't the time to wallow in regret. Dan had been body-snatched by a demon. And the psychic, Izzy Frankel, had some explaining to do. I spotted her standing near the front window. Striding over, I held out my hand. "You must be Ms. Frankel."

The tall, thin woman ignored my attempt at a handshake and stared at me curiously. She tilted her head to one side, shifting her long, frizzy gray hair over one shoulder. She pushed it back and narrowed one eye. "You harbor a lot of power, but it's too raw. You'll never be able to save him."

Mrs. T gasped from behind me. I glanced back. Kat held her steady with her arms wrapped around the trembling woman.

"How dare you frighten Dan's mom," I scolded Izzy, more than a little offended she'd dismissed my abilities so easily. "You don't know me. Or the people who'll be helping us."

For God's sake, I had my mentor, who happened to be the strongest witch I'd ever met, an entire coven, and an angel ready to fight the good fight. Not to mention a dreamwalking boyfriend, a ghost hunter, and two best friends who'd follow me into Hell if that's what it took to bring Dan back. What did this old fraud know anyway?

I took a step forward, invading her personal space. "As far as I'm concerned, you're the reason Dan's in trouble. You're in no position to criticize."

Izzy shrank back, grabbing the molding of the window frame. Her face turned ashen. "Every reading has consequences," she whispered. "I didn't know. I couldn't see…"

Cripes. I'd pushed an old lady over the edge. One I needed answers from. I reached out and took her hand. Her guilt penetrated my senses, weighing heavily on my skin, while her suppressed panic sent shock waves through my fingers. Ignoring the sensation, I pulled her over to the couch.

"Ms. Frankel," I lowered my voice. "Izzy, where did Dan get the portraits and voodoo dolls?"

Her deep blue-gray eyes, swimming with unshed tears, met mine. "I gave them to him."

"What portraits?" Mrs. T asked Kat in a hushed voice.

Kat murmured something back, and I was grateful when she led Dan's mom through the kitchen door. I didn't have the energy to explain how the souls and spirits of three sisters had been separated and then transferred into life-sized voodoo dolls and grotesque papier-mâché portraits. And that one sister, Meri, was a demon who possessed Dan through his connection with one of the portraits.

I sat back, stunned. "Why would such powerful relics be left in the care of a psychic?"

Izzy clasped her hands in her lap, staring at them. "I was there with the rest of the coven when Philip, Meri's mate, completed the soul and spirit separation. Not long after, I had a vision that one day a man would come for the portraits, and he'd bring with him the power to release your mother. The coven decided it was best if I watched over the voodoo dolls and portraits until that person materialized."

"A vision of Dan?" I breathed.

She slumped back. "Not exactly. The vision didn't reveal who, just that someone would come and everything would become clear. I couldn't believe it when Dan showed up that day. Déjà-vu hit me so strong, I almost fell over. It was the vision all over again." She held her hands palms up. "I'd seen him countless times over the years. He's my godson, you know."

I shook my head. According to Dan, she was just a weird old friend of his mother's.

She waved dismissively. "He didn't like to claim me because of my ability. He never wanted me prying—not that I'd ever invade his privacy on purpose."

Guilt bubbled up in my chest again. I'd pried. Many, many times.

"Well, I'd never once suspected Dan was the man who'd come for the sisters. If I had, I would have found a way to prepare him better. Lord knows I tried that day he came to the house, but he left so fast…there wasn't much I could do."

"Then he moved to New Orleans," I supplied.

"Yeah." She sighed.

I studied her, relaxing my vision so I could take in her aura the way Bea, my magic mentor, taught me. The light blurred to a streaky white then brightened as soft lavender glowed around the outline of Izzy's body.

It was the sign of an intuitive, but not a strong one. I blinked, and her aura vanished. "You said you were there when the sisters' souls and spirits were separated. Why? You're not a witch, are you?"

Her gray curls tangled as she shook her head. "No. Apparently my intuitive ability was enough to complete the circle. After I had my vision, Philip insisted I should be the caretaker of the dolls and portraits."

Philip. The angel who was Meri's mate and also the subject of her wrath. If only I could find him. "Izzy? Do you know where Philip lives?"

Her eyes widened in shock. "Dan didn't tell you?"

"Uh, no. I don't think Dan knew him."

"Izzy Frankel, stop right now!" Mrs. T shouted as she stormed in from the kitchen. "Don't say another word."

Kat rushed in behind her. "Mrs. T?"

"Not now, Katrina. I think it's time you and Jade went home. Izzy has said enough."

Izzy stood, drawing herself up, a full head taller than Mrs. T. "Renee, if you hope to hug your son again, you need to tell Jade. She can help."

"No," Mrs. T said in an icy tone. "She doesn't and she can't. The Boise coven can bring him back."

I whirled. Mrs. T knew about the coven? It wasn't exactly a secret, but witches didn't usually advertise their gifts to the laymen population either.

"If they couldn't bring Hope back, what makes you think they can do anything for your son?" Izzy asked with her arms folded.

Kat's eyes met mine. Her shocked expression mirrored my own. Mrs. T had known my mother disappeared from a coven circle this whole time and never said a word. Was she aware a demon had taken her too?

"We told Hope not to get involved. It's her own fault she ended up in Hell!" Angry tears streamed down Mrs. T's face as she turned to me. "It's your fault my only son is rotting there now."

She had known. Intense betrayal rippled through me. I clenched my fists to my sides, trembling with anger. For all those years, I'd thought Mom had just been missing. And all along Mrs. T knew a demon had captured her.

"Mrs. T!" Kat scolded in a hushed whisper. "It certainly is not. Jade didn't ask Dan to sacrifice himself for her mother. He did it because he's a good man. You need to give him credit for that. If, God forbid, he doesn't return to us, we need to honor him and his sacrifice. Not blame each other."

I shuffled backwards toward the door. Despite Kat's defense, what Mrs. T said hit a nerve. A big one. If I hadn't entered Dan's life, none of this would have happened. He'd likely be home safe, here on this very farm, right now.

"He did it for her," Mrs. T choked out between sobs. "She broke his heart, and he did it anyway." Dan's mother crumpled in Kat's arms and sank onto the couch.

Kat's eyes locked with mine as she silently mouthed a desperate plea for help. I kept retreating to the door. There wasn't anything I could do but leave. My presence was only making things worse.

I had my hand on the doorknob when Izzy suddenly jerked from a body spasm and then froze. Her eyes faded from deep blue-gray to a light gray mist.

The signs were familiar. My aunt Gwen is a psychic. I'd seen a trance a time or two. I dropped my hand and stepped forward.

Izzy's mouth worked as if trying to speak, but no words came out. A low, mewing sound reverberated from her throat.

I tensed, standing stock-still. Izzy Frankel looked like she'd been possessed.

All evidence of Mrs. T's recent breakdown vanished as she took Izzy's hand. Her touch seemed to calm the psychic, and the mewing stopped. "That's good, Izzy," Mrs. T soothed. "It's okay. Tell us what you see."

"Dan," Izzy wrestled the word from her lips.

"Very good. Let the rest out now. You can do this." Mrs. T stroked her friend's back. Her touch visibly calmed the other woman. I'd never seen such a thing before. One time I'd made the mistake of touching Gwen during one of her visions; I wouldn't be doing that again. The shock had startled her so badly, she bolted and almost ran right through a plate glass window.

Izzy's face relaxed, and this time when she spoke, she almost sounded like herself. "She has the power to bring him back. Her love will save him."

Her eyes turned back to deep blue-gray, and the trance ended. *Her love will save him.* Damn straight. She had to mean either Kat or me. Either of us would sacrifice almost anything for Dan.

I turned to Mrs. T. "Did you hear her? We won't stop until we have him home safe. You have my word."

The medium-built, plump woman, who shared the same thin lips and angular nose with her son, came to stand in front of me. Pain, the kind that wounds one's heart, brushed my senses. "I can't trust you."

Her words were an invisible blow. A rock-solid punch right into my soul. I opened my mouth then shut it. What could I say? I'd betrayed her son once already. Why would she think I wouldn't do it again?

Kat stepped up beside me. "Mrs. T? Do you trust me?"

"Of course I do, sweetie. You've always been there for my Dan."

My best friend sent Mrs. T a small smile. "Trust my word then. I know Jade better than anyone. She won't stop until Dan's safe. I won't let her."

Mrs. T searched Kat's face for a long moment. Something shifted, and I had the impression an interior wall was penetrated. She turned to me. "Don't let me down again, Jade. I already lost a daughter. I won't survive the loss of my son."

"A daughter...?" Dan had a sister? Why had he never told me about her?

A tremor of deep-seated sadness touched me. "You, Jade. You were my daughter in every way. When you and Dan broke up—" she swallowed. "When you left him, you left me too." She turned slightly away from me, with her shoulders slumped.

"I...Mrs. T?" I hadn't realized she'd suffered our separation, too. I'd missed her horribly, but I couldn't shake the sinking betrayal that she'd known about my mother and never said anything.

She shifted to gaze at me. A single tear rolled down her cheek. "Bring him back to me."

Izzy stepped up, forming a tiny circle. "Renee, I saw Philip there. You need to tell her. The information is powerful. The fact that Dan was taken, the reason why he could be taken. It matters. Give her all the tools she needs to rescue him."

Mrs. T's face went white. She froze and stared at a picture sitting on the mantle. It was one of Dan laughing, right after he'd graduated college. Kat and I had both been there that day. We'd been the cause of his mirth as we stood to the side, cracking jokes about his job prospects as an unemployable philosophy major. That day seemed like a lifetime ago.

Finally she turned, took a deep breath and met my gaze. "The angel, Philip, is Dan's biological father."

Chapter 2

An hour later, Kat and I sat in Aunt Gwen's sunroom, watching the storm drum against the windows. I cradled a hot mug of chai tea, trying to drive away the chill settled in my bones. Would Philip risk Hell to save his son? He hadn't for his mate, Meri, condemning the former angel into demonhood, a fate that had triggered a deep-seated need for revenge.

"Do you think Meri knows Philip is Dan's father?" I asked Kat.

Kat picked up the sterling silver talisman Dan's mother had pressed into her hands before we'd left. Her curly red hair fell over one eye as she ran her fingertips over the quarter-sized Celtic knot, almost resembling a sunflower. She sighed and clasped her fist tightly around the pendant. "It's doubtful. It seems to me if she'd known about the connection, she would have used him to hunt down Philip. Instead she used Dan to focus on her sisters."

I nodded. Twelve years ago, Meri's sisters had enlisted my mother to help them rescue Meri from Hell. Only they'd been too late. Hell has a way of quickly corrupting angels' souls. When they tried to banish her, she captured her two sisters and my mother, intent on letting Hell corrupt their souls as well. Only Philip had conducted a ritual to separate the three sister's souls from their spirits, trapping their spirits in voodoo dolls and their souls in portraits. With Meri neutralized, my mother had ended up in Purgatory.

But last week, with the help of the New Orleans coven, I'd rejoined their souls and spirits and freed the sisters from their immortal prison. Once Meri had materialized in our circle, her sole focus had been on finding her mate. First to reunite and then for revenge.

Kat was right. Meri would have used Dan to find Philip, had she known about their connection. Instead she'd tried to get Dan to destroy her sisters' spirits. Dan hadn't been able to follow through, thank goodness, but he'd gotten himself trapped in Hell in the process.

The tightening in my chest, which seemed to occur every time I thought of what Dan had done, returned. He'd risked everything to free my mom from Meri's clutches.

We had to save him. I wouldn't rest until we did. "Looks like we need to get on the first flight back to Louisiana."

Kat tilted her head toward the kitchen. "What about your mom?"

I sighed. "Gwen will take care of her."

"Girls," Mom called. "We forgot the French bread. Can your friend drive you to the store to pick some up?"

I rose, and Kat followed. We stopped in the doorway. "Kane ran out to overnight some paperwork for a client." In addition to owning Wicked, a strip club in the French Quarter, he was also an independent financial consultant.

My aunt Gwen paused from kneading her pie dough and wiped her hands on her red apron. She had on her signature red T-shirt and overalls. With her gray curls twisted into a bun, she looked every inch the homemaker farmer's wife. Only she didn't have a husband and she did all the farming. "You can take my car."

"In weather like this?" Mom gasped. "Jade doesn't have any experience driving in heavy rain."

Kat and I exchanged wary looks. "Mom—"

Gwen held up a hand, cutting me off. She moved to Mom's side and wrapped an arm around her shoulders. They didn't look anything alike. Mom's slick dark hair was pulled back in her signature ponytail. Her slightly slanted eyes were jade green, while Gwen's were hazel. Gwen had a good twenty pounds on Mom's slight frame. But most of all, Gwen looked the part of my mother, with slight wrinkles around her eyes, while mom could easily be mistaken for my sister. Spending thirteen years in Purgatory, where time stood still, would do that to a person.

"Don't worry, Hope," Gwen said. "I taught Jade all she needs to know about navigating stormy roads while you were gone. Just like Dad showed us."

Color blossomed on Mom's cheeks and she averted her eyes. She'd forgotten I'm a twenty-seven year old woman, not the fifteen-year-old she'd been torn from all those years ago. Again. "Of course. I'm sorry." She waved in my direction. "Go on then. Dinner will be ready soon. If you want garlic bread with the lasagna, you'd better hurry."

Gwen handed me her keys, and I smiled at Mom. "We'll be back before the table's set."

"Not too fast, young lady," Mom said. "Just because the speed limit is fifty-five doesn't mean it's safe to go that fast in this kind of weather."

"Yes, Mother." I rolled my eyes, but my smile widened to a grin. Damn, it was good to have her back.

After dinner, Kane and I sat on my old bed, propped up against the headboard. I tapped a few keys on my laptop. "There's a flight leaving at six a.m."

Kane ignored my statement and ran a hand down my neck. My whole body tingled. It was the first time we'd been alone in days. His hooded eyes met mine, then dropped, taking in the length of my body. I bit my lower lip to keep from licking them in anticipation.

"Stop," I whispered without any heat. We'd been at Gwen's for a week. With the close living quarters, we hadn't had any privacy. The physical separation only served to heighten our mutual needs.

He leaned in, barely brushing a kiss against my waiting lips. "You don't want me to stop."

Heat spiked, nearly melting my favorite Victoria's Secret panties. I pulled away just enough to get some air and sucked in a breath.

He smiled that knowing smile he gets when he's aware he's pushed all the right buttons. He closed the distance between us, but at the last minute, I brought a hand up, stopping him with a finger pressed to his mouth. "Rain check?"

We sat frozen for a few beats. Then Kane gently removed my finger and brought his lips to mine, slowly, artfully exploring with every delicious stroke of his skilled tongue. I melted into him, blissfully lost in his embrace.

When Kane pulled back, he pressed his forehead to mine and whispered, "Count on it."

"Huh?" I sighed, breathless.

He sat back. "Rain check."

The room came back into focus. My brain started functioning, and I remembered Mom and Gwen could walk in on us at any moment. "Right. Rain check."

Grinning, he focused on his laptop. "Now, what did you say about that flight?"

I checked the screen. "There's one at six a.m."

"We'd have to get up at four." He frowned and ran another search. "Here's another one at eleven. That will give us time to eat breakfast with your family before we leave."

I leaned over, squinting at the information on his computer. "Holy crap. The only seats left on that flight are first class. I can't afford the cushy real estate, and neither can Kat."

He got up and moved gracefully across the room to inspect my farmhouse photo collection covering one wall. "I've got points on my miles card. I can cover the tickets."

I plucked at the old quilt covering the bed. Eleven a.m. sounded a hell of a lot better than six. I narrowed my eyes. "You have enough points for three first-class, last-minute tickets?"

"Sure." He turned his rich chocolate-brown eyes on me. "It's my business card. The one I use for the club's expenses."

I wasn't sure I believed him, but if he used the card for the club's bi-weekly alcohol purchases, it certainly was possible. "All right."

He nodded and turned back to the photos. "Was this a school project or something?"

"No. I just always wanted to live in a grand, old, turn-of-the-century house. Something about the history intrigues me. I used to take pictures of them and imagine who lived there and what their stories were."

"I like this one." Kane pointed to one of my favorites. The white house had a giant wraparound porch and tons of windows. He crossed the room and took his place next to me on the bed. "We'll live in one like that someday."

I rumpled his dark wavy hair and laughed. "And leave New Orleans? Not likely."

He shrugged. "You never know."

"Sure. Whatever you say." I closed my computer. "I need to call Kat." She'd gone home to spend some time with her parents before we high-tailed it back to New Orleans.

"I'll get in touch with Lailah about tracking down Philip." Kane pulled out his phone, but I snatched it out of his hand.

"You don't need to do that. I can take care of it."

Two things: Lailah was Kane's ex-girlfriend and, even though she was an angel, I didn't trust her. I had good reason.

Last week we'd accidentally formed a psychic connection. Right before we'd left for Idaho, I'd caught her admiring Kane in a decidedly unangelic fashion.

While I appreciated Kane helping me, the thought of him calling Lailah, especially about my ex...well, call me ridiculous, but I'd rather walk through the swamps barefoot than ask Lailah for a favor.

"Jade," Kane warned. "You can't do everything yourself. Call Kat. In the meantime, I'll get in touch with Lailah. She can start getting a lead on Philip's whereabouts."

Over my rotting, gator-eaten body. Izzy had told us he was living out in the bayou. Dan was the only one who knew exactly where. Unless Hell had a one-eight-hundred number, someone was going to need to cast a finding spell. "Why does it have to be her? Why can't we ask Lucien?"

"You could, but Lailah has a lot more experience and she has a connection to Dan."

Lucien was the strongest witch in the New Orleans coven besides me. He had the skills to perform the finding spell, but Kane was right. He had almost no connection to Dan, and that mattered. Lailah was the better choice.

I raised my chin. "I can perform the spell from here."

Kane raised a skeptical eyebrow.

I made a face and jumped off the bed. After rummaging around in my suitcase, I pulled out my mentor's leather-bound spell book. "Bea gave it to me. She said I should take it since I'm the coven leader."

"If you're sure," Kane said.

"I just need a few minutes to locate the incantation." Sitting cross-legged on the floor, I quickly flipped the pages, searching for the correct section.

The old bed squeaked as Kane rose to join me.

A second later, Mom barged in. "Jade, you know you're not allowed to have boys—er…friends up here with the door closed." She grabbed the wooden desk chair and used it to prop the door open. "You don't want to disrespect your aunt."

Stifling a sigh, I waved my hand, indicating we were both fully clothed and half a room apart. "Mom, nothing's going on."

Kane caught my gaze. His lips twitched.

The man actually thought this was funny. I glared, daring him to utter even one chuckle.

He winked in my direction before turning to smile at Mom. "Ms. Calhoun. My apologies. I came up here to take a business call, and then Jade and I were finalizing our travel plans for tomorrow."

The anxiety swirling around my mother eased. She took a step forward and lowered her voice, "Oh, it's all right. It's not that I don't trust you two, but Gwen can be old-fashioned. You know how she is."

Unable to control myself, I snorted my disbelief and quickly covered with a cough. Gwen had tried to put Kane and me in the same room for our short visit, but my mother had insisted sharing a room wasn't appropriate. Since the house only had two bedrooms, Mom was bunking with Gwen, and I was in my old room.

That put Kane on the couch.

As if anything would ever happen on the squeaky bed from hell with my mother and aunt in the next room.

"Yeah, Gwen can be a little archaic sometimes." Hiding a smile, I brushed past Mom. "I'll be outside on the porch. I need to call Kat."

"Don't be too long, Jade. It's getting cold out."

It took all my willpower to not morph back into the moody teenager who would have answered "yes, mother" with a chip the size of Mt. Shasta on my shoulder. I shook my head and shrugged into a wool jacket. "I won't."

I left and headed off to the sunroom. Before I did anything else, I needed to call Kat. I sat in the same chair she'd occupied earlier in the day and touched her name in my phone.

She answered before it even rang. "What's up?"

"Kane found us seats for a flight at eleven a.m. They're first class, but he says his credit card points will cover all three of us. You okay with that?"

"First class? Free? Hell yeah!" Kat let out a whoop of exaggerated excitement and then lowered her voice. "I hope you have plans for a thorough thank you."

"Kat! Stop. Nothing's going to happen with my mom and Gwen here."

She sighed into the phone. "Yeah. That would be a mood killer."

"Listen, I'm getting ready to do a spell to find Philip, and I need something of Dan's to make a physical connection. Do you have anything? I gave everything of significance back to him after we broke up. The rest I tossed."

"Sure, the talisman his mom gave me this afternoon. Give me a moment… Hmm, that's weird. It isn't in my purse." A frantic rustling drowned out her next words.

"What?" I asked.

"Sorry, I can't find it. Hold on."

A soft thunk sounded, followed by more rummaging. I bit my lip and picked up a magazine on the end table. *Beyond the Barn.* Great. I tossed the farming magazine back down, and a shiny piece of metal caught my eye. "Kat?" I called into the phone.

"Just a minute," she called back. After a short pause, I heard a faint, "Crud!"

I picked up the silver pendant, fingering the familiar design. The letters engraved on the back were rough under my thumb. *DPT.* Dan Pearson Toller.

Dan had told me his middle name was a family name. I'd never imagined it came from Philip Pearson or that his dad wasn't his biological father. Had his dad known? It didn't matter now. Dan's dad passed away a few years ago, but I couldn't help but wonder.

"Kat!" I yelled.

"Sorry," she breathed into the phone. "I have no idea what I did with it."

"It's here. You left it in the sunroom."

"Thank God. You want me to come over and help with the spell?"

"Do you mind?" Kat didn't possess any magic, so she wouldn't be any help in that department. What she could do is help me focus and give me strength if I got carried away and used too much energy. And, let's face it, I'd been known to flub a spell or two.

"Don't worry. My parents already went to bed. They won't even miss me. See ya in five."

I put the phone on the table, picked up the spell book, and shuffled outside. While the rain still came down in sheets, the wind had finally died. I snagged a dry plastic chair from near the side of the house and placed it a few feet from the stairs leading to the back side of the farm.

Wrapping up in my wool coat, I took a deep breath. Mud and fresh pine filled my senses. Memories of Dan and me running through the neighboring woods flooded my brain. That night we'd walked under the brilliant moon, only to be caught in a late summer storm. Goose flesh popped out on my covered skin.

I no longer had feelings for Dan. We'd ended our relationship a few years ago, but I stilled cared about him. There was no way I'd let him spend eternity in Hell.

We had to find Philip. He was our best hope of tracking down Meri.

Magic fluttered against my breastbone, straining to do something. Anything. I opened Bea's spell book to the finding spell.

First step: *Secure a personal item of the missing person.* Well, the pendant didn't belong to Philip, but it was as close as I was going to get.

Second step: *Visualize the person of interest.* Tough to do, since I'd never met him.

Third step: *Light a candle to guide the journey.* Finally, an easy one. I ran inside and grabbed some matches and a candle sitting in the center of the kitchen table. It hadn't been lit yet, but Gwen wouldn't mind. She had plenty to spare. Psychics used them almost as much as witches did.

Back out on the porch, I pulled the small table in front of my chair and placed the candle in the middle. With an expert hand, I struck a match and lit the wick.

Fourth Step: *Repeat the incantation. Blow out the candle.*

That would complete the spell. I tapped my foot, impatient for Kat to show. It wouldn't hurt to practice a little, would it? Magic sparked to life in my chest. Practice was a good thing. According to Bea, I couldn't get enough. All righty.

I propped the spell book on the table and focused on the pendant clutched in my fist. Facing the flickering candle and the sheets of rain, I spoke, "From north to east to south to west, find the spirit, reveal its nest. Through brilliance and shadows, with nowhere to hide, reveal the angel Philip, with eyes open wide."

My magical spark warmed, sending a tingle through my limbs. I smiled. The practice had helped. Last week I would have supercharged the spell. Tonight, I'd given the incantation a gentle nudge. Was it enough?

The flame flickered once, then vanished, despite the absent wind. The familiar decaying muddy stench of the Mississippi river assaulted my senses as the rain stopped. The temperature shot up, making me sweat in my wool coat.

Moving toward the steps of the porch, I shed the jacket and gawked. The pine trees had cleared, revealing the New Orleans coven's circle. The one that sat among half a dozen giant oaks, very near the Mississippi river. In the middle stood Lailah, cradled in the arms of a man I'd never met. One I'd bet my life was Philip Pearson.

Chapter 3

Running down the stairs, I headed straight into the clearing. With dark brown hair, a stocky build, and an eerily familiar face, there was no way the man wasn't related to Dan. My gaze traveled to Lailah, lying limp in his arms, her face slack.

"Philip?" I cried as the man strode away, Lailah clutched to his chest.

I ran to catch up, but as he passed through the oak trees, the scene faded, leaving me standing ankle-deep in mud with rain soaking straight through my jeans and flimsy cotton sweater.

"Jade?" Kat called from the porch. "What are you doing out there?"

I stood frozen, terror seizing my limbs. Lailah was hurt. What had Philip done to her? My body started moving before my brain did. I tried to sprint back to the porch, but the mud trapped my feet in place, causing my upper body to jerk forward. Almost in slow motion, I tumbled and landed face-first in the gooey earth.

Sputtering, I looked up into Kane's handsome face. "Son of a...argh."

He offered a hand and pulled me to my feet. "Graceful," he said, his eyes crinkling with mirth.

"I need my phone." Frantic, I wrenched myself from his grasp and tried once more to run to the porch. My feet slipped and this time I would have fallen on my butt if Kane hadn't caught me.

"Whoa. Slow down there. I'll get you inside." Despite my protests, he lifted me into his arms and carried me in the exact same way Philip carried Lailah in my vision.

"Lailah's hurt," I said. "We need to call Bea or Lucien."

Once on the porch, Kane stopped next to Kat and set me back on my feet. "What do you mean, she's hurt?"

"She was in the finding spell vision."

"What exactly did you see?" Kat asked.

I moved to the door and eyed my phone sitting on the end table. Then I glanced down at my mud-caked body. "Can one of you grab my phone...and a towel perhaps?"

"Here." Kane handed me his Blackberry.

I shook my head. "No. Bea's number is programmed into mine."

"I have it." He flipped through his contacts and pulled Bea's number up.

Of course he'd have her number. She'd once helped him save me from a crazy ghost after he'd imprisoned me in another dimension.

I took the phone. "Thanks."

"I'll get you a towel," Kat said and disappeared into the house.

I hit send and cringed. My muddy fingerprint was front and center on Kane's black phone. "Sorry."

He shrugged.

Bea's phone rang three times before it went to voice mail. I hung up and started running through Kane's contacts, searching the L's. Lacy, Lailah, Landon, Liam, Lloyd. No Lucien. I scrolled back up to Lailah and hit send. It rang twice and went to voice mail.

"Double damn!" I tapped in a quick text. *Call ASAP. Jade saw something. Need to make sure you're okay.*

Kat appeared with a towel and my robe. "Here. You're gonna want to get out of that mess before going inside."

I glanced down once more. Yeah. Gwen would kill me if I tracked in a gallon of mud. So right there on the porch I started stripping.

"Jade!" my mother shrieked. "What's going on out here?"

I dropped my muddy sweater on the porch and faced my mother in only my bra and jeans.

"Oh my gosh." Mom rushed over, grabbed the towel out of Kat's hands, and wrapped it around me. "Get inside," she whispered harshly.

"Mom." I stepped back out of her reach. The towel fell. "I'm covered in mud. I need to get out of these clothes first."

Her face turned red and her fists clenched. "Honey, there are other people out here. Surely you can make it to the downstairs bathroom without causing too much of a mess."

Kat sent me an 'uh-oh' look and retreated to the safety of the shadows. Chicken.

I faced my mother and held a foot out. "Really? There's mud dripping from my jeans. I can strip right here. It's safer."

She shot a sideways glance and pointed toward Kane behind her other hand, as if he couldn't see what she was doing. How could he not? He was standing right next to me.

I suppressed a sigh. "Mom, I hate to break it to you, but Kane has seen me a lot more naked than this."

Mom's eyes started to bug out, but before she could say anything, Kane cleared his throat. "I'll go in and give you ladies some privacy."

I put a hand on his arm. "You don't have to do that."

He kissed the top of my head. "It's fine. I'll be in the kitchen."

Kane disappeared inside the house. I turned to my mother. "Mom, I'm twenty-seven years old. Please stop treating me like—" I stopped mid-sentence. We hadn't yet talked about her twelve-year-long disappearance to Purgatory. I hugged the towel to my now-shaking body. "Sorry. I know it's hard."

Mom stared at me for five very long seconds, then turned on her heel and quietly went back inside.

"Damn it." I sank into one of the white plastic chairs and buried my face in my now semi-clean hands.

"It'll be okay. You both just need time to adjust." Kat reappeared and pulled me to my feet. "Get out of the rest of those clothes. You're ice-cold."

The moment she said the words, my teeth started chattering. Up until then, I'd been too distracted to notice the temperature. With trembling fingers, I went to work on my jeans. Once jean-free and wrapped in my robe, I headed for the kitchen.

Kane sat at the table, two steaming cups of chai waiting. Instead of sitting in a chair, I curled up in his lap and kissed him. Thoroughly. Okay, maybe our make-out session was a little too risqué for Gwen's kitchen, but damn it, I needed a little heat. When I finally broke away, I whispered, "Thanks."

He smiled and pulled me to him again.

"Ahem," Kat said from the doorway.

I sent her a guilty smile. "Sorry."

"It's fine. But you just got a text." She held up my phone. "It's from Lucien. He says Lailah just showed up on his doorstep and she can't remember the last twelve hours."

Sleep eluded me.

I couldn't stop worrying about Lailah. Lucien was taking care of her so we knew she was safe, but what happened? Why had she been with Philip and how come she couldn't remember?

After what seemed like hours of tossing and turning, I finally got up. The cold hardwood creaked beneath my wool socks as I made my way down the hall to Gwen's office. Mom had been using the room to work on enhanced sleeping aids since she'd been home. I wasn't surprised. Adjusting to a normal life wasn't coming as easy as any of us hoped.

I turned a corner and spotted a glow underneath Gwen's office door. Relief flooded through me. Even though we were still adjusting to each other, Mom always had a way of soothing me. I knocked softly and cracked open the door.

"Jade?" Mom dropped a lit candle in a white bowl. Whatever contents she'd been working with went up in a whoosh of flame.

I grimaced. "Sorry. Didn't mean to startle you."

She doused the mini fire with water and waved her hand to clear the smoke. "Don't worry. I was experimenting. Why are you up so late?"

"Trouble sleeping. Actually, I was looking for one of your sleep enhancements."

She opened a small wooden box and pulled out a green pill. All of Mom's enhancements were green. What else would one expect from an earth witch?

She rose and pressed it into my palm. Not letting go, she squeezed my hand into a fist and clutched it. "I'm going to miss you, shortcake."

The suddenness of her emotion made my eyes mist. "Come with me?" I hadn't meant to ask her. It just popped out. How could I be so selfish?

"Oh, Jade." Mom's eyes filled with tears. "I don't think…"

"Never mind." I waved both hands in a 'forget it' motion. "I understand." And I did. She'd just gotten a second chance at life. How could I ask her to help me fight a demon?

Her intense gaze bore into mine. "I know you're going to do whatever you have to, but please, don't go running off into Hell without a solid escape plan…or two."

I gaped. This was the first time she hadn't treated me like an adolescent since we'd arrived in Idaho. "I won't."

"Promise me."

"I promise," I whispered, having trouble getting the words past the lump in my throat.

"And when you fight Meri—" her face turned sympathetic, "—keep in mind it isn't her fault she behaves the way she does."

I stepped back, shocked. "What does that mean?" Of course it was her fault. She'd stolen my mother and Dan and tried to hurt a bunch of other people I loved.

"She's a victim of circumstance. Try to remember she was a person once."

My eyes narrowed. Why was she defending her captor?

"Just listen to your heart. You'll understand." She folded me into her arms. "I love you. Don't ever forget that."

I buried my head in her shoulder, still confused and a little angry, but comforted by her touch all the same. "I won't."

When we broke apart, she tried to shuffle me back off to bed, but I paused. "Hold on. I have something for you." A minute later, I returned with a glass bead I'd turned into a pendant. I'd been meaning to give it to her before we left. With the vision of Lailah, I'd forgotten all about it. "I made this for you."

Mom turned it over in her palms. "It's full of your energy. Your love."

"You can feel it?"

She nodded, a look of wonder on her face.

Perfect. I'd never made a bead infused with magic before. This had been an experiment. "It's for protection. You wear it over your heart, and when you need an extra boost of strength, you can call on its power."

Immediately Mom removed the silver chain she always wore, added the pendant, and clasped the necklace around her neck. "It's beautiful. Thank you."

She gave me one last hug before sending me off to bed. As she shut the door behind me, I swore I saw tears streaming down her face. Happy tears, full of pride and love.

With the help of the little green pill, I drifted off within minutes. Normally Kane, being a dreamwalker, was waiting for me in my dreams. Almost every night, whether we were physically together or not, he appeared.

But tonight was different.

Someone was with me, but it wasn't Kane.

I lifted my heavy head off a cold cement floor and wanted to recoil, but my body wouldn't respond.

My head fell back to the cement, and I stared at Dan with bone-weary exhaustion.

He didn't look much better than I felt. He sat as far away from me as possible, his button-down shirt rumpled and stained with more than a few layers of grime. His usually clean-shaven face now had at least a week's worth of growth.

"Water?" I asked, my throat barely working from the dryness.

"It's behind you." Dan pointed.

"Oh." It seemed too much trouble to move.

A few beats went by. Dan sighed and retrieved the water bottle. He kneeled and carefully lifted my head. A black lock of hair fell over my eyes.

Hmm, odd. I have strawberry-blond hair.

Weird stuff happened in dreams.

Dan brushed it back and carefully poured the sweet liquid over my chapped lips.

"Thank you," I rasped when he released me.

He shook his head. "You'd better not be lying to me, or I'll take you to the devil myself."

A faint commotion intruded on my dream, and a moment later I opened my eyes to find both Kat and Kane staring down at me.

"Wake up, sunshine," Kat said, pulling the quilt off me. "We let you sleep as long as possible, but we have a ridiculously early flight to catch."

I glanced at the window. Still pitch black. "Does this mean we're on the six a.m. flight?" After finding out about Lailah's amnesia, I'd asked Kane to book the earliest flight he could find.

Kane handed me a steaming cup of java. "Yeah. Unfortunately." He checked his watch. "That means you've got thirty minutes."

I groaned and brought the mug to my lips. The aroma settled in my nose as I breathed in the dark roast. At least my boyfriend knew how to start me off on the right foot.

The flight was full and our last-minute tickets meant the three of us were separated. Lucky me. My ticket landed me in a middle seat with a young mom and a fussy newborn next to the window and an obnoxious, over-excited male who never stopped talking next to the aisle.

Not what I needed at the butt-crack of dawn.

"New Orleans is a beautiful city, but they really should do something about Bourbon Street," the man rambled on. "That place breeds sin. It's outrageous the city would condone people making money off corruption. I tell you, Bourbon Street and Las Vegas are the Devil's playgrounds."

I made a noncommittal sound, plugging my ears with the ear buds of my iPhone.

That didn't stop him.

He raised his voice and drawled on in his deep southern accent. "Young people like yourself have no hope of becoming productive members of society when you buy into all the immorality. Oh sure, I know you think it's all just in fun, but mark my words, someday you'll find yourself in Hell if you don't see the light."

Young people like myself? I eyed him. He couldn't be older than thirty. Attractive, too. Tall, medium build, brown eyes that would have been pleasant if he hadn't just insulted me.

I pulled the buds out of my ears. "Did you just call me immoral?"

He raised a skeptical eyebrow. "I didn't say that…exactly." His tone implied that was exactly what he meant.

"Excuse me." I shifted, trying to get further away from him, accidentally bumping the mom next to me. The baby started wailing again. I ignored her and turned my wrath on Mr. Judgmental. "You don't know me. I didn't ask for your sermon. If I were you, I'd stuff a sock in it before someone puts a pox on a body part. Preferably on one all you ignorant bastards have trouble keeping to yourselves."

So the lack of sleep, the baby crying for most of the last hour, and my anxiety over Lailah had zapped my brain. And my patience.

Anger rose from the depths of the man next to me, crawling over my skin. I cringed and shrunk into myself. His face twisted into a scowl and turned almost purple. Whoever he was, he clearly wasn't used to women fighting back. He reached up and hit the call for assistance button.

I turned away from him and focused on the baby. The mother had given up trying to do anything for the hysterical child. I closed my eyes, praying for calm, and took a deep, steadying breath. It wasn't going to work. I'd lost my last nerve.

A perky flight attendant with an easy smile materialized. "What can I help you with, sir?"

"I cannot sit next to this…*person* any longer. You'll have to find me a new seat."

"I'm sorry, sir." She frowned helplessly. "Our flight is full. There aren't any other seats available."

"There must be someone willing to switch," the man drawled, laying his southern charm on thick. "Tell them it's for Reverend Goodwin."

I held back a snort. Just my luck. I'd been seated next to a right-winged blowhard who currently topped the Nielsen ratings every Sunday morning on the cable station owned by his grandfather, the mega-media conglomerate powerhouse Fredrick Goodwin. What the heck was he doing in economy class?

The flight attendant's kind eyes narrowed and irritation radiated from her. "Sir, again, the flight is full. There's nothing I can do."

Goodwin raised his voice, clearly going for intimidating, but instead he sounded petulant. "First you overbook and I end up back here, in these sardine can chairs instead of in first class. Then you put me next to this disrespectful, foul-mouthed, unchristian—"

"Sir, there is no need for name-calling." She waved to someone at the back of the plane.

Goodwin wiped his brow and gestured toward the window seat, continuing his diatribe. "Not to mention she's upsetting that poor child. I have a lecture to give twenty minutes after we land. I can't focus here."

"Hey," I interjected. "I was just sitting here."

An official with a TSA badge on his arm joined the flight attendant. "Is there a problem?"

"Yes," Goodwin said, relief in his voice. "I need to be moved. This woman is causing a disturbance." He jerked his head in my direction.

"It seems to me you're the one disturbing the other passengers." He glanced at the flight attendant. She gave him a curt nod. Mr. TSA turned his attention back to Goodwin. "You'll need to come with me."

"Thank you." The reverend rose gracefully from his seat. "If you can arrange anything in first class, I'll be sure to put a word in with the man upstairs."

The officer sent him a steely glare. "Sir, you are now in the custody of the TSA until we say otherwise. Please step to the back of the plane."

"What?" Goodwin tried to back up, but with the flight attendant in his path, he didn't have anywhere to go.

"If you resist, you will be arrested. I suggest you step to the back of the plane."

I snickered, and Goodwin sent me a death glare. "Now, now, Reverend, that isn't very Christian of you."

The TSA agent gave him a nudge, and the pair disappeared to the back of the plane. My shoulders relaxed, and relief bubbled from the young mother beside me. "Sorry about that," I said.

She cradled her now-whimpering child to her breast. "Don't apologize. I wish I'd had the courage to tell him off. I'm sure part of the reason Katy is so upset is because that man was making me so mad. Babies sense these things."

Of course they did. People fed off other people's surface emotions all the time. They were the lucky ones. I had the pleasure of being up close and personal with everything they were feeling. Blocking it was exhausting. However, there was something I could do to help. "Can I hold her?" I smiled at the bundle in her arms.

"Um…" The mom glanced at her child and then tentatively held her out. The baby let out a wail she'd been barely holding back. "She's really fussy with strangers."

"Couldn't hurt to try." I took the swaddled baby and held her against my shoulder. She continued to cry, sobbing in loud hiccups. Rubbing her back, I cooed softly in her ear. "It's okay, sweetie. He's gone."

My magical spark warmed inside my chest, but I pushed it down. There was no need to spell the child. She just needed some calming energy. It would be better to take it from someone else and transfer it.

I could do it myself, but I still had issues with accidentally transferring my own essence. Not a good thing. If I gave too much away, I'd compromise my soul. Then blackness would take over, and I wouldn't be trying to get to Hell to save Dan. I'd gleefully try to take everyone I knew to the underworld, for good.

"Look at you," a familiar male voice said.

I glanced over to find Kane settling into the chair next to me. "Where'd you come from?"

He smiled. "I used to occupy the seat next to the TSA agent. Leave it to you to cause a scene just so you could get our seats switched."

I laughed. "Yeah, that's what happened."

Kane's easy calm settled over me. I reached out and touched his leg, letting his energy collect at my fingertips. After a moment, I gently nudged the calm through my body from one hand to the other. The baby's crying abruptly stopped and she laid her head on my shoulder, breathing steadily.

"Oh my gosh. You did it," the young mother whispered. She slumped back against the window and closed her eyes in relief.

"Thanks," I whispered to Kane.

He turned tender eyes on me, and when he reached up and gently smoothed the baby's pale blond hair, my heart melted.

Chapter 4

Kane pulled his Lexus to a stop in front of Lucien's single shotgun home. Bright red hibiscus blooms filled the flower boxes, and ornate stenciled vines decorated the door and window shutters. The house to the right had vibrant stained glass fitted to each of the front windows, and the house on the left was adorned with a number of handmade, brushed aluminum wind chimes.

The Bywater neighborhood, a few miles east of the French Quarter, housed a community of artists and witches alike. Lucien fit right in. He managed an art gallery and was the second most powerful witch in the New Orleans coven.

I jumped out of the car and ran up the steps of the small porch. The door swung open seemingly on its own. I stopped in the darkened doorway, squinting as I waited for my eyes to adjust. All the shades had been drawn to block out the mid-afternoon sun.

I took a tentative step. "Why is your living room impersonating a vampire lair?"

"*Luminarium.*" Lucien's voice sounded from deeper in the house. A soft light glowed to life through the archway of the next room. Shotgun homes don't have hallways. Each room is situated right behind the other, separated only by partial walls or doors.

With Kane and Kat on my heels, we made our way through the living room and straight into Lucien's office. The light he'd conjured floated near the ceiling, no fixture in sight. Lucien sat at his desk, his jawline stubbled and his blond hair uncharacteristically unkempt.

"Is Lailah okay? Where is she?" I asked.

"Other than not knowing what she did for twelve hours, she's fine. She's working on a recovery potion in the kitchen." He barely glanced in my direction before he turned back to the computer. "I'm researching a hunch."

I stopped behind him and peered over his shoulder. He'd typed *ancient memory charms* into the search field. "You think Philip spelled her?"

"Philip who?" He finally swiveled, acknowledging us.

"Philip Pearson. The angel I told you about. I saw him in my finding spell."

Lucien stared at me. "How can you be certain it was him? You've never met the guy."

"I'm sure." I crossed my arms over my chest, daring him to argue with me.

He took a deep breath. "Okay, but it would be better if you thought of that as a working theory for now."

Was he questioning my magic abilities?

I opened my mouth to protest, but Kane put his hand on my arm. "He's probably right. Until we verify his identity, we shouldn't make assumptions."

I didn't particularly like them ganging up on me. Who was in charge here?

"I'm done," a familiar female voice said from behind me.

I spun, finding Lailah in the archway that led to the back of the house.

"The potion's ready," she continued. "Jade? I could use your help." She turned and disappeared into the room she'd come from.

"Kat, can you fill Lucien in on what we learned from Izzy?" I asked.

"Sure." She sat perched on a wood-framed futon and crossed her legs.

Kane leaned closer. "Do you want me to go with you?" he whispered.

I shook my head. Absolutely not. Kane would only be a distraction for both of us. "Have a seat. I got this."

Before he could protest, I escaped into the next room. Then stopped dead in my tracks.

It appeared one had to go through Lucien's bedroom to get to the kitchen. To the left sat a wrought-iron queen-sized bed, covered by a gorgeous lilac comforter with delicate embroidered orange blossoms. On the nightstand sat a vase of fresh-cut daisies. A couple of bright 3-D, acrylic floral paintings brightened up the opposite wall. I moved, intending to join Lailah, but paused next to his open closet.

I couldn't help myself. As far as I knew, Lucien didn't have a significant other. But the room was so…feminine. Was he hiding someone? A quick glance told me if he did, her clothes didn't mingle with his. Only dress shirts and suits lined his closet.

"Jade?" Lailah called.

Oops! I glanced back toward the office. A low rumble of voices filtered through the doorway, and I prayed they hadn't heard Lailah. Fearing someone might investigate, I scooted into the kitchen.

"It's about time. What were you doing?" She set a bowl of clear liquid on the table.

I bit my lip, trying to turn my thoughts off.

It didn't work. Lailah started to laugh. "I know, right? His bedroom is unbelievable."

"Umm…"

"With that décor, he's going to have a hard time convincing a potential date he isn't already attached."

No man I'd ever known would intentionally choose lilac. A woman most definitely had done his decorating. *Maybe he does have a girlfriend.*

"He doesn't," Lailah said, taking the thought from my mind. "Stop that." I sat at the table. "What do you need me to do?"

Her face turned from curious and playful to dark and brooding. "Since the memory charm is for me, I can't invoke it myself. It might backfire. All you need to do is repeat the incantation and infuse the potion with a drop of your blood."

"Blood?" I stood abruptly, knocking my chair over in the process. "No way. I'm not performing blood magic."

Her exasperation filled the kitchen, making me want to retreat through the back door.

She sighed. "You're not going to leave. I have answers you want. Just invoke the charm so we can get on with this."

"Stop reading my mind," I demanded. "I don't read yours."

She raised an eyebrow.

Okay, so I did sometimes. But she wasn't making any effort to stay out of my head.

"I can't help it. You keep projecting," Lailah said.

"Ugh! Is there any other way to retrieve your memory without involving my blood?"

"No," she said quietly. "None that I'm aware of." Her entire demeanor changed to one of a frightened woman in need of help. Desperation clung to her aura. "Please, Jade. I need to recover my memories. I can't go through this again."

Cripes. This was becoming a habit for her.

Last week, while Lailah was assigned to save Dan's soul, the demon Meri used the connection to form a tie with Lailah. Meri had then gone on to compel Lailah to poison Bea and seduce an unwilling Kane. A side effect of the compulsion was memory loss. Lailah had no recollection of any of her evil doings. Being faced with more forgotten hours must have scared the hell out of her.

She eyed me. "Now will you do the blood spell?"

My resistance cracked. Even though a shiver crawled up my spine, I shrugged. "Yeah, okay." I slid into the heavy wooden chair and dragged the bowl in front of me.

Lailah handed me a thick white candle. "Declare your intentions before you light it."

"I know." Since Lailah was an angel, her magic allowed her to wield spells without following all the ritual steps. I couldn't.

Well, technically I could, but the results were usually disastrous. The last time I'd worked a spell on the fly, I'd ended up mentally connected to the very last person I wanted privy to my thoughts—Lailah.

"Sorry. Just a reminder." She sat back and closed her eyes. "By the way, reading your mind isn't a picnic for me either."

"Stop talking about it," I snapped. "If you can't block me out, just pretend you can't hear me."

She mumbled something that sounded like, "If only that were possible."

I didn't say anything, demonstrating my point, but in my mind I shouted, *See how that works? Try keeping your unwanted comments to yourself next time.*

She snorted.

I turned my attention to the candle. "Goddess above, hear my words. When my blood falls, Lailah's memories will be restored." I plucked a match from the box and, with a slight nudge of my inner power, I willed it to light.

A small flame appeared without so much as a spark.

Satisfied, I lit the wick. "While this candle burns, let the flame be a symbol of protection. Guide my magic, let it do no harm, seek no harm, or cause any harm."

The flame brightened, growing tall and strong.

"Good." Lailah passed me a sheet of paper with a handwritten incantation. "Now say this and then add a drop of blood to the potion."

I grabbed the small ceremonial dagger lying next to the bowl and spoke the words. "From the purity of the white witch, let my blood be the sacrifice of stolen memories. Restore what was taken. Fill the void left in the angel Lailah. Let her mind be whole. With these words I pay the price."

I swiped the dagger across the fleshy pad of my thumb and winced. Blood pooled, oozing from the wound. Grimacing, I tilted my hand and let one lone drop drip into the bowl. My thumb throbbed, and I quickly bandaged it with a tissue. "Did the charm work?"

Lailah groaned, laying her head down. "No. You must have done something wrong."

"Um, wrong? I did exactly what you told me to do. Maybe it was your potion." I scooted forward and stared into the bowl. My blood droplet sat in a small bead on the top of the now-solidified liquid. Resisting the urge to use my finger to mix it, I picked up the bowl, rocking it back and forth until the thin film broke. My blood spread in spidery veins, weaving its way slowly through the liquid.

Darkness swam at the edge of my vision. Damn it all. Not again! I would not pass out. Not this time. Since moving to New Orleans, I'd formed a bad habit of losing consciousness every time I got involved with something mystical.

I sat and held my head in my hands. The blackness faded. But when I focused, I was no longer sitting in Lucien's kitchen.

Double damn. *Here we go again.*

Sitting on the floor in the middle of a brightly colored living room, I reached forward, picking up a black candle, thought better of it, and replaced it with a white one. I imagined a lit wick, and the flame burst to life, illuminating a pink rug and red couches.

Ready to finish the spell, I held my arms out. Surprise rippled through me. The hands attached to my arms weren't mine. In fact, the arms weren't mine, either.

I mentally groaned.

The short skirt paired with leggings and the belted blouse I wore meant one thing; the body I mentally inhabited was Lailah's.

*Oh, for the love of…*A man strode into the room, his eyes a very familiar shade of pale emerald green. When he spoke,

I gasped. Though no one heard me, since I only existed in Lailah's mind.

He sounded exactly like Dan. He had to be Philip Pearson.

Lailah sat, staring at him as if she'd been spelled into submission. And when Philip ordered her to stand, she did.

"Angel of the Light, lead me to his last location," Philip said, his voice commanding and cold.

Lailah moved toward the door. When she brushed past him, he touched her lightly on the shoulder and whispered, "I know you're in there, witch. Stay out of Lailah's memories. Your magic doesn't work here."

My world spun and my stomach lurched. I groped to clutch something. Anything to make the spinning stop. Abruptly, the chaos ended. I found myself back in Lucien's kitchen, my fingernails clawing at the shiny table.

I blinked and relaxed my fingers.

Lailah stared at me, mouth open. "You…"

"What?" I stiffened.

"Why were you in my memory?" She stood, anger streaming off her. "Can't you do anything right? I told you to invoke the memory charm, not modify it or spell it. Geez, Jade. Keep your magic to yourself next time. Who knows what kind of lasting effect this will have."

"Excuse me?" I rose and met her toe to toe. Last week, as the leader of the New Orleans coven, I'd been tasked to reinstate Lailah's magical ability. She'd been in a magical time out after she'd accidentally poisoned Bea. Unfortunately, I'd gotten a little overzealous and ended up sharing part of my magical spark with Lailah. That's what caused our psychic connection. Believe me, it wasn't a mistake I was likely to make again. "The only magic I used was to light the match. If the charm went wrong, it's on you. All I did was what you asked. Nothing more, nothing less."

"The potion worked. You were there. My memory came roaring back…to you." She stepped forward and pointed a finger at me. "All I got out of it was your thoughts!" Her voice rose until she was almost shouting.

Blood rushed to my ears, and I took a step back before the altercation became physical. I clenched my fists to keep from turning her finger into a pretzel.

"Problem?" Lucien asked from the arched doorway.

"Oh, no. Nothing at all," Lailah mocked. "Except your coven leader messed up a basic memory retrieval charm." She paused, eyeing me. *If you spent less time in Kane's bed, you'd have more time to learn your job.*

"What did you say?" I cried.

"You heard me." She tossed her honey-blond hair and left the room.

I had to do something about our psychic connection. Soon. Sensing emotions was one thing, but direct thoughts? Not acceptable. Especially when the person in question clearly didn't like me, just as much as I didn't like her.

Lucien picked up the glass bowl and carried it to a utility sink near the back door. He dumped out the contents and went to work on sterilizing it. "What happened with the memory charm?"

I stared out the window at the fading afternoon sun. "Something odd."

He chuckled. "Something's always odd when you're involved."

I shrugged. "I guess so, but this was different. I only used magic to light a match and that was before I even stated my intentions. I don't see how I ended up sucked into Lailah's memory. Or how Philip managed to force me out."

Footsteps caught my attention. I glanced back and a wave of relief washed through me. Kane. The man had a way of putting me at ease just by being present. "Where's Kat?" I asked.

"Talking Lailah down." He draped an arm around my waist. "Want to fill me in?"

Lucien placed the now-clean bowl back into the cabinet and motioned for us to follow him outside. The balmy November air warmed my skin, but when Lucien's expression turned grave, my limbs turned to ice.

He locked his green eyes on mine, intense and worried. "I think Lailah's been possessed again."

Chapter 5

Before my brain processed what Lucien said, Kane spoke. "What makes you think that?"

"Jade infiltrated her memory. The breach suggests a weakening in her aura. With her memory loss, I'm almost certain she's been compromised."

"Meri's back?" I breathed, clutching Kane's arm. He tensed, and I tightened my grip. I'd just gotten him back from her clutches. I wouldn't let her have him again.

"Not necessarily. But the only being strong enough to penetrate an angel's aura is a demon or another angel."

"Philip?" My eyes widened.

Why couldn't angels be good? Was nothing sacred?

Lucien shook his head. "Probably not. We don't know if the person you saw in your vision was Philip. Angels don't turn on each other. They save their energy for demons."

I stared at a weed forcing its way through the patio bricks. Prior to Lailah poisoning Bea, she'd been acting strange. I'd known something was off about her, but none of the coven members dared entertain the idea an angel could be less than... well, angelic. Look what happened to her. She'd been controlled by a demon.

My gut told me the mystery man was Philip. Until someone proved otherwise, I'd work under the impression he was up to no good. No one was going to be a victim of possession on my watch.

I disengaged from Kane and put on my best coven leader attitude. "I need you to help me with a finding spell for all angels within a two-hundred mile radius. In addition to locating Philip, we still need help rescuing Dan. Can you do that?"

Lucien retreated to the back door. "I'd rather not. Angels can get nasty when their privacy is compromised."

So much for being the nice boss. "Too bad for them. Unless you have an official angel contact list handy, when the coven meets at midnight, we're performing the spell."

He pursed his lips and took a deep breath. "Don't say I didn't warn you."

"It's settled then." I swept past him and tugged Kane into the house. "Let's go before he comes up with another argument."

Kane stopped in the middle of the kitchen. "We can't leave Lailah here. What if she *is* possessed? You're the only one powerful enough to do anything if she goes off grid."

Damn it all if he wasn't right. "Fine. You do the honors of telling her. If I do it, we'll have another fight on our hands."

Lailah silently fumed all the way back to Kane's house. I would've happily ignored her, but she kept throwing mental insults in my direction.

At least she was creative. Whoever heard of an angel calling a coven leader a magic-stealing twat waffle?

After dropping Kat off at her apartment, Kane pulled to a stop in front of his shotgun double, Victorian-style home on one of the quieter streets in the French Quarter. I already had my hand wrapped around the door handle when Kane pushed a button, triggering the automatic door locks.

"Before we go inside, I'd like to make a request," Kane said.

Lailah's curiosity crawled up my neck, making me long for a shower. After her mental assault, I didn't want her energy anywhere near me. I eyed Kane suspiciously. "And that would be?"

He turned to catch Lailah's eye and then stared pointedly at me. "A truce. Until we're sure Lailah isn't compromised, the three of us are stuck together. I know after what happened at the club..." he trailed off, no doubt deciding now wasn't the time to talk about the make-out session the pair of them had in Kane's office.

Sure, they'd both been under the influence of a demon at the time, but that didn't mean I'd magically gotten over my shock of seeing them together. Logically, I knew I shouldn't be mad. Too bad my inner self was still pissed. At Lailah. Probably because she still wanted to get him between the sheets.

"For Goddess' sake, Jade. I do not!" Lailah yelled from the back seat. "Kane, open the damn door. I have to get out of here."

"And go where?" I asked coolly.

"Bea's house. She can babysit me. I don't want to intrude on your love nest."

"No. Bea's still recovering." My mentor and the former leader of the New Orleans coven was the most powerful witch I'd ever met. Under normal circumstances, Lailah would be fine at her house. But only a week had passed since Bea came perilously close to losing her soul. The last thing she needed right now was another crisis. "You're welcome here. Besides, we need to learn to work together."

She closed her eyes and leaned against the window. "Fine, but we'd better find a way to get out of each other's heads or else this will never work."

"Agreed." I held my hand out.

She hesitated for a moment. I waited patiently. She knew if she touched me, I would be able to read her emotions and hear her thoughts more clearly. It wasn't an easy thing to share with someone. Especially the someone who dated your ex. She squared her shoulders and clasped my hand.

"Truce," she said.

Relief flooded from her. The tension in my shoulders eased, and I sent her a tentative smile. She didn't want to feud any more than I did.

We'd make this work. Somehow.

"Can we get out now?" I asked Kane.

He snorted. "You could've left any time you wanted to and you know it."

"True. But I try not to magic my way out of every situation." I grinned and let a bit of my magical spark fly. Instantly the locks clicked open.

Lailah laughed. I joined her on the curb, and we walked to the house together, leaving Kane to grab the luggage.

Kane was called away to meet with a client shortly after we arrived, leaving Lailah and me alone. Perfect. With her in his house, all I could think about was the pair of them sharing his bed sometime in the distant past.

I longed to be holed up in my glass studio right about then making beads. Nothing put my mind at ease faster than losing myself in the miniature creations. It was my sanctuary, the one place I could go and block out everything and anyone who bothered me. But I couldn't leave Lailah alone.

To keep my mind occupied, I grabbed Bea's spell book and escaped into the kitchen. There had to be some reference to severing a psychic link. The sooner I got Lailah out of my head, the better.

"You're not going to find anything," Lailah said.

I jerked. Damn, she was a quiet angel. Wood floors combined with mid-heeled boots should have alerted me to her presence long before she made it to the open doorway. "How would you know? I thought you didn't work spells the traditional way."

She half-shrugged. "I don't, but that doesn't mean I'm not educated. I come from a family of witches, you know."

"You do?" How had I not known this? Because we weren't friends. Our relationship was defined by one mishap after another. First an exorcism, performed by Lailah, had sent

Pyper, one of my best friends, into a coma. Then while Lailah had been controlled by a demon—through no fault of her own—she'd poisoned Bea, sexually assaulted Kane, and then abducted him to Purgatory.

It's no wonder I didn't have the warm and fuzzies for her. Still, she was Bea's friend and employee. I'd decided that was enough to give her the benefit of the doubt. That didn't mean it was easy for me.

Her brow creased in disbelief. "Angels are born into magical families. My father is a witch, and his mother is an angel."

"What about your mom?" I got up and headed for the refrigerator. After retrieving the pitcher of sweet tea, I filled two glasses and returned to the table.

Lailah sat in my chair, flipping through the spell book, a blank expression on her face.

I set one in front of her and sat. "Lailah?"

"Hmm?"

"Are you okay?"

Her usually guarded emotions slipped past her barriers, prickling me with detachment. Her emotional walls snapped in place and she glanced up. "Fine. Thanks for the tea."

"You're welcome." We sat in silence, sipping our drinks. I took the hint. She didn't want to talk about her mom.

After spending years not knowing what happened to my own mother, I sympathized. It had never been a topic I'd been comfortable with myself. Whatever it was, I'd respect her privacy.

She picked up the pen and started scribbling in the notebook I'd left open. "There's an old spell my father used to use to keep psychics from delving into his future. We might be able to modify it to terminate our connection."

I frowned. "He spelled himself on the slim chance he'd run into a psychic?" Statistically, the odds of witnessing a real seer experiencing a vision were incredibly small. Microscopic. Most people would never experience such a thing, unlike those of us who grew up with one in the family, like I did. The exceptions were people who sought out psychics.

She smiled. "Dad is…eccentric. He closely guards his privacy." Her smile vanished. "He has his reasons."

Okay. Dan and I weren't the only ones with weird family secrets. "All right. Have you ever modified a spell before?"

"Of course." She pulled her mussed hair back into a bun and secured it with the pen. "It's Witch Chemistry one-oh-one."

I swallowed the lump lodged in my throat and tried to ignore the flash of inadequacy running through my brain. I could barely do any spell, much less modify one.

Oh, I had the power. Plenty of it. That was the problem. I didn't know how to fully control my magic. "Maybe we should consult Bea."

She stopped writing and stared at me with hardened eyes. She let her irritation shine through her emotional armor. "I know what I'm doing. Do you have any idea what I do for Bea at The Herbal Connection?"

"Help customers? Stock the shelves? Deal with vendors?" That's basically what I did at The Grind, the café Pyper owned.

She gritted her teeth. "You think I'm a retail clerk?"

The Herbal Connection is a retail shop. What was I supposed to think? "Umm…"

She stood with an exaggerated huff. "I do the R and D on all the spells she offers. You know the charm when you first walk in? The one that custom-tailors a scent to each patron? I invented it. Me. Not Bea." She flung a hand in frustration. "I know what the hell I'm doing."

She stormed off, swallowing her last thoughts. Of course, I heard them anyway. *Unlike you. If you don't kill someone before we find Dan, it'll be a fuckin' miracle.*

Ouch. I don't know what shocked me more. Lailah—an angel—using the F word, or finding out she'd invented the soothing scent spell. Every time someone walked into The Herbal Connection, the scent in the air changed to whatever made the person most happy. My scent shifted from a sea-salted breeze to Kane's fresh rain cologne. The first time I'd entered the shop I'd been very impressed and had assumed it was Bea's spell. My assessment of Lailah and her abilities did a one-eighty. It appeared I had a lot to learn about the angel.

Despite my attempts to apologize and offer dinner, Lailah stayed locked in the guest room until right before we left to meet Lucien and the rest of the coven.

Even then she ignored me.

I tried one last time. "Kane brought po'boys. There's one in the refrigerator for you."

"No, thank you," she said, but her interest brushed against my psyche. I stifled a sigh and grabbed the sandwich anyway.

"In case you get hungry." I held the shrimp sandwich out.

She eyed it and then nodded. "Okay." She turned to Kane. "Thank you, that was thoughtful."

"No problem." He smiled and offered an arm to each of us. "Shall we?"

And even though I wanted to smack him, I said nothing as we both grabbed an arm and the three of us headed to meet the coven.

Chapter 6

The air blowing off the Mississippi held a slight chill, and I shivered as we made our way through the old oak trees to the coven circle. A faint trace of oil and gas mixed with the muddy stench of the river. I covered my nose with the sleeve of my sweater and wished for Lailah's soothing scent charm.

The trees gave way to the hidden clearing. Candles flickered brightly around the edge of the coven circle, illuminating Lucien and Rosalee as they placed more candles in the center.

"What's all this?" I gestured, indicating the massive amount of tea lights.

Rosalee, a tiny, wide-eyed witch in her early twenties, faced me. She held up a diagram. "We're creating a map of the two-hundred-mile radius you want to search."

"With candles?" I asked.

Lucien crossed the circle, careful to not knock over any tea lights. "Yes. See how we marked each city?"

Rosalee passed me the diagram. I inspected it, finding a candle marker in the circle for every decent-sized city within our target area. I nodded.

"After we work the spell, if any other angels are near, their image will materialize over the candle, representing the city they're closest to. That will give us a starting point." Lucien pulled the diagram from my grasp and compared it to the scattering of candles on the ground. "I think we're almost ready."

"Really?" I glanced around. "Where's the rest of the coven?" There were thirteen of us. Spells had a much better success rate if the entire group was present. We could work the spell with the three of us and Lailah, but I'd have less of a collective to draw from. It was likely our reach wouldn't cover as much distance as I hoped.

Lucien spied his watch. "They're on their way."

"Jade!" a familiar voice cried. I spun, finding Kat stalking toward me. "Why didn't you call me? You're searching for Philip and you didn't say anything?"

I stared at Kane, my eyebrows raised in question.

He shook his head and held his hands up in a 'not me' motion.

"Sorry, Kat," I said. "It's just an information-seeking spell. I figured I'd fill you in on the details tomorrow."

Irritation swirled around her and then dissipated. She had an uncanny ability to control her emotions, something most people never got a handle on. "Please. Have you ever conducted a spell that didn't go wrong in some fashion?"

"Hey! That's not fair. I banished bugs from Kane's yard. Bea taught me." I eyed the silent man beside me. "Right?"

A sheepish smile spread over Kane's face. "Sort of."

I groaned. "What?"

"You banished them, but when they came back, they tripled in number. I had to call the exterminator." He grabbed my hand and squeezed lightly. "You never see them because they're dead."

"Crap," I muttered. The spell was supposed to temporarily relocate any vicious type of bugs. You know, fleas, chiggers, red ants. When humans left the yard, they'd come back. My blunder had resulted in a mass genocide of bugs. Icky bugs, but still.

Kat stifled a laugh. "See? You need moral support."

The words 'shove it' were on the tip of my tongue, but I quickly decided it was good to have her around. She was my best friend and had just as big a stake in finding Dan as I did. "Hey, how did you know the coven was meeting?"

"I told her," Lailah said from beside me.

I jumped. She hadn't spoken once since we'd arrived. I'd almost forgotten she was there. "Why?"

She shrugged. "Does it matter? It's not like it was a secret." She walked off in Lucien's direction.

"Did she call you?" I asked Kat.

"Yep. A couple of hours ago. She had some questions she wanted answered." She fingered the sterling silver, oak tree pendant at her throat. Kat was an accomplished silversmith; she'd made the piece herself. "The coven thing just came up. I don't think she was trying to interfere."

"It doesn't matter." I lowered my voice. "What questions did she ask?"

Kat didn't get a chance to answer. Right then the rest of the coven burst through the trees. Friendly chatter filled the air as they each made their way to their specific spots on the circle.

"Showtime," I said.

Kane grabbed my wrist, stopping me before I could join the coven. He pulled me to him and clamped his mouth over mine. The hot fierce kiss heated me to my toes.

"What was that for?" I asked, breathless after he released me.

"Luck."

"With luck like that, what could go wrong?" I quipped. Then frowned. "Sorry. Bad choice of words."

He shook his head and walked toward a wrought iron bench set in front of one of the giant oaks. Kat gave me a hug and joined him.

"Okay. Let's do this." I turned to Lucien. "Do you have the incantation ready?"

He pulled a folded piece of paper from his jeans pocket. "This should do it."

I focused on the other members, noticing for the first time their casual wear. "No robes?"

He raised one pale eyebrow as his gaze traveled the length of my body.

"Yeah, yeah. I'm not wearing mine either. It's at home, and I haven't been back to my apartment since we landed."

He smiled. "Relax. You were right when you told Kat this spell wasn't a big deal. Really minor in the grand scheme of things. It should only take a few minutes, and then we'll have a plan."

He moved to take his place on the circle, but I touched his arm to stop him. "What about the angels we locate? You said they'd be really unhappy to have their privacy invaded. 'Angry angels' doesn't sound minor to me."

"True. But you'll only have to worry about that once you catch up to them."

"Well, that's something." I followed Lucien and took my place at the northernmost point of the circle. Emotions sparked from the members, everything from excitement to boredom to indifference. And maybe even a little irritation. I'd probably be annoyed if my coven leader sprung a meeting on me at the last minute, too.

I clapped my hands and cleared my throat. "Thank you, everyone. I'm sorry if I ruined any plans, but I wouldn't have asked if it wasn't important."

Most of them murmured a casual "you're welcome" or "no problem." Only one stayed silent, and the irritation I'd felt grew.

Emotional energy is distinct. I can recognize it much the same way I can identify a particular voice or scent. I followed the thread of irritated energy with my mind to a young male witch. Before now, he'd almost always been ecstatic to be working with the coven.

"Joel?" I asked. "Everything okay?"

"Sure…I mean…yeah. Fine," he stammered, confusion joining the swell of frustration taking over his body. He ran a nervous hand over his face and shuffled his feet.

Rosalee left her post and took Joel aside. She leaned in to whisper in his ear. He nodded, but made eye contact with no one. I bit my lip. His mood hadn't improved in the slightest.

Rosalee wrapped an arm around him, giving him a half-hug, and spoke again. This time whatever she said brought him a reassuring calm. She stepped back, grabbed him by both shoulders, and stared him in the eye. "Ready?"

His gaze found mine. "Yeah."

"Okay." Rosalee moved back to her spot next to me. "Let's find some angels."

Hmm, what could that have been about? Whatever it was, I made a note to thank Rosalee.

I extended my hands to her and Anne, a tall, graceful witch in her sixties. When we touched, the circle glowed to life, fueled by the coven's collective power.

Lucien's voice rose clear in the still night. "Goddess of the light, send your protection to our circle. Guide us in our quest for knowledge. Keep us sheltered from the power of the black. Our hearts are pure, our intentions sound. From north to south to east to west, blessed be in our quest."

The coven echoed his prayer, strong and unified.

The magical spark jumped to life in my chest. The warmth spread through my limbs, sending electric shocks vibrating through my core.

Alive. In this state, I could do anything.

But right now, all I needed to do was say the spell Lucien had dug up for me. "From here and there, to near and far, Angels of this night, show yourselves with all your might."

The circle brightened, turning glaring white, almost blinding me. I squinted, trying to make out the activity within the circle. Faint familiar energy pulsed, energy not attached to any of the coven. It grew stronger, calling to me with its purity. Tears of emotion sprang to my eyes. I blinked them back, waiting as the shadows materialized into translucent forms.

Rosalee's hand tightened on mine, and someone gasped from across the circle. The brilliant light slowly separated, seeming to funnel into two beings. As they formed distinct shapes, my attention stayed trained on the one closest to me. The energy, so intimately familiar and yet foreign, held me captive. I couldn't place the signature, but something inside me recognized it all the same.

A blanket of electric blue magic flashed over the circle and then vanished. The candles winked out, leaving us standing in the dark, transfixed on the two glowing figures.

The one nearest me met my gaze.

His stocky build and pale emerald eyes were exactly as they'd been in Lailah's memory. I'd been prepared for that. But I had no way of knowing his emotional signature would touch the part of my heart I'd locked away a long time ago. So familiar to the Dan I'd known and loved for all those years. Pure. Welcoming. Good.

I swallowed the sob forming in my throat and took a deep, ragged breath. He wasn't my Dan. Not that Dan was mine anymore or even that I wanted him. But this man—Philip, Dan's biological father—had all the emotional goodness I'd loved so much in the teenaged boy I'd grown up with. He brought back all the hopes, dreams, and fears of the young, scared girl I'd been.

With one incantation, I'd been transformed into someone I'd hoped to never be again.

"Philip," Lailah said from right behind me.

Standing next to the candle indicating the city of New Orleans, Philip inclined his head. "Lailah."

She broke my grasp on Rosalee's hand and pushed through our arms into the circle. "It's protocol to announce your presence to the resident angel when you come to town. You know that."

"My apologies. You are, of course, correct."

"Had you not invaded my space and taken my memories, I'd be inclined to let you off with a warning. Instead, I think I'll command your cooperation and bind you to me until a formal inquiry can be conducted."

Philip took a moment to study her, amusement coming off him in streams. "You think you possess such power?"

"Yes. And I'll prove it as soon as I find your sorry ass." She sounded more exasperated than angry. How well did they know each other?

He chuckled. "I look forward to the challenge."

Lailah stepped back, annoyance clouding her emotions. She turned her attention to the other angel and groaned. "Jade, we have the information we need. You can let the spell go."

I followed her gaze to the second angel. He was turned away from me, hovering over the candle representing Baton Rouge. Great.

While the capital city wasn't too far away, it was the second largest city in southeast Louisiana. It could take days to find him.

Sighing, I let the magic drop and waited for the angels to disappear. Instead, they floated to the ground and their images shifted from translucent to solid flesh.

"Umm…" I stared at the second angel's profile. He rubbed his temples in confusion. "Looks like the spell didn't go quite as planned. Instead of illusions, we summoned them *body* and spirit."

The coven erupted with questions and gasps of surprise.

Lailah took a second to assess the situation and then advanced on Philip. She snapped her fingers and said, "By the bond you created, you're now bound to me until your secrets are revealed."

A silver band appeared from thin air and wound its way around his wrist. He frowned and plucked at the cuff. "That wasn't necessary."

He moved forward, reaching for her, but she jumped from his grasp and took up position beside me. "Don't mess with me, Philip. I'm in no mood." She glared at him. "Did you notice what this witch did? She transported you here. Do you have any idea what that means?"

He relaxed his stance and smiled. One of those cocky, shit-eating ones. "Yes. Do you?"

She ignored his question and yelled in my mind, *Jesus, Jade! You could've killed someone with that stunt. People die during magical transportations.*

I flinched, more from the fear and worry behind her reprimand than the actual words. What had I done?

The other angel finally spotted me and found his voice. "You! How dare you bring the gates of Hell to my feet with your blasphemous witch magic?"

"Mr. Goodwin," I said to the reverend I'd met on the plane hours earlier. "It appears you are a messenger of God after all, in the form of an angel."

"Jesus," Kane whispered from behind me.

My thoughts exactly.

Chapter 7

"Jonathon," Lailah said, her voice thick with disdain. "To what does the wondrous state of Louisiana owe the pleasure? Here to condemn us all to Hell again?"

"You know him?" I whispered.

Later, she scolded me through our connection.

I glanced in her direction, but her eyes stayed glued on Goodwin.

"Now, Lailah," he drawled. His entire demeanor shifted as the tension and anger vanished from his face. Candlelight glowed around him, bouncing off his sun-kissed bronze skin. "My only mission in life is to save souls. Looks like God has a new assignment for me."

"And who exactly do you think should be the unfortunate recipient of *your* attentions?" She raised her chin and crossed her arms over her chest.

Reverend Goodwin kept his intense gaze trained on her as he moved across the circle. Lailah took a step back.

When he didn't stop, she put her palm out, holding him at arm's length. "That's close enough."

A flash of amused determination flickered in his energy. "We'll see."

The rest of the coven started to clump together, whispering quietly among themselves as Kane and Kat walked up behind me. Philip moved off to the side, silently watching the exchange between Lailah and Goodwin.

I cleared my throat, ready to come to Lailah's defense, but Kane wrapped an arm around me and shook his head. What did he know that I didn't?

"Your assignment?" Lailah persisted.

A slow grin spread over his perfect features. "You, of course."

She scoffed. "Back off, Goodwin. I don't need to be saved. If I did, you'd be the last person I'd ask for help."

His grin vanished and his face hardened. "You've made that perfectly clear on previous occasions. Your refusal doesn't change the fact that you and your coven of magic abusers summoned *me* here. You know how this works. Everything for a reason. I'm sure my orders will be waiting for me back at the hotel."

Lailah's thoughts burst into my mind as if a dam had broken. *Egotistical, useless, good-for-nothing piece of angel turd. What did I ever do to deserve this? How could I have ever thought he was my mate?*

I stifled a gasp. *Your mate?*

Get out of my head, Jade! She turned her icy blue eyes on me, anger and frustration consuming every inch of her aura.

Sorry, I mouthed and pressed closer to Kane. Her mate? I'd recently learned angels really did have soul mates, and once found, they were bound together for eternity. I glanced at Goodwin and shuddered. How awful to be connected with someone so…dogmatic.

I think the words you're looking for are 'judgmental and intolerant.'

Now who's in whose head? I pulled away from Kane and joined the uneasy members of my coven. We were all still a little wary since battling a demon.

Joel, the young male witch Rosalee spoke with earlier, shifted from foot to foot, twisting his hands. I lightly touched his arm and pushed a tiny bit of calm in his direction. It wasn't an energy transfer. More like a suggestion.

Instantly he stopped fidgeting. Hmm, easily controlled, that one. I'd have to keep an eye on him in sticky situations. "Don't worry. This seems like personal business between the two of them. I'm certain Lailah's soul isn't in danger."

"You sure?" Joel glanced in her direction, his worried eyes resembling a lost puppy.

Stifling the urge to pat him on the head, I nodded. An angel's main job was to protect souls from danger. I'd been under the impression their mission was human souls, but Lailah had been through a terrible ordeal. It wasn't totally inconceivable an order would come down from the angel council to protect one of their own.

"Then why are there three angels in New Orleans?" Joel clenched his hands into fists and narrowed his eyes as he stared at me. "You're not telling us something."

The rest of the coven went silent with his accusation. Distrust pressed on me from all sides. I turned to Lucien, silently asking if he knew what was going on.

He gave me the slightest head shake and stepped up next to me in a display of support.

Together we faced the witches. Though none of them were as powerful as either of us, combined they could do some damage. Especially if their power was aimed at someone without any magical defenses.

Kane and Kat moved to stand beside me.

"Jade," Rosalee said, her voice laced with a dangerous edge. "What exactly is going on here?"

"Please, everyone stay calm." The coven's unease ratcheted up, making it hard for me to breathe. My gaze found Rosalee's. "I don't know," I gasped out. "We already explained what we were doing. But the spell didn't quite work as planned."

Pain shuddered through my chest. I clutched my breast bone with one hand, wishing I had healing abilities that didn't require brewing a potion.

"Jade?" Kat's hand rested on my shoulder. Her loving energy circled me, creating a thin shield from the coven. I could still sense their hostility, but at least it wasn't suffocating me anymore.

I placed my hand over hers and squeezed. My best friend always knew what I needed. Kane's concern brushed against my psyche, but he stayed still and silent. I appreciated that, knowing he would rush to my defense if I asked. This was my coven. My problem. A white knight wasn't going to help.

Standing straight with my shoulders back, I summoned as much poise and calm as I could muster. "I don't know what caused this sudden breach in trust, but rest assured I'm not hiding anything. We were only supposed to summon the image of any angels nearby. It wasn't our intention to transport them here. As witches, we're taught all spells carry risk. The place, people, and intentions of everyone involved matters when spell casting. Not everything is going to go right when we have so many variables within the collective."

I paused and met the eyes of each of the eleven suspicious members standing before me. "We are a coven. Trust matters. I trust you. I trust Lucien. The question is, do you trust me?"

I held my breath. I'd only been their leader for ten days. In that time, they'd almost lost Bea, the beloved former coven leader, and they'd been subjected to a demon from Hell. Thankfully we'd defeated the demon and saved both Bea and my mother, but we'd lost Dan in the process. To have any chance of finding him, I'd need their help.

"No," Alan said over the grumbling crowd.

"Not me," someone else cried.

"Why should we?" Rosalee asked with defiance. "You've done nothing but cause us trouble."

"Rosalee!" Lucien scolded. "You don't believe that."

Her eyes blazed from caramel to almost black as she advanced on us, her arms raised.

"Enough!" A loud boom sounded, and Philip appeared out of thin air right in front of me. A second ago he'd been across the clearing.

Silence filled the night, each of the coven members gaping at the impressive transportation spell.

I glanced back at Lailah, still standing where I'd left her moments earlier. Goodwin stood beside her, eyeing the scene with mild interest. Turning around, I gave Philip my full attention.

He stood, legs slightly apart with his hands resting on his hips. Power and authority streamed off him. "All of you, remove yourselves from the circle."

When no one moved, he barked, "Now."

I couldn't tell if he put magic behind the command or if he'd just startled them into action. Either way, they all marched out of the circle, toward the giant oak trees. On the way, their normal chattering started back up, and I even heard some laughing.

What the hell?

"Want to explain?" I asked Philip.

He gestured toward the retreating coven. "Ask them."

I shot him a look of disgust and jogged to catch up with Rosalee. "Hey, hold on a second."

She stopped and waited.

"Talk to me. What was that about back there?"

Her brows pinched in confusion. "What was what?"

I frowned, searching her emotional energy for clues. No anger. No frustration. Only mild concern. For me.

"Are you feeling okay?" she asked, moving closer. "Do you need an energy pill? Magic sometimes drains me if I'm not careful." She started rummaging around in her designer purple handbag.

I put my hand on her arm to stop her. "Rosalee, I'm fine. Do you not remember what just happened?"

She tilted her head to the side, and a bit of worry clouded her eyes. "Did the spell not work?" She glanced past me. "Are those not the angels you were looking for?" Before I could answer, she called to the other members. "Guys, hold up. Jade might still need our help."

"No, no. Don't worry about it. Go on home or whatever your plans were." I waved them off just as Lucien joined us. "Something's not right," I said to him.

"I noticed." He jerked his head back toward the circle. "Philip's still not talking, and Goodwin's hitting on Lailah. At least, I think that's what he's doing. Doesn't look like he's getting very far."

The Reverend Goodwin was following Lailah around as she picked up candles, talking nonstop. Her silence seemed to only egg him on. On the other side of the circle, Kat appeared to be badgering Philip, no doubt about Dan. Kane stood next to her, embodying the role of a protective older brother. Good. She'd be safe with Kane…unless Philip spelled him.

"Guys?" Rosalee asked. "I'm totally in the dark here."

Right. "Can you just tell me what you think happened tonight?"

She frowned and straightened her spine. "What's wrong?"

I raised my shoulders and hands in an 'I don't know' motion. "That's what I'm trying to find out."

"Well." She glanced toward the circle. "Lucien said the opening prayer. You recited the incantations, and then those two angels showed up. Lailah seems to know both of them, but that makes sense since she's an angel. After they appeared, you told us we could go. End of story. Except for the fact the two guys are physically here when we only tried to summon their images. But things happen, right?"

Lucien and I shared a wary glance. "Yeah, things happen," I said.

She ran a hand over her dark hair and pushed her bangs to the side. "There's more, isn't there?"

I nodded. "Yeah, but we can talk about it at the next meeting. First I need to figure out exactly what happened."

"You sure? I can stay and help if you want." Her gaze drifted to her watch, but she shook her head, as if talking herself out of leaving.

"No, it's fine. You go ahead." I gave her a quick hug, truly appreciating the offer.

When I let go, she met my stare, her light brown eyes wide. "Call if you need anything."

"I will. Thanks." As she left, the image of her blackened eyes flashed through my mind. I'd only seen that particular effect two times before. And both were caused by black magic. I grabbed Lucien's sleeve and tugged. "Come on."

Once we joined the remaining group, Goodwin sent me a look of contempt and said, "You're back."

"And you're still here," I snapped, wishing he'd go away. There was no way we'd be able to work together.

"Transportation is hard to come by in the middle of the night. My rental car is still in Baton Rouge. One of you—" he glanced at Lailah, "—will need to drop me at the hotel."

We both ignored him. I turned to Philip and crossed my arms, positive he was the cause of this mess. "They don't remember anything. I think you have some explaining to do."

Lailah froze, a candle clutched in each hand.

"You seem to be making a habit of modifying people's memories lately." I sidestepped, putting myself between Philip and Kat. If he tried anything, I didn't want her on the receiving end.

Philip's face hardened. "I don't have that particular ability. Even if I did, I certainly wouldn't use it."

"But you did with me, last night," Lailah spat. "Jade saw you when she did a tracking spell. You were the only other person there. Then you showed up on my memory recovery. Twelve hours I lost."

He turned in her direction, his eyes softening. "I was there, but that's not why you don't remember."

Her lips pressed into a thin line.

"Why then?" I asked, breaking the silence.

"It's the circle." He gestured around the clearing. "It's been compromised."

"What?" I took an unconscious step backward, putting distance between me and the circle.

"It's tainted. All spells performed here have the potential to do serious harm." He stopped and turned back to me. "They can't remember because they were infected by the circle's magic. It took over their conscious thoughts, with only one goal in mind."

"And that would be?" A pit the size of a crater formed in my stomach.

"Destroy the one who tainted it."

I stopped breathing and forced out, "Me?"

"Yes." Compassion and no small amount of apprehension radiated from him. "Your magic tainted the circle. Your black magic."

Chapter 8

Chaos erupted. Everyone spoke over each other while I stared at Philip, frozen in shock. He met my gaze, a trace of sadness in his pale green eyes. One blink and the emotion vanished, replaced by stony determination.

Goodwin's voice rose above the others. "We need to bind her. Now."

"Jonathon, don't be ridiculous," Lailah scoffed. "Clearly Jade isn't posing an immediate danger. No need to be drastic."

Magically binding me would keep my soul from being corrupted. It would also put me in a coma. Forever. Unless someone managed to neutralize the black magic. And I was the only witch I knew strong enough and stupid enough to attempt such a thing.

Goodwin stalked toward me, and I glared at him. Bind me first and ask questions later, huh? Yeah, not gonna happen.

Kat and Lailah appeared beside me, each flanking one side.

Kane stepped in Goodwin's path. "Turn around and walk away."

"Who are you?" Goodwin asked, impatience lacing his voice.

"The guy who's going to send you to your own special version of Hell if you don't get the fuck away from my girlfriend."

Goodwin started to glow, magic building around him. He took a small, challenging step toward Kane. "Go ahead and try."

"Jonathon!" Lailah barked. "Back off."

Neither of the men acknowledged her. Kane's arms flexed, and Goodwin's magic rippled. Jonathon raised his arm, ready to throw the magical equivalent of a punch.

"Kane!" I cried as he took a swing at an honest-to-Goddess man of the cloth. Not that Goodwin didn't deserve it.

A bright white light materialized between them and forced them a good five feet apart before either could strike the other. Kane stumbled and grimaced as he clutched his thigh—the same one Meri had stabbed during his stay in Purgatory—but he managed to stay upright. Goodwin tripped over his own feet and landed on his backside.

They both stared at me.

I raised my hands. "I didn't do it." Jerking my head toward Lucien, I added, "That's his magical signature."

Lucien stormed over and positioned himself in front of me, power still brimming at his fingertips. "Enough. We're not binding Jade. At least, not until we figure out what's happening."

Goodwin scrambled to his feet, a challenge already forming on his lips.

"One more word and I'll curse you," Lucien snapped, an icy calm radiating off him.

I'd never seen him work so much magic by himself. Something suspiciously close to pride welled in my chest. My second in command was growing stronger.

Philip, who'd stayed back assessing the dynamics, moved and whispered something to Lailah. She tilted her face up, studying him. Finally she looked away and cleared her throat. "Maybe we should all go somewhere and figure this out."

A wave of exhaustion washed over me. I brought a steamy cup of coffee to my lips and leaned back into the overstuffed loveseat in Kane's living room.

The three angels hovered in the corner, arguing in hushed tones. Kane sat next to me, silently keeping an eye on Goodwin.

Kat perched on my other side in a wooden chair she'd snagged from the kitchen. Her anxiousness was actually making me nauseated. To keep my dinner down, I raised my imaginary glass silo, blocking everyone's emotional energy. My stomach settled, and I sighed in relief.

Lucien paced back and forth in front of us, his brow creased in thought. "If what Philip said is true, why didn't I turn on you?"

"You think Jade's tainted?" Kat sent him a hard stare.

"No. I mean, I don't know." He paused and glanced at Philip. "We can't take anything he says at face value. He's a stranger. A demon's mate, even. He could be helping Meri."

My head started to pound. I rubbed two fingers across my skull. "He's not helping Meri. He shunned her after she fell, remember?"

"That doesn't mean he hasn't changed his mind." Lucien stopped and turned his attention to the angels. "What are they arguing about?"

Can she be saved? Lailah's thoughts slipped into my brain.

With a heavy sigh, I leaned against Kane. "They're trying to decide what they're going to do with me."

"What does that mean, what to do with you?" Kane asked, caressing my arm.

I met his worried mocha-colored eyes. "If it's true I've been corrupted by black magic, then I'm a threat to not just the magical community, but all the people around me. They're trying to come to an agreement about the best way to handle it."

"And?" Kat asked.

"Goodwin's proposing to send me to Hell. He's of the mind that I'm a lost cause." As far as he knew, there wasn't a way to reverse threads of black magic. Once it took hold, it would eventually eat your soul. Then the only safe place for me would be the fiery underworld.

Except, I'd saved Bea, the former New Orleans coven leader, from the hold of black magic just one week before.

"That's crazy!" Kat stood and stalked across the room. "Jade is not a lost cause. I can't believe you're making plans for her

future when we don't even fully understand what's going on."
She placed her hands on her hips, her feet spread wide. "The
three of you have some explaining to do before we go any
farther. Philip, we'll start with you."

His pale emerald eyes crinkled in amusement and he shot
her an easy smile. "You've got spunk."

She stepped back, clearly caught off guard, a troubled expression on her face. I could almost hear her thoughts. The easy
reaction to Kat's outburst was so eerily familiar to the way Dan
used to behave, I had to steady my own shaken emotions. Her
expression cleared, replaced by a sense of resolve. "Enough. Tell
us exactly why you think Jade's been compromised. And if so,
why didn't Lucien turn on her?"

Philip grabbed his coffee mug off the mantle and moved to
sit across from me on one of the overstuffed chairs. He took a
sip and glanced at Lucien. "He's stronger than the rest of the
witches. When the threads weave their way deeper through
the circle, eventually he'll be affected." Dan's father turned his
steady gaze to me, staring intently into my eyes. "Normally
angels work under the radar, but I'm going to need your
cooperation if we have any chance of defeating the evil we're
up against. I believe it would be to your detriment to keep my
purpose here a secret."

Did he already know about Dan? Was he here to save him?
A small tingle of hope formed in my chest.

"A week ago, I got the call your soul is in danger. I've been
assigned to you," Philip said, still holding my gaze.

Kat gasped.

Lailah stared at him, realization dawning in her eyes. "That's
why you allowed the spell to physically transport you into the
circle, isn't it?"

He nodded. "I needed to be there to defuse the situation."

"Well, you didn't need to bring me along for the ride,"
Goodwin scoffed.

Philip shrugged, barely acknowledging his complaint.

"I still say she's too dangerous," Goodwin said, his demeanor suddenly calm. "But since you've been assigned to her, I'll give you three days until I file a report with the National Order."

This time Philip nodded. "Understood."

"Good." He turned to Lailah. "I'll see you soon, mate."

"Don't count on it," she said with an air of disgust.

A second later the door slammed closed, rattling the windows.

"The National Order?" I asked Lailah.

"It's the angel's council. They govern souls. If yours is compromised, they have the power to order you bound."

"Oh." Three days until I potentially had a whole mess of angels deciding my fate. Peachy.

Lailah stared at Philip. "You still have some explaining to do. What happened to me for twelve hours last night?"

"Sorry about that." He sighed, weariness suddenly showing in his tired eyes. "I had to put you in a temporary trance to stop you from using the circle. I've been watching it ever since the black magic breach last week. I needed to make sure you weren't part of the problem. After your trip to Purgatory, I couldn't be sure."

"Someone noticed a breach?" I asked. Were people watching everything we did? More pain pulsed over my right eye.

"Not someone. Me." His voice hardened. "I arrived the day after you battled Meri."

Lailah reached over and grabbed his hand. "I'm sorry. That must have been a shock when you assessed the circle."

He gave a short nod of acknowledgement and turned back to me. "What Lailah said is true. The council could order you magically bound if they deem you dangerous enough. But it's worse than that. They oversee all magical beings, witches included. If they decide you are a willing black magic user, but your soul isn't compromised, there could be serious consequences."

"Such as?" I asked, fear creeping into my heart.

"They could imprison you and strip you of your power."

A shiver crept up my spine. I'd almost used black magic while battling Meri. It had been right there at my fingertips. I would have unleashed it on her if it hadn't been for Kane and my friends bringing me back to myself.

The wall clock clicked over to two a.m. I said nothing and concentrated on the second hand, making its way steadily around the face. Tick. Tick. Tick.

"But how did this happen?" Lucien asked. "I've never heard of a circle being compromised before."

"None of us have ever met a witch as powerful as Miss Calhoun." I could barely hear Philip's reply over the ticking clock ringing in my head.

More voices joined his. They rose and faded in and out of my awareness. Someone was yelling. I think it was Lailah, but I couldn't follow what she was saying. All of it blurred through my mind. A chill crept over my skin, leaving me numb.

A hand squeezed mine, and warmth penetrated my exterior. Kane. I studied him, finding concern and worry troubling his chiseled features.

"Get me out of here," I whispered.

Kane stood and pulled me to my feet. "Jade needs to process. You're all welcome to stay here if you like. But I'm taking her home for the night."

Philip moved in front of the door. "I can't let you do that. It's too dangerous."

Lailah, of all people, came to my rescue. "Let them go. Jade hasn't shown any signs of her aura eroding. It's glowing white, tinged with the faintest trace of purple, right now. No black in sight. And Kane can take care of himself."

One of Lailah's specialties was reading auras. She'd once identified a black shadow attached to Pyper. If anyone could see erosion, it would be her.

"That's against protocol." Philip didn't move.

"So is leaving your mate stranded in Hell and not even asking for help to free her." Lailah's blue eyes flashed with defiance. "Yeah, I know everything that went down with Meri. If you don't want me to bring it to the NO's attention, you'll let my friends go for the night."

I stared at her as if I'd never met her before. Why was she threatening a powerful angel? Especially in order to help me? *Because no matter what, we're friends. Even if we don't act like it. You don't deserve this. Go home. Spend time with Kane. We'll deal with everything tomorrow.*

Tears threatened to burn my eyes. I didn't know why, but Lailah using the word friends after all we'd been through touched me. For much of my life, friends hadn't come easily. Now that I had a group I counted on, I held them closely guarded in my heart. I hadn't trusted Lailah before. But she trusted me. I made a mental vow to not make that mistake again.

About time, Lailah's cheerful voice rang in my head.

Philip reluctantly moved away from the door, anger shooting from him in Lailah's direction.

Kane pulled me outside. I sent Lailah one last mental message. *Thank you.*

Duke, my ghost dog, jumped and drooled pools of dog slobber upon our arrival. If he'd been solid, he would've knocked me over despite my five-foot-seven frame. "Down, Duke," I commanded.

"He missed you." Kane pulled me into the room and nudged me to sit on my sagging secondhand couch.

"Yeah."

His footsteps echoed over my wide-planked pinewood floors as he headed to the kitchen on the other side of the room.

I closed my eyes and leaned back into my lumpy couch. What seemed like only a second later, Kane appeared with a toasted, buttered bagel, a glass of water, and some ibuprofen. I gulped down the pills and nodded toward the bagel. "Where'd that come from?"

"I ran down to the café after checking out your condiment holder over there." He nodded to my refrigerator.

Not knowing how long we'd be gone, I'd intentionally tossed all perishables. The last thing I wanted to come home to was a penicillin farm. "You left?"

"Just for a second." He kissed my temple. "You fell asleep."

I took a few bites and then set the bagel down. After the scene at Kane's house, I wasn't at all hungry.

Kane pulled me up from the couch. Instead of leading me toward the bed, he steered me to the bathroom. Inside, the sweet aroma of jasmine filled the tiny room. He'd run a bath and filled it with my favorite bubble bath.

I smiled. "Perfect."

He bent his head and touched his lips to mine, kissing me slowly and tenderly. His love radiated through that kiss.

I pressed into him, sliding my hands up his back, gently biting his lower lip before sinking deep into the kiss. His clean rain scent, mixed with the jasmine in the air, sent a dart of desire straight to my center. I pulled back, tilting my head to look up at him. "It's been a while."

"A week," he mumbled as he bent to nibble my ear.

An intense shiver tingled over my skin. The anxiety and implications of what I faced in the coming days made me want to lose myself in him.

With my eyes closed, I leaned back, giving him full access to my neck. He trailed hot kisses as his hands came up, unbuttoning my shirt. The cotton fell open, my breasts spilling over the top of my black lace bra. He cupped them together, gently kissing the exposed skin. They instantly became heavy and my nipples ached, impatient for attention.

Burying my hands in his thick, wavy black hair, I moaned with pleasure. I felt his lips curve into a satisfied smile, and then his tongue darted under the lace, flicking the hardened tip of my right nipple. I pressed into him, demanding more.

In one quick motion, my shirt and bra fell to the floor. His lips closed over my left breast, sucking hard, while his hand kneaded and teased the other. I gasped, and he scraped his teeth over my sensitive tip. Ripples of glorious heat slithered through me.

"Kane," I said, my voice thick.

Raising his head, he moved his hand to my hip and pulled me against his hard body. "Yes, love?"

"Take me to bed."

His brown eyes turned molten chocolate with heated passion. I didn't have to ask twice. He lifted me easily and carried me into the other room.

Taking his time, he liberated me of the rest of my clothes. First my jeans, and then he placed both hands on my waist. Inching his way down, he slowly lowered the last of my garments, kissing a trail to my belly. Kneeling on one knee, his hot breath mingled with the heat between my thighs.

I sucked in a breath and waited. Days. It'd been days. He hadn't even visited me in my dreams while we'd been gone. My real life reactions to Kane's dreamwalking was entirely too personal considering I'd been sharing a bedroom wall with family.

He ran firm hands along my legs, pressed a soft kiss to my inner thigh, and then looked up at me.

I quirked an eyebrow.

A low rumble sounded in his chest as he rose. "The next time I touch you, I want you lying down."

"Oh?"

His lips turned up in a predatory smirk. "What I have planned, your muscles can't be trusted to keep you upright."

I took a tiny step forward and slipped my hands under his shirt. "What if I have my heart set on seducing you?"

His gaze turned intense. "What the lady wants, she gets."

"Good," I murmured and pressed my palms against the concave of his hips. God, I loved touching him there. I slowly brought my hands up, pressing fingers to his corded muscles. He raised his arms, and a second later I pulled his shirt off.

I took in his beautiful form. Over six feet tall, slightly tanned, and the body of a man who knew his way around the gym. He was gorgeous. I placed a soft hand over his heart, knowing that was what I loved most about him.

Abandoning any pretense of seduction, I wrapped my arms around him, holding tight. He was mine and I was his.

His strong arms came around me, and he whispered, "I love you too, pretty witch."

"I know," I whispered back and brought my lips to his for another slow, tender kiss. But as soon as our tongues met, the spark reignited. That intense heat flooded through me again. I reached for the button of his jeans and seconds later we were both naked. His hard length pressed against my belly, forcing a strangled moan from the back of my throat.

I leaned back.

His eyes were glinting again as he watched me. "Lie down, Jade."

The gruffness in his voice sent shivers of anticipation to all the right places. I did as he asked.

He hovered over me, and I pulled him to me, flesh on flesh. Tension shot through my starved body. Our lips met, tongues darting, teeth scraping.

Heat burned my insides, pulsing with his desire.

I reached down, closing my fingers over his velvety shaft.

His breath hitched, but he grabbed my wrist and gently pulled my hand away. "No. Tonight I worship you." He kissed his way down my body, his tongue dancing over my skin. And this time when his lips brushed against my thigh, his tongue followed.

Wet and quivering, I gripped the sheets as Kane spread my legs. He paused just for a second and blew a hot, tantalizing breath, marking my center. He lifted his head and watched me as he ran a slow and deliberate finger against my opening. I raised my hips, more than ready.

He smiled up at me and plunged his fingers into me. A small cry escaped my lips as his mouth closed over my most sensitive spot, his tongue stroking in tandem with his clever fingers. Intense pleasure pulsated, blurring my thoughts to nothing but the pressure building beneath Kane's expert touch.

My breath came in short gasps as the dual sensations mixed into one fiery, intense flame. Tiny shockwaves rippled through my core as my muscles tensed. Kane paused, and when I whimpered, he plunged his fingers again, simultaneously scraping his teeth over my sex. Pleasure exploded through me, liquid lightning electrifying every last nerve. I let out one last cry as my body turned languid and utterly satisfied.

Kane rested his head on my belly, tracing circles over my hip. I placed a hand on his head and ran my fingers through his tousled hair. A few minutes later, Kane rose and positioned himself over me, silent. Waiting. With a tiny nod, I welcomed his thick, hard length into my tender flesh.

We came together, him filling me and me taking every last inch of him. Slowly his hips started to move. I rocked with him, intense need building once again. His hands moved to my hips, holding me still as he thrust hard and deep, over and over again, until his breath became ragged. His fingers dug into my flesh, and I let go, crying out as the wave took me over the edge. Muscles tensing, he buried himself in me one last time, a guttural groan rumbling from deep in his throat.

His grip eased. He pulled me close, still buried deep, and kissed my shoulder. Resting his cheek against mine he said, "I'm not letting anyone take you from me. Ever."

A bittersweet pulse fluttered in my heart. I brushed my lips over his ear and whispered, "I'm counting on it."

Chapter 9

We held each other, silent, as our breathing returned to normal. After a few minutes, Kane rolled away and sat up, planting his feet on the floor. He grabbed my hand and tugged. "Come on."

"Where?"

"Bath time." He stood and grimaced as he flexed his right leg.

"You okay?"

He smiled. "Yeah, just stiff. A soak will help."

Trailing Kane into the bathroom, he flipped the hot water on and climbed in the antique claw-foot tub. He propped himself up against the back, knees raised, and patted the water, inviting me in. Bubbles clung to his chest.

I gazed at Kane submerged in the bubble bath. How could I resist? I lowered myself into the lukewarm water and leaned against him. The scalding water rushing into the tub burned my toes. Swirling the water to equalize the temperature, I closed my eyes and heaved a heavy sigh.

"Want to talk about it?" Kane ran his hands lightly over my arms.

I pressed my toes to the faucet and shut the water off. "I don't know what to think."

"About which part?"

A lot had happened. Jonathon and Lailah were possible mates? How creepy was that? I actually felt sorry for her. No wonder she fantasized about Kane. And then there was Philip. Could he be trusted? If what he'd said was true…

"The part about my soul being tainted." A small tremor ran the length of my body.

Kane tightened his arms around me as if shielding me from any harm. "There isn't anything wrong with you. If black magic is eating away at your soul, don't you think one of us would notice?"

I shrugged. "What about the circle? I did tap black magic when I battled Meri. Thank the Goddess I didn't use it." I paused, mulling my thoughts. "Do you think when I released the darkness, the circle absorbed the magic?"

He paused and ran his thumb over my cheek. "You'd better talk to Bea."

My mentor, Bea, was the former New Orleans coven leader. During a battle with Meri, she'd sacrificed herself to the soul-eating magic in order to save the rest of us. We'd had to magically bind her into a coma to keep her from turning all evil-witch, but we'd managed to bring her back, whole and pure. At least, we thought we had.

Kane was right. Bea was the person to ask.

"First thing tomorrow," I said.

Kane kissed the top of my head. "You mean later today." He gestured to the sun-shaped clock on the wall.

Four a.m. We'd been up for twenty-four hours. My eyes watered with fatigue. I stood and reached a hand to helped Kane up. "Time for bed. We need at least a few hours sleep before we start the next round."

In my own bed, with Kane beside me, sleep was almost instantaneous. But instead of Kane waiting for me in dreamland, I found myself lounging on a king-sized bed, covered in purple silk. I glanced around at the windowless room. The lavish cherry wood furniture shone to a high gloss, matching the wood-paneled walls. The placed screamed dark and elegant. Where was I?

A door in the form of a hidden panel swung open. A silver tea cart emerged from behind the panel, rolling silently over the thick carpet. A pause, and then…Dan appeared. What was he doing in my dream?

"You need to eat." He stopped the cart next to the bed and locked the wheel.

"Just some tea. I'm not hungry," my dreamself said.

He gave me a stern look. "You've said that every time I've brought food to you. You need your strength."

I pressed into the pillows. "For what? They don't appear to be interested in letting us out of here." Confusion swirled in the back of my consciousness. Who was I referring to and where were we?

He poured a cup of black tea and doctored the Earl Grey with a lump of sugar. "We'll find a way." He handed me the cup and tucked a lock of black hair behind my ear. Black hair? I glanced down at a silver knife on the tray and caught a glimpse of my reflection. Gray eyes, long, thick hair, angular nose.

Meri.

I was dreaming I was Meri, and Dan wanted to help me.

"I need you to get strong. Dad's waiting for us," Dan continued.

A heavy sadness settled in my chest. "Philip doesn't care what happens to me. Forget about me and save yourself."

He sighed. "Let's not argue this again. You know I'm not leaving without you."

I stared at my slim fingers wrapped around the tea cup. "Fine, but it's going to take a lot more than apples and cheese slices to gain any substantial energy."

"It's a start," he said and disappeared through the panel door.

My eyes flew open to the early morning light, sweat dampening my brow. I sat up holding my head in both my hands. What the hell?

"Jade?" Kane murmured beside me and ran a hand down my back. "You okay?"

I lay back down and snuggled into him, comforted by his touch. "Yeah, I'm fine. Just a weird dream."

He pulled me closer and kissed my neck. "Go back to sleep, love."

Snuggled in his arms, my safe place, I squeezed his hand and willed myself to drift back into oblivion.

A loud banging tore me out of my restless sleep. I bolted upright and through blurry eyes spotted Kane answering the door, half-naked in only his faded jeans.

Pyper, my boss and Kane's best friend, strode into the room, her dark hair layered with bright pink streaks flying behind her. She wore a black jeans and a hot pink blouse, a few shades darker than her freshly dyed locks. Without a word, she picked up the remote and turned the TV on.

"Is everything okay at the café?" I rasped out as I sat up, covering my bare body with a blanket. Pyper had given me time off from my job at The Grind while I dealt with finding Dan. But my impromptu absence had left them severely shorthanded.

"It's fine. Holly has everything covered." She pointed to the television and ordered, "Watch this."

I blinked, trying to focus on the small nineteen-inch screen. A tall, thin, Hollywood-type, blond reporter stood in front of a giant oak tree, speaking into the camera. I tugged the blanket around myself and got up to move closer.

"Standing with me," the reporter said, "is the well-known evangelist Reverend Jonathon Goodwin." The camera lens zoomed out and Goodwin came into view, projecting a self-important smile. "Reverend, this morning you filed a complaint with the city that last night, here in this clearing—" she gestured and the camera panned, revealing nothing other than the coven's circle, "—a group of so-called witches performed some sort of dark magic."

"That's right, Sybil." Goodwin nodded. "I did."

The reporter's eyes went wide with curiosity and mock disbelief. "That's quite an accusation, Reverend. Do you have any proof?"

"Obviously there are the burn marks in the shape of a pentagram and the circle surrounding it. That's a sure sign of the Devil's work."

"The Devil?" Sybil's eyebrows rose. "I thought you said witches were the culprits?"

Goodwin's tone turned condescending. "Where do you think the dark magic comes from, Sybil? We, as a society, need to come together to fight against these misguided individuals." He stared straight into the camera. "Tonight at six p.m., I'm hosting a rally in Jackson Square. I urge all of God's children to join me in protest of such evil doings."

"One more question, Reverend?"

He nodded.

"Rumors of witchcraft in New Orleans have been circulating for years. Why battle the practitioners now?"

Goodwin's eyes turned hard. "The great city of New Orleans has been a breeding ground for social and moral indecency for years. God has sent me. It's time to stand up for what's right. With no moral stronghold on the city, the youth are being corrupted. We must all seek to follow God's word. That means the impropriety of Bourbon Street must be challenged, youth need to be educated on right and wrong, and dark magic users need to be neutralized. Evil comes in many forms. If we want a safer New Orleans of tomorrow, the time to act is now."

A cheer went up from somewhere off camera. My stomach turned, and I couldn't help but wonder if he'd brought his own sound track.

"There you have it, New Orleans," Sybil said cheerily. "Tonight at six p.m., join the reverend in Jackson Square to fight moral indecency and dark magic." A smile blossomed on her full lips. "If we're lucky, maybe a boy with a scar on his head will show up and fight the evil for us. This is Sybil Tanner for WNNO, signing off until tomorrow. Back to you, Mike."

The newscast flicked back to the studio where another reporter started a rundown on the weather.

Shock paralyzed my limbs as thoughts raced through my brain. Witches weren't a secret. People knew we existed and that we could produce spells, though most assumed we were harmless or fake. We liked to keep the big stuff under wraps. Non-magic users were too much of a liability.

Damn Goodwin! He'd announced to the whole city where the coven usually meets. Outed our circle.

I stalked across the room and yanked my coffee pot from the machine. "He called us out on live TV so we couldn't go back there and use a tainted circle."

"He couldn't have just asked?" Kane pulled a T-shirt over his head.

I yanked on the faucet with more force than I'd intended, and the handle came off in my hand. Water sprayed straight up, drenching me. "Son of a demon's whore!"

Kane calmly reached under the sink and had the water turned off in no time. I hadn't even known the shut-off knob was there.

"Someone want to fill me in on the creepy Bible-thumper?" Pyper said, handing me a towel.

"He's a TV evangelist from Georgia." I eyed the coffee pot longingly. No water, no coffee. "I was unlucky enough to get assigned a seat next to him on the plane. Surprise! It turns out he's an angel, too."

"Not just any angel," Kane said, handing me a Diet Coke from the fridge. "He says he's Lailah's mate."

Pyper's mouth dropped open and a small sound got caught in her throat. She coughed. "Excuse me?"

"Weird, right?" My phone started vibrating. I glanced at the screen and answered. "Bea?"

"Jade?" My mentor's worried voice came through the line.

"Thank goodness. We've got more problems." I scooted over to my dresser and started pulling out clean jeans while Kane and Pyper huddled together, Kane filling her in on the night's events.

"I can see that, dear," Bea drawled, her accent heavier than normal. "How did Goodwin get mixed up in this?"

I winced and gritted my teeth. My fault. Again. "Uh, we were searching for any other angels in the area and…well, had I known we'd summon Goodwin, I never would have asked the coven to work that particular spell."

She sighed. "Angels come in all different sizes and shapes, unfortunately."

I threw a clean T-shirt on the bed on top of my jeans. "I have to talk to you about something. In person. Is now a good time?"

"Of course. And Jade?"

"Yeah?"

"Don't work any spells, no matter how benign for the time being." She ended the call before I could say anything else.

Yikes. Had Lailah already filled her in? I grabbed my clothes and headed for the shower. "I'll be ready in ten minutes," I told Kane.

Thirty minutes later we pulled up to Bea's Garden District carriage home. The small white house gleamed in the November sunshine.

"Something's different," Pyper said from the backseat of Kane's Lexus. She'd insisted on tagging along and left Holly in charge of the café.

"It's the flowers," I said, eyeing the vibrant rows of blooming marigolds in front of her porch. After banishing a spirit to Hell, Bea had been too weak to tend her gardens over the summer. It had taken three months of practice, but I'd finally found my magical spark and restored her energy. "I'm glad she's getting back to normal."

"Yeah, but for how long?" Pyper climbed out of the car.

A chill crawled over my heart. There was no doubt I'd need Bea's help, even if Philip was wrong about me. One doesn't go into Hell and expect to get back out again without a witch casting an anchor spell on the other side. And Bea was the only one I knew powerful enough to handle such advanced magic.

Kane put his hand on my thigh and squeezed lightly. "You all right?"

I took a deep breath. "I think so."

He leaned in, pressing a soft kiss to my temple. "I'll be by your side no matter what."

Emotion bubbled in my chest. I nodded, too afraid to speak. A moment later, Kane got out of the car, then walked around to my side to open my door. I took his hand and stood on shaky legs. "Thanks."

Determined to find out if I was, indeed, a vessel of black magic, I forced myself to put one foot in front of the other. If anyone had the skill to detect the taint, it would be Bea.

"They're here," Lailah called from the front door.

Philip appeared behind her, his face pinched with impatience. "Finally. We've been here for hours."

I waved at Lailah and sent Philip a cold stare. Who cared if he'd been waiting on us?

Lailah nodded a greeting as I brushed past her to join Bea in her dining room.

"Be nice, Philip," Lailah said. "We're going to need to work together, especially now that Jonathon's in town."

I sat next to Bea, noting her freshly dyed auburn locks. She was every bit the southern lady in her beige linen pants and violet silk blouse. Strong and confident, exactly as she had been the first time I'd met her. "Did you see the news?"

She nodded and passed me a notepad. A simple incantation filled four lines.

"What's this for?" I asked.

Her sympathetic brown eyes stared into mine. "It's the spell to let us know if your soul has been tainted."

Panic rushed through my limbs, and without thinking, I pushed the notebook out of my reach.

"Jade, you don't have anything to be ashamed of. After our encounter with Meri, I should have thought of this sooner, but I wasn't quite myself, and you were out of town. We'll do the incantation together. We're both at risk. If what Philip says is true, we could both be compromised."

Her words held little comfort. "No one sent an angel to watch over you."

A small, bitter laugh escaped her lips.

Startled, I turned to give her my full attention. "Bea?"

"Why do you think I put you in charge of the coven?"

"You had to. You were being consumed by black magic."

She closed her eyes and shook her head. "I had the opportunity to take the position back when you offered. It was my right and, to be honest, my duty. As powerful as you are, you have no business running a coven. You barely even know the proper way to conduct a smudging."

I said nothing. She was right. I'd spent my entire adult life shunning the magical community, not knowing I had power. Just recently, I'd been forced into embracing my witchy side. But I knew next to nothing and almost everything I attempted ended in disaster.

Bea studied her aging hands. "You see, Lailah works for me because she was sent to watch over my soul."

My gaze flickered between Lailah and Bea. Finally I focused Lailah. She hadn't done a very good job. A few weeks ago she'd almost killed Bea with poison. Lailah winced. I sent her an apologetic smile then eyed Philip. What kind of mess could I expect from him?

"Wait," Pyper said, breaking the silence. "Lailah is your guardian angel?"

Bea nodded.

"I thought she was assigned to Dan." My heart squeezed. Did that mean Dan was already lost? I stood, knocking the chair over with a loud crash to the floor. "Why didn't anyone tell me?"

Philip moved to stand beside me. "Guardian angels are usually kept secret."

"You didn't seem to have a problem telling everyone you're mine." I glared at him, frustrated I couldn't sense any of his emotions.

He shrugged. "They're in danger. They had a right to know."

One. Two. Three. I sucked in a breath and mentally finished counting to ten. It didn't help. Through clenched teeth, I asked, "And Dan? Is he...I mean, since he's gone, does that mean...?" I couldn't bring myself to say the words.

"He's still assigned to me," Lailah said with a huff of impatience. "I *am* capable of watching over more than one soul at a time. For the record, I've been assigned to Bea for about a year now. Long before Dan was put on my radar."

I gaped at them. "But why?"

Bea placed a reassuring hand over mine and squeezed. "Because you were coming, dear."

Chapter 10

Holy shit. What was I? Destruction central?

Well, so far, Lailah had been all but useless. I'd been the one to cure Bea when she'd compromised her life energy after banishing Roy to Hell. I'd also been the one to save her from Meri's black magic.

What had Lailah done besides expose Pyper to a demented ghost, get Kane kidnapped into Purgatory, and poison Bea? Some angel she was. Hopefully Philip didn't share her talent for fucking up.

Anger lashed out at me from across the room. I raised my eyes to Lailah's slanted gaze. *You're forgetting a few details*, she spat in my mind. *Like how without my help, Bea never would have been able to banish Roy, or how Kane would still be in Purgatory if I hadn't brought him back. You're far from perfect yourself, Jade.*

Shame seized me. I'd forgotten she could hear my thoughts. And she was right. She was hardly to blame for all the crazy we'd been subjected to. I took a deep breath. *I'm sorry. Bad day. I'm not thinking rationally.*

Obviously. She turned her gaze from mine, a twinge of despair seeping through her anger.

Shit. I was a terrible person.

"Jade." Bea gently laid her hand on my arm.

I eyed the fingers pressing into my wrist, only looking up when she said my name again.

"None of this is your fault," she continued.

Shaking my head, I clamped my mouth shut. I didn't want to argue with her, but it was clear if I hadn't moved to New Orleans, none of this would be happening.

But if you hadn't, your mother would still be missing. This time it wasn't Lailah intruding in my head. It was my own subconscious reminding me of at least one good thing that had come of all this.

My gaze traveled to Kane. Okay, two good things.

Bea shifted beside me. "White witches attract those who seek power. Considering your magical strength, it's not a surprise you'd be at the center of such chaos."

I gave Bea my full attention. "What about you? Why did Lailah only show up months before I appeared? You're plenty powerful."

Bea stifled a soft chuckle and cleared her throat. "I have lived a long life. Lailah isn't the first angel to appear on my doorstep."

"I'm not?" Lailah perched forward on the loveseat.

Bea gave her assistant a small smile. "Like I said, I've got a lot of years behind me."

Kane and Pyper were staring at Bea, no doubt just as curious as Lailah and I were about Bea's past. But now wasn't the time for memory lane.

"Okay. So I attract trouble. I guess I'd better get used to putting out fires." I sucked in a breath and steeled myself. "I need your help."

"I know." Bea eyed the delicate watch on her wrist and stood. "Ian should be ready for us now."

"Ian?" Pyper glanced around, nervous energy coming off her in microbursts. "He's here?"

Ian was Bea's nephew, a semi-professional ghost hunter and Pyper's current love interest. Last I'd heard, they'd been on a date or two. Since Dan had disappeared, I hadn't exactly kept up with all the details. Judging by the anxious crinkle of Pyper's eyes, maybe things weren't going as well as I'd thought.

Bea plucked her elegant, cream-colored leather purse from a side table and shook her head. "No. He's pulling some strings to get the crowds cleared from the circle."

I leaned forward in my chair. "Why?"

Bea pulled her front door open. "It's where we're going to test Philip's theory."

Kane moved to stand behind me and rested his hands on my shoulders. "You mean, to see if Jade's tainted with black magic?"

"Exactly." Bea took a few steps and called over her shoulder. "Hurry, now. We've only got a short window of time."

I don't even remember leaving Bea's house or climbing in Kane's car. Ten minutes later, I was sitting in a parking lot surrounded by yellow caution tape stamped with *production studios #13.*

"Someone's filming a movie?" I asked as Kane grabbed my hand and pulled me from the car.

"That's what it looks like."

Somehow we'd been admitted past the metal barriers holding back a small crowd. They held protest signs that read *Jesus hates magic* and chanted, "Banish the witches, remove the evil. Save the people of New Orleans."

I rolled my eyes. Goodwin had certainly reached his target audience this morning.

Three production trucks were lined up together, blocking the path leading to the circle. A couple of workers with headphones milled around with clipboards.

One of them, a woman wearing a Saints ball cap, scanned the parking lot and then waved us toward an RV sitting off to the side. "Hurry," she said. "You've got less than an hour."

"Wait!" Kat came running up behind us. "Ian called and said to meet here."

Damn Ian. I'd hoped to keep Kat out of whatever we were going to be doing today. Her love for Dan made her too volatile. Given the chance, Kat wouldn't hesitate to put herself on the front lines. Hell, it's what I planned to do, and she knew it. No way to make her go home now.

Her running shoes barely made a sound on the cracked pavement as she caught up to us. She'd dressed the part at least. Jeans, a long-sleeved T-shirt, and sensible shoes. I, on the other hand, hadn't taken the time to plan decent footwear. The platform wedges I'd slipped my feet into had been right next to my bed. I hoped I wouldn't have to do any running. My ankles would never survive.

Out of breath and red-faced, Kat fell in step with me as we followed Pyper and Kane. "That's twice you haven't called me," she huffed out.

"Sorry." Guilt formed a small ball in my stomach. "After we saw the newscast this morning, everything happened so fast. I didn't have any idea we'd end up here. Besides, Bea is only going to confirm or deny Philip's claim."

"Only." She stopped and turned serious eyes on me. "You think I don't know how scary this is for you? Don't even try to push me away like you usually do when crazy crap is going on. Because I'm having none of it." I opened my mouth to defend my actions, but she shook her head and slipped a hand through the crook of my arm. We started walking again. "Nothing you can say will change my mind, so don't bother. No matter what happens, I'll be here."

Her fierce determination kept me silent. I wanted more than anything to order Ian to take her home, but I knew none of them would leave. *I* wouldn't. Why would they? Friends. Can't force them to bend to your will. Well, I could…with the right spell. I shook my head and banished the thought.

"Did Kane hurt his leg?" Kat asked.

"No. I don't think so." I frowned, noticing a slight limp in his gait. "He said his thigh was stiff. Maybe he pulled a muscle."

"He should take one of Bea's healing herbs."

I let out a noncommittal grunt. I sort of felt the same way about enhanced healing herbs as I did about prescription drugs: only taken as a last resort.

Kane disappeared into the shadows of the old oak trees and a sudden familiar energy brushed my conscious. I clutched my chest, trying to stop the pounding of my heart. "Come on," I whispered to Kat as I tugged her into the canopy.

My focus narrowed on the dirt path cluttered with patches of grass. Her long legs quickly outpaced mine and she disappeared into the circle clearing. I stopped in my tracks, alone in the middle of the oaks.

Each person's energy was distinct, unique to them. If I knew someone well, I could sense the person anywhere.

Dan was with me in the trees.

I spun, lowering my barriers, trying to latch on to the fading thread I knew belonged to him.

"Dan?" I whispered into the shadows.

"Jade!" Kat called.

The sound of her voice broke my concentration, and Dan's energy fled. I ignored her, running through the small clump of trees. If Dan was within half a mile, I'd find him. I sent my awareness out, but Kat's worried impatience slammed into me.

Muttering a curse, I retraced my steps back in her direction, careful to keep an open eye. I sensed nothing but Kat and a faint trace of my friends already gathered near the circle. Had I imagined Dan's signature? It was possible, but somehow I didn't think so.

"What are you doing?" Kat asked when I stepped into her sightline.

"I thought I felt someone, but I could be wrong."

"Oh." Mild concern crossed her features. "They're waiting for you, but I'll take a look around."

I started to shake my head, not wanting her to wander around alone. Then I changed my mind. "Can you get Ian to help you? Two is better than one."

She nodded and disappeared back into the clearing. I opened my senses and sent out a probe, still searching for Dan. Barely a thread of energy materialized. Too faint to identify, the tenuous connection was suddenly cut off as Kat and Ian neared.

Deciding not to get Kat's hopes up, I stifled a sigh and said nothing. How could I have sensed Dan? I'd seen Meri take him to Hell with my own eyes. The whole damn coven had witnessed the scene. Even though Meri's power had been compromised later, he wouldn't have been able to escape Hell on his own. Could he? He *was* the son of an angel. Was he trying to reach me somehow? First the dreams and now this. Except I had no idea how to contact him. I made a note to ask Bea.

Kat returned with Ian at her side. His six foot, lean frame towered over her average height. He wore his signature all black jeans, T-shirt, and Converse shoes. Somehow that tiny bit of normalcy comforted me.

"Go." Kat gave me a gentle nudge. "There isn't much time. We'll do a search for any rubberneckers."

"Bea's ready for you." Ian patted my arm awkwardly and flashed me a tight smile, sympathy shining from his light blue eyes. "I'm sure everything will be fine."

Who could argue after that enthusiastic endorsement? I gave him a flat smile of my own and turned, finding Kane waiting for me at the edge of the tree line. His serious eyes and crinkled brow told me he'd been watching me.

"Ready?" he asked, snaking an arm around my waist.

"I think so." His solid form steadied me. "I noticed your limp. Leg still aching?"

"Yeah, I'll get a healing pill from Bea later before she slips one in my drink."

I laughed. Bea had been known to spell my tea every now and then when she thought I needed a boost. Since I usually stubbornly refused to take her pills, she improvised. What could I say? I didn't trust magic. Too often things went wrong. I was happy to wait out my particular ailments.

Kane didn't have my hang-ups. He'd willingly take whatever she gave him.

"In fact, if I keep hanging out with you, I'm probably going to need to stock up," he teased.

I mock-punched him in the arm. Still, I didn't argue. As Kat has been known to say, weird shit happened around me and healing herbs were just about as tame as one could get.

The wind shifted, bringing with it the stench of decaying river rot. The awful smell always reminded me of death. Of road kill left on the side of the road, baking in the sun after a thunderous rainstorm. I took shallow breaths, trying not to gag. Even Hell had to smell better than that.

"There you are," Bea called from the northern most position of the circle. "I need you to stand in the middle of the pentagram. And Kane, stand directly across from me in the southern position."

"Why?" I gripped Kane's arm and pressed close, as if to shield him from the answer.

"We can't use members of the coven because of what happened last time. They're too sensitive to magic. Kane, Pyper, and Kat are the best choices to complete the circle since they're who you're closest to."

"What about Philip?" I glanced around for my so-called guardian. "And Lailah? They didn't come?"

Bea shook her head. "They had council business. Besides, we don't need them for this. I've got it covered."

"It's fine." Kane gently pulled his arm from my death grip and took his place on the circle.

"Good. Pyper, you take the eastern point," Bea ordered as she picked up a black pillar candle.

I wanted to argue. I wanted to grab them both and tuck them away in Kane's house until this was over. Not that I didn't think they could take care of themselves. They'd both been victims of paranormal craziness in the not-so-distant past. If anything happened to either one of them, I wouldn't be able to function. Enough was enough.

But Kat and Ian reappeared before I managed to formulate a response. Kat shook her head, indicating they hadn't found anyone, then took the western position without being asked. Clearly they'd discussed the procedure while I'd been in the trees. She sent me a determined look, obviously bracing for the coming argument. I let out a long breath, knowing I'd lose this round.

Please, Goddess. Keep them safe. Do what you will with me, but protect them from the darkness.

"What's Ian doing?" I asked as I slowly dragged my feet to the center of the pentagram.

"I'm keeping watch in case anything goes awry." He held a small electronic device that looked suspiciously like one of his ghost-hunting EMF readers. A green light came on after he flicked a switch. He nodded and moved to stand next to Kane. "I'm ready."

I placed my hands on my hips and stared him down. "What are you doing?"

Ian fiddled with a knob on the black piece of equipment, and when no one answered me, he finally made eye contact. "Oh, you mean me. I told you, I'm keeping watch."

"No, Ian." I didn't bother to temper the impatience in my voice. He had a bad habit of studying every last odd occurrence that went down in my life. Even though his readings were sometimes useful, it didn't stop me from feeling like a lab rat. "What are you doing with that thing?"

A blush crept over his cheeks. "You never know when some readings might come in handy. Do you mind?"

The contrition in his voice, combined with the cloud of anxiousness clinging to him, pushed my irritation aside. Why was I so moody? This was what Ian did. I should expect it by now. Heck, I'd even asked him for help on more than one occasion. I waved a dismissive hand. "It's fine. I guess you just caught me off guard. Don't worry about it."

The slight tension in his shoulders eased. He nodded at Bea. "Better get started. The production crew can only cover us for twenty more minutes."

"No movie?" I asked.

Ian shook his head. "Not here. They're filming something uptown at the college. I called in a favor."

Shame washed over me for being irritated at him. My reaction to his reading was due more to my own issues with the paranormal. Ian was one of the good guys. I caught Pyper staring at me, her eyes narrowed accusingly. I sent her an apologetic smile and focused on Bea. "Let's get this over with."

"Face me," Bea said and held up her candle. "After I say the incantation, light this with your mind."

I nodded. "What is the goal of the spell? How can we tell if I'm tainted?"

"Don't worry. You'll know when you see it."

Standing in the middle of the pentagram, surrounded by my loved ones, I should've been nervous. This was the moment I'd find out if my soul was in danger.

Instead, I concentrated on the love filling my heart. These people were my family. Emotion welled in my chest. After years of trusting no one but Kat and Aunt Gwen, I never thought I'd be part of such a group. They'd be by my side no matter what.

Bea closed her eyes and held the candle straight out toward me. "From the points of north to south to east to west, let the glow of the candle represent the inner light. With the spark of flame, search for the hidden darkness."

Her eyes flew open, dark brown pools of intensity. Magic pulsed from her in tight, controlled waves. She held her power back, waiting for me. My spark rose from my chest and rushed through my limbs, pulsating at my fingertips.

I raised one hand and aimed for the black pillar. "Ignite."

The candle sprang to life, a perfect tapered flame glowing bright in the afternoon sun.

Small threads of apprehension bubbled from my friends surrounding me, but I couldn't tear my gaze away from the flame, now growing larger with each caress of the gentle breeze.

"Search now," Bea rasped, her voice husky and strong.

Tendrils of gray smoke rose from the mini-inferno and snaked its way around the circle. Kat shuddered as it passed through her. Pyper stood rooted to her spot, as if to ignore the intrusion. Kane's body trembled as it invaded him. And then the smoke shot straight at me.

Icy probing fingers pressed into my skin, reaching deep into my body. I writhed, blinded by the smoke, clutching my chest as something resembling an ice pick stabbed my heart. I cried out in terror, debilitating fire burning through my veins.

But no one heard me over the gut-wrenching scream coming from the east.

"Pyper," I called, stumbling in her direction. My skin warmed, erasing the icy pain, and the smoke vanished, giving me a clear view of Pyper's empty spot on the circle.

I spun, catching a glimpse of her hot-pink-streaked hair. She was on the ground, arms around Kane's shoulders. Black, translucent ropes had wrapped around his limbs, binding him to the earth.

"Kane?" My voice came out weak, useless.

"Jade." His eyes met mine just before he slumped backwards in Pyper's arms.

Chapter 11

Numb with horror, I stared at Kane and Pyper. I could tell by the exaggerated movement of her lips that she was yelling at me, but I was trapped in a cone of silence. The world stopped momentarily until Bea's words flashed in my mind. *You'll know when you see it.*

Somehow my feet managed to move. One step. Two. Then three. Pyper's terror broke through my protective walls. Noise rushed into my brain. I couldn't decipher any of it.

Kane's soul was in danger.

I fell to my knees beside him, hands stretched out. Darkness had threatened to take Kat once. I'd redirected the corrupted magic to myself then; I could do the same now. My power erupted from my fingertips, causing thin black threads to peel off the ropes binding Kane. They clung to my hands and crawled up my arms in an intricate net, weaving a tight pattern around my skin.

Invisible knives stabbed deep into my muscles. I focused my magical spark, welcoming the intrusion. I'd fight it one way or another.

Desperate to free Kane, I grabbed the ropes binding his wrists. A fiery ball of energy hit me in my chest the moment I touched them, knocking me back and breaking my hold on the tainted magic. No!

Frustration consumed me as my breath came in shallow gulps. I grasped clumps of rough grass, my hands twitching with the effort. "Kane?"

"He's fine," Bea said from somewhere nearby. Her face came into view and her auburn hair fell forward. "Sorry to hit you so hard with that spell, but anything less and I wouldn't have been able to free you both."

My vision swam. I blinked. Her calm words didn't hide the concern strumming through her. I propped myself up on my elbows and glanced over at Kane. He was sitting up, clutching his wounded leg, face white. I crawled to his side. "What happened?"

His dark, serious eyes met mine. He looked down and removed his hands from his leg. A blackened, singed hole in his jeans revealed a puncture in exactly the same spot Meri had stabbed him with a wooden stake when she'd taken him to Purgatory.

My mouth went dry. I tried to swallow and forced out, "I thought the wound had healed."

"It had."

Pyper whipped off her cotton blouse, leaving her in a skimpy camisole, and started tearing the hot pink shirt into strips. With deft hands, she quickly bandaged Kane's oozing wound and tied the ends into a neat bow.

"Nicely done, Pyper." Bea inspected her handiwork.

"What happened?" I asked again, this time getting to my feet.

"Not here." Ian scanned the clearing. "We've run out of time. The production company has to leave, and if Goodwin finds us here, we're going to end up in the middle of a media circus." He extended his hand to Kane.

Kane stared at it, and for a second I thought he'd refuse. But he grabbed on. Ian hauled him to his feet. I sighed in relief and moved to wrap an arm around his waist, supporting him as we walked.

He gritted his teeth each time he took another step. By the time we reached the oak trees, sweat beaded on his agony-riddled face.

"This is stupid," I muttered, pausing as I kicked my platform sandals off and tried not to think of any toe-hungry bugs that might be crawling around. I'd be damned if I let Kane suffer one more minute. Healing charms were my mother's specialty. I'd seen her do them a thousand times as a child. All I needed was a little earth magic. "Hold still," I told Kane.

He leaned against the nearest tree and let out a breath.

"That's good." I pressed my toes into the dirt and called my magic to the surface. My second sight slid into place, revealing his aura. The bright gold was marred only by the blackness pulsing around his wound.

Earth magic tickled the bottom of my feet. I embraced it, ignored Kane's flinch when I placed my hands over his thigh, and said, "Ancient oak, lend your healing strength. From your deep roots, I ask only what you can give. No more, no less. By the power of the earth, mother of goodness, I command thee."

Pure, clean magic rushed through my limbs and collected in my palms. With one touch, green-tinged white light fused with Pyper's pink dressing, glowing in the shadow of the oak. Slowly the light started to fade. When the charm winked out, the aura around Kane's wound faded from black to an unattractive shade of burnt orange.

"Any better?" I asked, hopeful.

He pushed away from the tree, tentatively taking a step. This time he didn't grimace. "Much."

He started off ahead of me. I studied the oak. Its newly wilted leaves blew sadly in the gentle breeze. I touched the trunk. "Thank you. Recover quickly."

After jamming my feet back into my shoes, I trotted the short distance to where Kane stood waiting for me.

"That was some impressive magic." He took my hand and kissed my palm before wrapping it in his.

I forced a smile. The wound wasn't cured. The burnt orange tinge was already growing darker. But I'd take what I could get...for now.

I sat on Bea's sunflower-print couch, Kane's head in my lap, as Pyper tended to his wound. She'd split his pant leg open and was just about ready to disinfect it with hydrogen peroxide.

"You might want to grab hold of something," Pyper said.

Kane's hand tightened around mine.

"Not a good idea. I don't think my poor bones stand a chance against your grip." I gently pulled my hand from his and offered the thick coven manual I'd been flipping through.

Ian snatched the book first and passed it to Bea. I glared at him.

"What? She needs to find a spell," he said.

Bea had insisted we meet back at her house. Then she'd driven like a retired stock car racer, running red lights and cutting people off. Now she was frantically searching for an incantation—for what, I had no idea. She wouldn't say.

Ian handed Kane a throw pillow.

Kane stared at it then shook his head. "I'll be fine."

"Suit yourself." Ian retreated and stood near Kat, who was pacing a small circle in front of the stairs to the second floor.

I smoothed Kane's hair back from his temple, trying to distract him. His leg had started to throb only moments after he'd settled into the passenger's seat of his car. Maybe I could summon a numbing charm. Too bad I needed the spell book for that. I sighed. "Bea, isn't there anything we can do for him right now?"

Before she could respond, Pyper poured the disinfectant over Kane's wound. His whole body tensed as he bit back a groan.

"Ice," Bea said.

I tried to shimmy out from under Kane's head, but he'd gone rigid, pressing into the sofa and my thigh. "Ian? Ice?"

He nodded and disappeared into the kitchen.

"Found it!" Bea hurried over to the couch, holding the spell book open. "Pyper, can I take your spot?"

Pyper glanced at Kane's wound, patted around the edges with a clean towel, and stepped back. "Can I bandage him first?"

"We'll take care of that in a second. Right after I spin the containment spell." Bea set the book on her wooden coffee table and pushed up her sleeves.

"Why didn't my healing charm work? Did I do something wrong?" I shifted slightly, worried I'd made matters worse.

"The charm did its job. The problem is with the black magic. It grows like cancer. No ordinary healing charm can do anything but create temporary relief."

"Cancer?" Pyper breathed.

Bea patted her arm. "It was just an example to help you understand what we're dealing with. The containment charm will keep the curse localized until a more permanent solution can be reached."

"And what would that be?" Kane asked, pushing himself up into a sitting position. He twisted and rested his foot on the coffee table.

"We'll have to find one." She turned to me. "Jade, your power is a distraction. Can you join Kat near the stairs?"

My protective instincts kicked in. The last thing I wanted to do was leave Kane. But I trusted Bea. She'd never failed me before. With no small amount of trepidation, I did as she asked.

Kat clutched my hand and whispered, "Where's Philip?"

"I don't know," I said absently, not caring in the least.

A mixed ball of her frustration and anxiety pounded on me from all sides. Immediately I raised my glass silo barrier, blocking her out. I was too drained to worry about her mental state at the moment.

She tugged on my arm. "He was wrong."

"Huh?" I kept a close eye on Bea as she waved a crudely wrapped smudge stick over Kane's leg and murmured a chant I couldn't hear.

"He said you were compromised with black magic, but it's Kane. Not you."

Pyper turned and stared at Kat then fixed her gaze on me.

"No, he's not," I argued. That was impossible. Utterly unthinkable. "Didn't you notice the web that tried to attack me when I was at Kane's side? It just got sidetracked on its way to me."

Kat stood with her back straight, shoulders squared, and shook her head slowly. "The smoke made it to you and rebounded to Kane. Don't you understand? It's that wound Meri gave him. She scarred him. With black magic."

I shifted back, bumped into the bottom step, and lost my balance. Pain screamed from my tailbone as I landed on the stairs. Tears burned the back of my eyes, and one fell before I managed to blink them back. "Damn, that hurt," I said, trying to cover my emotions.

She was right. Kane needed help. Angel-type help. I grabbed my iPhone and sent Lailah a text: *Urgent. Get to Bea's now. Hurry.* Our mental connection only seemed to work when we were physically near each other.

To the left, a ball of mist materialized from the unlit smudge stick Bea still held. It trailed the path of Bea's hand and, with a flick of her wrist, shot to the hole in Kane's thigh. From my spot on the stairs, I couldn't see what happened, but the misery eased from Kane's face. He sagged into the couch, relief apparent in his posture.

Bea leaned over and traced a finger over Kane's leg. "Can you feel that?"

He shook his head, staring at his leg. I stood, craning my neck for a better view.

"How about this?" She pressed her fingertips right above his kneecap.

"No."

She frowned. "I may have given the spell a little too much juice." She moved her hand to his calf and pinched.

He jumped and shifted his leg out of her grasp. "Stop, that tickles."

She chuckled, and my shoulders sagged in relief. Thank the Goddess.

I moved and sat next to Kane. He wrapped an arm around my shoulder, pulling me close. I pressed my cheek against his chest and held on.

A second later, he planted a kiss on the top of my head. "Thank you," he whispered.

I pulled back. "For what?"

"The healing charm. I know you don't like using magic if you don't have to."

I waved an impatient hand. "It's nothing. You know I'd do just about anything—"

"It *was* something," Bea interjected. "Impressive, even. You took an amazing amount of energy from that oak. Enough you should've killed it."

"But—"

This time she raised a hand. "But you didn't. You exercised a control I've not seen in you before. It was a perfect piece of magic."

"Then why didn't it work?" I chewed on my lip.

"It did." Bea shifted, blocking Pyper and Kat from my view. "But Meri stole your magic from him."

I froze, heart pounding. "You mean...?"

"Meri's found a way to regain her strength."

"From Kane," I said.

"*Through* Kane," she corrected. Her intense amber-flecked eyes softened as something close to pity brushed my psyche. "And you're her source."

Chapter 12

I pulled away from Kane, trying to distance myself from him. His arms tightened around me, but I ducked out from under his grasp.

Frustration swirled around him as he stiffened. "Jade—"

I shook my head, cutting him off. My stomach clenched with fear.

Meri was hurting him and getting stronger because of me.

"How is that possible?" Kat asked Bea, face pinched in confusion. "I thought Meri was weakened when Jade banished her back to Hell."

"It's the wound," I said. "She marked Kane when she took him and Lailah. She has a connection to him." I met Bea's eyes. "And because Kane and I are so close, it's a connection to me too, right?"

"Yes." Bea handed me the spell book. "Take it. Study. Learn all you can. You're going to need it."

The weight of the book settled in my hands, heavier than I'd remembered. I got to my feet and moved toward the front door.

"Where are you going?" Kane asked in a low voice. Tension strummed off him, brushing against my skin.

I longed to reconnect with him, send him some calming strength. Instead I opened the door. There was only one thing to do. "I need to find Philip."

Before I could talk myself out of it, I ran outside. I didn't look back, but I sensed Kane following me. His frustration reached me as I ran down Bea's driveway toward the wrought iron gate.

I had to put distance between us. The stronger Meri got, the more pain he'd endure and the more danger Dan would be in. I couldn't risk it.

I rounded the corner and spotted the streetcar. No way was I going to catch it while wearing my platforms. I kicked them off, scooped them up with my free hand, and sprinted, jumping on at the last second before it rolled down Saint Charles.

Glancing back, my eyes locked with Kane's. His frustrated expression turned to one of sad understanding as the car rumbled down the avenue. All too quickly, he disappeared from my view.

I shuffled to a seat in the very back, stuffed the book in my purse, and then closed my eyes.

Kane. I was poison to him.

I shook my head, banishing the thought. Phone. I needed my phone. With shaking fingers, I scrolled through my contacts and landed on Lailah's number.

"Where are you?" she asked after only the first ring.

"Kane already called you?"

"Kat did. They're worried."

They should be. I was. "I'm headed to your house. Philip's there, right?"

"No, but I know where he is."

"I thought he was bound to you? What about that charmed silver?"

She let out a long breath. "He's here to watch over you. I did that because I was mad he didn't tell me he was in town. I took it off him last night."

Her halting tone told me there was something more personal going on, but I let it go. "Oh. All right. Where can I find him?"

"Meet me on the riverfront in twenty minutes, in front of Jackson Square."

"He's at the rally?" Son of a… The last thing I needed right now was a giant crowd. My emotions were running rampant. I'd never be able to function properly with a riled-up mob of people.

"Yes. He's doing damage control. But after that, I have no idea where he'll be, so if you want to catch him, this is your best shot."

I groaned. "Fine. See you soon."

She hung up without saying goodbye. I sent Kane a text, letting him know I was okay and that I'd call him later. Talking to him right now would be too hard.

Once again strapped in my platforms, I hopped off the streetcar on Canal Street and walked the four blocks to the waterfront. A horn blared, indicating the ferry's departure on its return trip to Algiers Point. I longed to be lounging against the rail, headed for the quiet neighborhood across the river. Instead, I climbed the steps to the riverwalk and moved toward Jackson Square.

Only a few tourists strolled along the famed Mississippi. I sighed in relief and quickened my steps. But as I neared the rally, a swell of hate pricked my skin. I dug my nails into my arms, struggling not to scrape them over my irritated flesh.

Damn evangelist. I forced myself to keep putting one foot in front of the other and didn't stop until I reached the wrought iron railing directly in front of Jackson Square and the Saint Louis cathedral. Sickening rage and judgment filled the air.

In the center of it all, Jonathon—an angel—stood watching. And he thought *I* was evil?

I let the poison batter against me. Took my time experiencing their inner turmoil. Darkness filled me. My heart ached, and I had trouble breathing. Gasping for air, I pushed the toxic emotions from me. My glass silo snapped in place and my mind went numb.

"That was dumb," Lailah said from behind me.

I didn't bother to turn around. "It helps to understand who you're fighting."

She joined me at the rail and waved a hand at the mass of people below. "You're planning to spend energy on this?"

I turned to meet her bright blue eyes. "Goodwin needs to be stopped. How can you, of all people, tolerate this?"

She frowned. "It's not my place."

For once, I couldn't hear her thoughts in my head. I didn't know if it was because I had my barriers up or if she was blocking them from me. I was both relieved and annoyed. The one time I actually wanted to know what was going on in that head of hers, and I was blocked. "He's spreading hate."

Her face hardened and her eyes narrowed. "Look, Jade, just drop it, okay? We don't have time for this. You, Dan, and Kane are in serious trouble." She stared past me and jerked her head toward something behind me. "There's Philip."

I spun. My soul guardian was striding away down the stairs in the direction of the French Quarter. I grabbed Lailah's hand. "Let's go."

My glass silo disappeared and all the righteous excitement crawled over my skin. But that wasn't what stopped me in my tracks.

Lailah tugged on my hand. "Come on. What are you waiting for?"

I tightened my grip, holding on as her fear flooded my awareness. "What is it? What are you so afraid of?"

"Not now!" she cried and tore away from my grasp. "I'm going after Philip. You can do whatever you want." She ran, weaving in and out of the swelling crowd.

"Shit," I mumbled and followed. Why in the world hadn't I worn more sensible shoes? The uneven bricked sidewalk threatened to turn my ankles with each step.

Don't think about it. Eyes trained on Lailah, I kept her blond head in my sights and tried my best to not barrel anyone down. I followed her across Decatur, and I'd just passed into the gates of Jackson Square Park when someone grabbed my shoulder.

"Where's the fire?" the man slurred.

His stale beer breath made my stomach turn. I stepped back. "Excuse me. I need to catch up with my friend."

"I'm sure she'll wait. Reverend Goodwin is just getting started." He casually draped an arm around me as he tried to guide me toward the corner of the park. "Come have a drink with me and my buddies."

Buried anger boiled in my chest as I twisted away. "I said no."

"I don't remember asking." He laughed. "Why else does a pretty girl like you come to New Orleans? We'll show you a good time, sugar."

Another man, tall and thin with a low ponytail and yellow teeth, flanked my other side. "Don't worry, one shot of Uncle D's moonshine and you won't even remember me putting my tongue down your throat."

Gag.

I stepped back, but the pair had me surrounded. I glanced over my shoulder, not finding Lailah or Philip anywhere. Son of a… There was only one thing I could think to do. My fingers started to tingle, and I reached out, zapping their wrists. Magic burst from my fingers in an electric jolt. Beer Breath cried out as he tumbled backwards, while Yellow Teeth grunted.

"What the fuck?" Yellow Teeth snarled, and then his eyes widened. "You're a damn witch."

"What?" Beer Breath exclaimed from his spot on the grass.

I took off as the pair stumbled after me, yelling at the top of their lungs. "Witch! Get her!"

The crowd parted for me as I ran. They stared with confused eyes, either not hearing or not comprehending my attackers' accusations.

"Stop her," Beer Breath managed to gasp out.

No one did. Thank the Goddess.

Then somehow, someone on stage got wind of our pursuit, and over the loud speaker, Goodwin's voice boomed. "Good people of New Orleans, it appears one of the offenders is here in the park. Please join me in a prayer."

I ducked behind a bush as a chorus of boos rose, drowning him out. A few shouted obscenities, but when a small group started chanting, "Burn the witch," my hands started to shake.

I had power, but if the crowd turned into an angry mob, I couldn't take them all.

"Quiet now. Shh," Goodwin continued. "Violence isn't the answer. Always remember, hate the sin, not the sinner," he added with no small amount of charm.

That smooth voice and all the righteous bullshit he spewed made me want to throw a magic ball right at his perfect face. Who was he to judge?

Damn angel.

"But forgiveness does not equal a free pass. We must help this poor soul."

Cheers rose, and Goodwin's smile brightened.

"I have a mission for you, my loyal followers. A contest, if you will. All you need to do is find the witch and bring her to me unharmed, and you'll be rewarded on my next program as an honored guest."

The supporters collectively lost their minds. Fist pumps and cheers rippled through the park. I rose from my crouch, deciding hiding would only make me look guilty.

Goodwin's eyes met mine.

We held each other's gazes just long enough for him to wink. Then he turned to someone on the stage and acted as if he'd never seen me. The bastard had used me as a pawn to rile his troops.

With Lailah and Philip long gone, I turned my back and headed toward a different exit. I didn't get ten yards when a large, squat woman stepped in front of me, blocking my path.

"I know who you are," she said.

Magic coiled in my chest. I couldn't take everyone, but I'd go down trying. "I'm sorry. I'm in a hurry, would you excuse me?"

"People are waiting for you that way. Your best bet is to leave from behind the stage." She pointed a stubby finger. "Go. I'll hold them off as long as possible."

I peeked behind her. Sure enough, Beer Breath and Yellow Teeth were scanning the crowd. When had they gotten past me? Probably while I'd been distracted by Goodwin's speech. With no other options, I gave the lady a grateful smile and thanked her, then took off for the stage.

Great. It was the last place I should be. My butt started vibrating, making me jump. The phone. I didn't take time to answer it, just kept moving.

The people in front were even more rabid than the ones milling around in the back. That was good though; they all kept their gazes fixed on Goodwin, nodding and shouting out *amen* every other second. I couldn't decide if I wanted to vomit or bash some skulls.

"We'll take back the city," Goodwin promised the crowd. "Purge the streets of Wiccans, drug dealers, and thieves."

Wiccans. Idiot. Talk about religious persecution. I longed for a magical duel with the angel in question. What I wouldn't do to hit him with a powerful indigestion spell. No-good, self-important troublemaker.

I abandoned my mental insults when I spotted the entrance to backstage. Right behind the bouncers was an opening clearly marked Exit. I had to get to that doorway.

Except the large, squat woman came up behind me and stopped me in my tracks when she whispered, "Wait."

"Why?"

She grinned and pulled out a microphone. "I've got the witch."

A sinking realization washed over me. Shit! I'd been played. I spun, heading for that open gate, but a man strongly resembling the woman stepped in my path. My only option was to show the world my power by zapping them, or—

An ominous rumble vibrated across the sky, bringing with it the darkest rain cloud I'd ever seen. The sun vanished and in the space of maybe ten seconds, the skies opened, sending fat, pounding rain over the city.

Philip appeared at my side out of nowhere. "Move," he ordered. "Now."

Chapter 13

"Did you cause that?" I asked as Philip dragged me down Saint Peters Street. Rain soaked through my cotton shirt, making gooseflesh pop out over my skin.

"No. Jonathon did."

I wrapped my arms around myself, trying to keep warm. "Why? Is this his idea of a sick joke?"

Philip stopped under a balcony. "He had to do something before the crowd tore you apart."

"It's his fault they were after me in the first place," I cried.

He stared down at me, impatience clinging to his wet body. "No. It's yours. You went into a volatile crowd and used your magic. He did his best to keep you safe. Why do you think he asked them to bring you to him?"

"So he could pray for me? Make me an example? How should I know?"

Philip took a step forward and shook his head. "Pay attention, Jade. Jonathon is interested in people leading moral lives. Fire and brimstone are his methods of influence. He has no desire for anyone to get hurt. Especially not you. The only reason he called you out is because you were in danger. You might not like his approach, you might even loathe it, but this was your fault. You had no business showing up at that rally."

I glared, teeth chattering. I didn't give a flying shit what Philip said. Jonathon was fostering violence. "He did this. He went on television and basically said witches are evil. His words make people distrust each other. Why me? Why now? All I did was ask for help."

"You were the perfect catalyst for his cause." Philip took off down the street again.

I followed. "And that is…what? Burning witches at the stake?" I ducked under another balcony and pressed against the wall to escape the pounding rain.

He paused. "Mobilizing the masses. Creating press. Keeping the donations rolling in. He's nothing without a platform."

"Oh, he's something, all right."

Philip gave a noncommittal shrug and we walked on in silence.

We crossed Bourbon Street, moving deeper into the residential area, and I finally asked, "Where are we going?"

"Lailah's."

Relief mixed with trepidation. If I went anywhere else, Kane was likely to show up. Of course, nothing was stopping him from looking for me at Lailah's. He did know where she lived, after all. But he probably wouldn't guess I'd be there.

I hated that I was hiding. Hated that I couldn't be near him, touch him, and most of all, that my presence actually caused him to suffer. I had to stay away. It would just be too hard to see him, knowing we couldn't be together. Not while Meri could get to me through him, anyway.

I'd never been inside Lailah's house before. The pale pink, single shotgun Victorian had a small front porch and a two-person swing, painted turquoise with white daisies. A pair of bright pink flip-flops and a yellow mug that said *Shoes are a girl's secret to happiness* had been left on the porch.

"Are you sure this is the right place?" I pushed my sopping hair out of my eyes and scowled as a trickle of water dripped down my back.

Her place seemed so girly. And not at all what I'd expected.

Philip nodded, and the door swung open. Lailah filled the entry, holding two giant, hot pink bath towels. Since when had she taken a shine to so much color? In contrast, she wore a faded green peasant skirt and a black tank top.

"Here." She handed us the towels and shooed us in the door. "Some of them might be following you."

I glanced back at the fat raindrops and darkened streets. Not likely. I wrapped the plush towel around my shoulders and kicked off my shoes, leaving them on the porch.

The vibrant colors of the living room assaulted my vision, and I almost stepped back outside. A bright red couch covered in multi-colored floral pillows sat against the wall. On either side, two end tables had been painted with distorted faces and psychedelic flowers. And to top it off, a hot pink shag rug covered her oak floors. A sense of déjà vu settled over me. It dawned on me I'd been there once before in Lailah's memory.

The place was much brighter in person. I struggled to keep from shielding my eyes. How could anyone think in such a room?

"Follow me," she said and led us to the back of the house.

We passed through a door into a soothing bedroom, done in white and mint green. If it were possible for my eyes to sigh in relief, they would have.

The kitchen, to my surprise, was pure elegance, with its black painted wood floors and gorgeous white cabinetry. Fresh red lilies sat in the middle of her black and white checkerboard table. It was beautiful, but I couldn't shake the feeling we'd just walked through some version of a funhouse. I eyed Lailah, trying to decide if her decorating indicated some sort of manic disorder.

"How are you going to work this?" Lailah asked.

"Huh?" I tore my gaze from the lilies and watched her fill an old-fashioned teapot.

Philip searched her cupboards for mugs, appearing very much at ease in her home. I narrowed my eyes and studied them. A slight brush of an arm as Lailah moved past him.

No subtle adjustments for personal space. Brief moments of unshielded eye contact.

Lailah had something going with Philip.

Stop, Jade, Lailah scolded in my head. *It's none of your business.*

What about your mate? I accused.

That's definitely *none of your business. Drop it.* She turned to Philip. "Sooner's better than later."

"True." Philip placed a tea bag in each cup. "But she isn't ready. If we send her unprepared, we'll lose both of them."

I waved a hand from my position at the table. "Excuse me. What are we talking about?"

They both ignored me.

"What will happen to Kane?" Lailah picked up the teapot and filled the matching red cups with steaming hot water.

Philip closed his eyes for a moment and took a deep breath. "He'll be tied to her forever unless Jade succeeds."

Lailah placed one of her delicate hands on Philip's forearm. A trickle of pity and compassion radiated from her. "I'm so sorry."

He shook his head. "It's for the best. It should have happened years ago."

"It's not your fault. No one expected you to be the one to do it."

I stood. "Do what?"

They both turned, expressions surprised, as if they'd just realized I was still in the room.

Philip spoke first. "Annihilate Meri. It's the only way you'll stop her from destroying you and Kane." He moved to stand next to me and placed a gentle hand on my shoulder. "Even if you keep your distance from Kane, eventually her poison will spread and…he won't survive."

Fear squeezed my heart. Kane was in serious trouble. I'd known it, obviously. But I hadn't let myself consider the consequences. He could die. The image of Kane, cold and lifeless, flashed through my mind. Terror rippled through me.

I clenched my fists and straightened my spine. No way was I letting the evil spawn take Kane from me. "How long does he have?"

Philip frowned. "It's hard to say. Keeping your distance from him helps, but now that the wound is festering, you probably have less than a week."

"Are you saying I have to go—" I swallowed "—to Hell?"

"Yes." His voice turned low, full of regret.

Meri had said Philip didn't come after her. I couldn't help but wonder why. Hadn't he loved her enough? Were there other factors beyond his control? Whatever happened, I wouldn't let his mistakes stop me. Not if it meant losing Kane.

"She's going to need help," Lailah said gently.

"I know." Philip paced the tiny kitchen. "This time I have no choice."

He stood with his back to us, hands on the counter. I glanced at Lailah. "What's he talking about?"

She shook her head, indicating now wasn't the best time for questions.

Philip turned around with hardened eyes. "I'll have to send you to Meri—to Hell— and help you destroy her."

I sat in Lailah's color-overload living room, staring at my iPhone. I'd envisioned performing some sort of spell to bring Dan back from Hell. And while I'd considered it a possibility that I might have to navigate the gates of the underworld, I hadn't truly believed it was an option.

Now, after Philip's explanation, I realized it was my only option. If I didn't go in and find Meri, Kane would slowly lose his soul. If I tried to summon her, she'd siphon all my strength straight through him.

The phone vibrated. Another text from Kane: *Where are you?*

I'd sent him a text earlier letting him know I was safe but hadn't relayed any other information. The phone buzzed again.

This time it was Pyper: *Put him out of his misery and call him already.*

I typed back, *Soon.*

It wasn't that I wanted to avoid him. On the contrary, I longed to curl up in his arms. I just didn't know what to say. There was no way he was going to be okay with me sacrificing myself for him. And there was no way I wasn't going to do it.

I hit contacts and pressed call.

"We're ready. Say the word and we'll be on our way," Gwen said over the line.

"I need…Mom." I swallowed back a sob of emotion.

"I'll put her on the phone—"

"No." I struggled to keep my breathing normal. "Just get her here."

"You got it, sweetheart. We'll be on the next flight out."

I hadn't wanted to ask my mother to come. She needed time to recover from her twelve long years of being stuck in Purgatory. She had all the signs of Post-Traumatic Stress Disorder. Making her relive her experience could cause all kinds of awful consequences to her mental health, but she had information none of the rest of us did. A virtual roadmap of Hell.

Lailah appeared, holding a violet blanket and matching pillow. Did the woman have anything in a neutral color other than clothes? "Here," she said. "Philip and I will be in my room if you need us."

I raised an eyebrow. *Sharing a bed?*

She ignored my mental question. "There's a new toothbrush in the bathroom, and I laid out some pajamas for you to borrow." She retreated toward her room.

"Did you know Philip is Dan's father?"

With her back to me, she paused in her doorway. "Does it matter?"

"Not really."

She glanced over her shoulder. "Yes, I knew."

My chest tightened with irritation. "Did it ever occur to you that might make him more susceptible to Meri's magic?"

Her lips pressed into a thin line as she clutched the door frame, knuckles white. "How was I supposed to know Meri was Philip's mate? Or even that both of us were being controlled by her? Don't you think I'd have done something different if I'd known?"

Meri had managed to possess Dan through a portrait her soul had been trapped in. Using Dan's energy, she found a way to eventually control Lailah, as well.

"One would think so," I said.

She winced when my tone came out colder than I'd meant it to.

I bit the side of my cheek. "Sorry."

"Whatever. Good night."

"Wait." There was something else I had to know. "Have you been in touch with Philip this whole time?"

She shook her head. "No one ever knows how to find Philip unless he wants them to." The door shut silently behind her, leaving me alone in the living room.

I sagged against the velvet couch and closed my eyes. I didn't mean to be so short with Lailah. I couldn't help myself. The mind-reading, her soul guardianship over Dan, and her history with Kane grated on my last nerve. She was too close to me and the people I loved. Somehow, I had to move past my possessive tendencies. We all needed as much help as we could get.

Pulling my feet up under the blanket, I wrapped it around myself and then grabbed my phone once more. I tapped Kane's name and typed, *Meet me in my dreams.*

I didn't wait for a response. He'd find me. He always did.

The couch was surprisingly comfortable and, despite the stress of the day, or perhaps because of it, I instantly fell into a deep sleep.

Sunflowers. Everywhere. The moonlight shone down on a cloudless night, highlighting the sleeping blooms. Movement rustled the stalks behind me. I spun and smiled when I spotted Dan, his eyes alight with mischief and lips turned up in a goofy smile.

He held his hand out. I moved forward to take it. Just as our hands joined, he tugged me to him and locked his right leg behind mine, tumbling us both to the ground. We landed with him lying on top of me, his lips inches from mine.

"Hello," I said, breathless.

His grin widened. "Sorry about that."

I laughed. "No, you aren't."

His expression turned serious and the grin vanished as something primal stirred in his eyes. His voice came out deep and husky. "You're right."

My eighteen-year-old heart sped up, thumping rapidly, and I stopped breathing. The sunflowers swayed back and forth in the light summer breeze, casting long shadows over us. Even if anyone came looking, they wouldn't find us. Not at that hour.

I stared at Dan's lips and licked my own. "Dan?"

"Yeah?" He shifted, easing his weight off me as he laid on his side, still staring down at me.

"Kiss me."

He brought his hand up, softly caressing my cheek. I rested my hand over his and gazed up at him with lovesick adoration.

His emotions mirrored the ones swelling through me and when he dipped his head, lips brushing mine, a tiny tear of happiness fell down my temple.

Everything shifted and suddenly I was standing in front of Kane's house, alone, staring at his front door. The same large moon hung in the sky, but I was no longer the young eighteen-year-old I'd been moments before. I waited a few beats for the lingering teenage emotions to fade away.

Kane. The man I loved was inside. Loved. With all my heart. Dan was in the past and had been for some time.

I took the steps and the door swung open to darkness. I poked my head in. "Kane?"

He sat on his overstuffed coffee-colored loveseat, sipping from a mug. "Sorry to interrupt."

Ah, crap. I'd been dreaming of Dan. Again. But not just any dreams. This time they were memories. Right down to the last detail. But why? Was it because I was so focused on finding him? Maybe I was slipping into his dreams? No, that was impossible. Neither Dan nor I was a dreamwalker. That was Kane's specialty. "Sorry. I don't know why he keeps showing up in my subconscious."

He set the mug down. "The mind is a powerful thing."

"True enough." I stepped into his house and shut the door behind me. I moved to take the seat beside him, but thought better of it and perched on the edge of his couch. "How's your leg?"

I eyed his thigh, but I couldn't see anything through his dark denim jeans. It wouldn't have mattered. This was a dreamwalk. Kane had the power to alter any damage and probably had.

"I took a few painkillers. It didn't help." He glanced down and then met my eyes. "Is there something you want to tell me?"

Righteous indignation shot through me. "I told you it was just a dream. I can't be expected to control those, can I? Dreamwalking is your thing, not mine."

"Jade," he said with no small amount of impatience. "I meant about today. About why you took off without even talking to me? Or why you ended up almost caught in Goodwin's media frenzy? And why you're at Lailah's house instead of your own...or mine?"

I stared at my hands clutched in my lap. "I'm not sure being here with you in a dreamwalk is safe."

His tone softened. "Safe from who? You or Meri?"

"Both," I whispered and met his concerned gaze. "I'm the one she's drawing power from. You're the catalyst. Don't you understand? The longer I stay away from you, the safer you'll be." Tears started to flow, unchecked down my face. "I've lost so many people in my life. I can't stand to lose you."

Kane moved to my side and wrapped his arms around me. "Don't think for one moment I'm going to let you fight this alone."

I choked back my tears and tried to pull away, but he only held on tighter. With my face buried in his shirt, I said, "I'm sorry. I shouldn't have run like that. But Kane—" I tilted my head up, "—in order to destroy her, I have to go to Hell. You can't follow me there. With her mark on your leg, it's too dangerous."

"Fuck that." He kissed me, lips urgent and demanding.

My hands gripped his arms and I held on, desperate for this last moment together. It didn't matter what I said. He'd find a way into Hell. He had all the connections I did, and worse, if he found a way to summon Meri, she'd take him. No, I'd have to go on my own. Soon.

He broke the kiss. "Promise me we'll work out a plan, together."

I bit my lip, not wanting to lie to him. But then I nodded anyway.

"Good. Because I'm not losing you, either. Remember that."

Chapter 14

"Hey, shortcake," my mom's voice filtered in through my sleep-filled haze.

"Hmm," I murmured, but didn't move.

A hand stroked my tangled mane. "Wake up, sweetheart."

I blinked, squinting in the morning light. More shocking pink and red tones startled me awake. I sat up in one quick motion. My walls weren't red. Where the hell was I?

Then I focused and my gaze landed on my mother, sitting on the brightly painted coffee table next to Lailah's red couch. I threw my arms around her and hugged tight. "You're here."

"Of course we are. You called. We came."

Over her shoulder, I spotted Gwen standing near Lailah's front door. She gave me a smile and waved a hand, indicating we'd connect a little later. A twinge of guilt sliced my gut. Gwen had been my parental figure for the last twelve years. I pushed the feeling aside, enjoying the moment with my mother.

Lailah appeared, holding a tray loaded with a carafe, bright pink coffee mugs, and something that looked suspiciously like beignets. "Good morning, Jade. Did you sleep all right?"

Her smirk told me she knew damn well Kane had dream-walked me. I pretended I didn't notice. "Fine. Thank you."

"Philip's in the shower. After he's dressed, we can work on a plan of action."

I rubbed my eyes and stifled a yawn. "Okay."

She disappeared back through her bedroom door, closing it behind her. Just how close were those two angels? Obviously close enough to share a bed. I couldn't help but wonder how Goodwin, her supposed mate, factored in.

Gwen sat beside me and gave me a one-armed hug.

Warmth filled my heart, and I smiled. "Did you two hijack a plane or something? How did you manage to get here so soon?"

"Your mother worked a little magic." Gwen grabbed one of the small plates with a beignet and nibbled on a corner of the powder-sugar covered donut.

"As in, cast a spell?" I asked, impressed. "How does that work?"

Mom shrugged. "I gave the airline a nudge to find us seats on the red eye. It was nothing."

"It wasn't nothing," Gwen said after she swallowed. "'Impressive' is the word I'd use."

Mom fidgeted and shifted uncomfortably. Her unease brushed my skin momentarily before she raised her emotional barriers.

I couldn't understand why the topic of her using a spell made her uncomfortable, but her reluctance was obvious. I let it go. They were here, and that's all I wanted. I held one hand out to my mother and the other to Gwen, holding on tight to both of them. Mom shifted forward and sat on the couch next to me.

"I need help," I said.

"Anything. You know that." Gwen patted the back of my hand.

"With what, shortcake?" Mom hedged as if she knew what was coming.

I took a deep breath, not sure I had the nerve to say the words. They stared at me, Mom's jade green eyes troubled and Gwen's hazel ones curious, but wary. The words flew from my mouth. "I need information on Hell. Specifically, the easiest way to get in."

"What?" Gwen cried. "No. No way. We'll work a summoning spell to get Dan back."

Mom drew her hand back and regarded me with hooded eyes.

"Can you help?" I asked her.

"No." Gwen jumped off the couch. "She can't help. Even if she could, I forbid it." She clenched her hands into tight fists at her sides. "You hear me, Jade? I forbid it."

I slumped back into the couch, not able to summon the energy to argue.

"Gwen," Mom said quietly. "Can you give us a minute?"

My aunt turned to my mother, eyes wide and her mouth half-open. "You want me to leave?"

My gaze traveled between the pair. Gwen, with her gray hair and shocked eyes, appeared very much the mother figure, whereas Mom didn't look a day over thirty. Still, in that moment, she exuded authority.

"Yes, I need a moment with Jade," Mom said, her voice firm.

Gwen struggled to keep her heartache hidden. She failed. We were too close for me to not notice. I wanted to hug her, tell her to stay, demand she be kept in the loop, but something about Mom's steely demeanor silenced me.

With a reluctant glance in my direction, Gwen stepped out the front door. I imagined her sitting on the turquoise swing, silently battling her frustration.

Mom paced over the shag carpet as if collecting her thoughts. Then she stopped abruptly, her feet spread, hands on her hips. "Is he worth it?"

"Excuse me?"

She took a step closer and peered at me through hardened eyes. "Is he worth risking your life? Getting into Hell is easy. It's the getting-out part that's a problem. I'm asking if he's worth losing everything. Think about what you're giving up. Your aunt, your friends…and me." She stepped back. Her features softened as she dropped her defenses, letting me experience the regret and longing swirling in her. "It's been twelve years, Jade."

I stood, suddenly filled with anger. Who was she to ask me such a question? She'd performed blood magic for some stranger and ended up leaving me all alone when Meri had taken her to the Underworld. I'd been just a few weeks from turning fifteen years old and my life had changed forever. "Yes, he's worth it. Both of them are."

"Both?"

"You're unbelievable." God, she didn't even know about Kane's wound yet. Which meant she hadn't been asking if I was willing to sacrifice myself for my boyfriend. She'd been asking about Dan, the person who'd traded his life for hers. I stalked to the front door and yanked it open. "Gwen, can you come back in? I think our mother-daughter talk is over."

"Of course." She got up and tucked her arm through mine. As we moved back into the house, she whispered, "You all right?"

I didn't bother to keep my voice down. "No. Dan is in Hell. Kane has been marked by Meri, and she's using him to siphon power from me. No one knows how long he can endure such an invasion. And Mom would like me to forget about everything so we can rebuild this family. What do you think?"

"Jade." Mom sighed. "That isn't what I said."

"Sounded like it to me." I flopped back down on the couch, arms folded, scowling.

Gwen joined me. "I know this is hard. You're strong. We'll help you through it. No matter what. Right, Hope?"

"I..." Mom backed up, her hand clutching her neck. "I don't think I can. I'm sorry." Regret and shame brushed me as she ran past us and out the door.

Damn. That hadn't gone at all the way I'd planned. How could I be so blind? Mom wasn't strong enough after her own ordeal to help with this. I squeezed my eyes shut and shook my head. "We should probably go after her."

"She'll be fine," Gwen soothed. "She's not going anywhere."

"I guess I have some pent-up resentment." I picked up one of the small plates, just to do something with my hands.

"No kidding," Lailah said, leaning on the door frame from her bedroom.

I clutched the plate. How long had she been there?

"A few minutes," she said.

"Damn it, stop doing that."

She shrugged. "I don't have the experience with mental barriers you do." She walked into the room, and Philip followed her.

He extended his hand to Gwen. "Nice to meet you, Ms. Calhoun. Hope has told me a lot about you."

"Philip, I presume?" Gwen stood and shook his hand. "My sister's been anxious to see you again."

A shadow fell across his face as he took a step back. "Yes, I imagine she has."

Lailah glanced back and forth between the pair of them, confusion streaming off her. "You know Jade's mother?" she asked Philip.

"We met a long time ago."

His obvious discomfort only made me more curious. But I had more pressing issues to deal with. "She's outside. You can see her whenever you like."

"In a bit," he said. "We have things to discuss first."

"Let's go into the kitchen," Lailah said, leading the way to the back of the house.

I lingered, letting the three of them go before me, and then peeked out the front window. Mom sat motionless on the swing, her face void of emotion. Almost catatonic. I opened the door. "Mom?"

A film seemed to disappear and her expression came alive again. "Hey, shortcake."

"Are you okay?"

"Fine. Just enjoying the fresh air."

Nothing about her tone or easy smile implied she even remembered the altercation we'd had a few minutes ago. "I'm sorry about what I said."

She pushed at the ground with her feet, giving the swing a slight nudge. "Mothers and daughters bicker sometimes. It's normal and in the past. Everything's fine."

Bickering? We'd had a disagreement about going into Hell. What was normal about that? "Not quite everything. We're meeting with Philip and Lailah about what to do next. Do you want to join us?"

The swing started to slow, and she gave the ground another push. "Not right now. I'll be here if you need me."

"Uh, okay. If you change your mind…" The sudden switch in personality left me at a loss for words. One moment she was my kick-butt witchy mom. The next she was a space cadet don't-have-a-thing-to-contribute mom. Gwen had warned me she'd have trouble adjusting. I sighed. "We'll be in the kitchen."

She nodded and stared down the street.

I retreated back into the house, worry tightening in my chest. We had to get her help. Soon.

In the kitchen, Gwen motioned for me to take the seat next to her. I shook my head and stood, staring down at Lailah and Philip. "How are we going to do this?"

"Do what?" Lailah asked.

"Get into Hell."

Silence.

Their eyes met and a silent communication passed between them.

"You're Dan's father," Lailah said to Philip. "Your connection should be enough to help you find him wherever he is."

He lifted his chin in acknowledgement. "But you're his soul guardian. You've been bound magically. That's a stronger tie. We might locate him easier if you cast the finding spell."

Lailah shook her head. "Doubtful. Nothing is stronger than a blood bond."

He narrowed his eyes. Reluctance seeped off him as he nodded slowly. "You're right."

"We should get to work on a plan." Lailah picked up her phone. "I'll call Lucien—he can rally the coven. We'll need backup to open the Hell gates."

"Wait," he said. "My first priority is to Jade. I shouldn't even consider letting her go, but if I don't, Meri will drain her." He ran a frustrated hand through his dark hair. "I can't lose one more soul to the darkness." The words came out clipped and angry.

Lailah sent him a sympathetic look.

I stiffened. "Can't lose *another* soul. How many have you lost?"

He jerked. Anger and shame filled the room as he lifted his gaze to mine. "Three."

Crap on toast! He'd lost three people. One was too many. What did this mean for my chances?

"You're not being fair, Philip," Lailah said. "Dan wasn't yours. *I* lost him."

"Does it matter?" He got up and moved to the window over the kitchen sink. "I knew something was off, but I didn't press the issue, figuring you were there to help. How could I have known Meri would get to you too? She's my mate. If I'd saved her, none of this would have happened." Grasping the basin, he closed his eyes and bowed his head.

I gave him a moment to collect his thoughts and then asked the question I'd been holding back. "Why didn't you?"

He met my gaze with his hardened one. "I had a son to watch over."

My heart sped up. An agonizing respect for Philip's devotion to his son made me regard him through new eyes. Philip had given up his true love for him. Did Dan have any clue his real dad cared that much? I hoped so.

"Seems it was all for nothing," Philip continued.

"Not nothing," Gwen said. "Dan risked his life for the woman he loves."

"Gwen." I shook my head. Now wasn't the time to bring any of that up.

She waved her hand, dismissing my warning. "He's a good man. With your help, Jade will find a way to bring him back."

I stared at her. She stared back. Something in her tone and the glint in her eye told me she knew more than she was saying. That she'd seen something. But I knew better than to ask. Psychics usually don't share their visions. It's too dangerous. Too easy to veer off-course and make a difficult situation worse.

Her words put the fire back in my belly. I was ready to fight, and I needed all the information I could get. "Philip, who was the third person you lost to Hell?"

Nobody said anything for a second. Gwen and Lailah shared a glance, and suddenly I understood. They both knew who he'd lost. That meant only one thing. "You were my mother's soul guardian."

He took a deep breath. "Yes."

"You didn't try to stop her from summoning Meri, knowing Meri could've already turned demon?" His mistake had gotten my mother and Meri's two sisters trapped in Purgatory for twelve years.

His neck flushed red as the blood crept toward his face. Guilt overwhelmed his emotional energy and he forced out, "I'm the one who taught her the blood spell."

Chapter 15

An angel, my mother's soul guardian, had taught her blood magic. Magic that comes with terrible consequences. Magic that ended up costing me my mother. For twelve years, I'd had no idea what had happened to her.

I stood so fast I almost knocked the wooden chair over. The buried resentment of those twelve lost years manifested, and I was ready to explode. I opened my mouth, but no words came out. Outrage seized my brain.

The floors creaked behind me, and I spun. My mother, with her shoulders straight and her witchy nerves of steel demeanor, stepped into the kitchen. She put a light hand on my arm. "Don't blame Philip. He was only trying to help."

"But—"

"No. I was going to do the spell with or without him. He did what he could to keep me as safe as possible." She wrapped an arm around my waist. "I think you know a little something about being stubborn when it comes to people you love. Is anyone going to stop you from helping Dan?"

A memory flashed in my mind. In the middle of the Idaho coven circle, my mom summoned Meri, only to find out she'd already turned demon, and then stepped up to sacrifice herself in order to save the members.

It was exactly what I would have done. It's what I would do. I just couldn't understand why she'd done the spell in the first place.

"Why did you risk leaving me?" I asked her, my voice small, child-like.

Mom hugged me tight and whispered, "Meri was my friend."

I stiffened and pulled back in horror. "You...you knew her?" Is that why she'd been defending her when we'd been back at Gwen's? Could she not see Meri was beyond help?

"Yes. She and Philip moved from Idaho when you were little. No reason you'd remember them. Meri was a very close friend." Her gaze shifted and landed on Philip. "They both were."

He rose from his chair, bittersweet love running through him, and pulled Mom into his arms. I barely heard him whisper, "I'm so sorry, Hope. You have no idea how much I've agonized about that night."

She leaned back, tilting her head up and gave him a reassuring smile. "I'm pretty certain I do."

Philip let go. He stared at her, taking her in, as if to make sure she really was standing right in front of him. He clasped both her hands. "I would've done anything. Tried anything I could think of. Except..."

"I know." She put an arm around me and pulled me close. "You had to stay to take care of my girl. And Dan."

"Wait, what?" I jerked out of Mom's embrace and turned to Gwen. "What's she talking about?"

My aunt glanced at Mom and Philip and then back at me. "He's always been your soul guardian, honey."

Now I was pissed.

Why had I just met this man? He was Dan's father. My angel. And the person who'd been at the center of all this craziness. Frustration and intense betrayal jumbled my thoughts.

I couldn't focus. I did *not* need this right now. We needed to find Dan and free Kane.

Lailah got up and moved to my side. "Come with me."

"Where?" I forced out as she dragged me to the back of the kitchen.

"Outside." She pulled the screen door open and nudged me onto her deck. "Let's get some fresh air."

I stopped in the doorway. "I don't want air. I want answers."

"I know. Just move."

My feet responded on their own, and the next thing I knew, we were alone in her tiny barren backyard. Good Goddess, her house was a mystery. The deck gave way to a dry patch of dirt and weeds. "Why don't you have any plants or a lawn?"

"Really?" She threw her hands up. "That's what you want to talk about? My yard? If you must know, I was in the process of redoing the landscaping. Then demons started showing up."

"Oh."

"Yeah, I've been a little busy."

"Tell me about it." I took a seat on the deck steps and stared at a white rock, shining up from the dirt.

She stood behind me at the rail, unease running through her.

"Just say whatever you have to say." A red fire ant scuttled around the rock. I resisted the urge to crush the toe-biting, evil creature.

"You should know angels don't usually reveal themselves to their charges. And in Philip's case, there was Dan as well, making things even more complicated."

I twisted, wanting more of an explanation. How come Philip left Dan's mom? Why was Philip never around if he was watching over Dan? Why all the secrecy?

"Sorry, that's their business and not for me to disclose," Lailah said, obviously hearing my thoughts. "What's important is Philip has been your guardian all these years, and if you want to help both Dan and Kane, you're going to have to trust him."

I turned back around and eyed the ant crawling over a withered leaf. "I trust you."

"You do?" The surprise in her voice made me chuckle.

"Yes. It's shocking, but I know you're not going to let either of them suffer at the hands of a demon." I got to my feet and met her gaze again. "You may not care about me, but you do care about them."

She bowed her head and gave it a tiny shake. "I care about you." Her lips quirked. "You just irritate the hell out of me."

Surprised at her candor, I laughed. "Fair enough," I sputtered, still chuckling. "You push my buttons as well." I held out a hand. "Truce?"

"Truce." She took it and right before she let go, a faint shock ran the length of my arm.

"What was that?"

"A little magic to seal the deal." She tilted her head toward the door. "Come on, we need to work out a spell if we're going to get you into Hell today."

"Today?" My heart sped up.

"No time like the present."

I followed her back into the kitchen to find Mom bent over the table, sketching. Peeking over her shoulder, I asked, "What's this?"

"Knowledge." Mom pointed to a maze she'd drawn. "A map of Meri's section of Hell."

I touched the edge of the paper. "You know I'll do whatever it takes to save Dan. Including destroy Meri."

Mom straightened. "Of course. I wouldn't expect anything less from a daughter of mine. But just because you can, doesn't mean you should. Nothing is black and white."

Biting my tongue, I shrugged a half-hearted acceptance of her advice and turned back to the map. "Looks like I have some work to do."

"I don't think this is going to work." I tossed the notebook down on the bar and longed for a Guinness. The bottles lined up against the wall mocked me. Stupid club filled with alcohol. A little liquid courage would go a long way to calm my nerves. Too bad booze and spells didn't mix.

Pyper grabbed the book and thrust it back at me. "You haven't even tried."

"We're running out of time." Lailah gestured to the digital clock glowing beneath the counter.

Pyper craned her neck and nodded. "Yeah. Kane will be back within the hour. If you plan to use the club's dark energy, you need to get started sooner rather than later. Because once he shows up, the shit's gonna hit the fan."

Besides the spell, the biggest obstacle we faced was finding a portal into the Underworld. Ideally we'd use a coven circle, but since ours was under a constant media watch, that wasn't going to work.

Bea's house was full of old mystical power after generations of witches residing there. It would've been my next choice, except I wasn't willing to risk her sanctuary to any rogue demons.

I didn't particularly like the idea of using Kane's club, Wicked, either, but we were out of options.

A few months ago, Bea and Lailah had joined together to banish an evil spirit. According to Lailah, the club was now magically marked as a portal. We only needed to make sure and open it near Dan. Otherwise I'd likely get lost in an entirely different dimension.

"Ugh." My nerves clamored away at my confidence. I glanced over at the stage, where Philip, Lucien, Kat, and Rosalee stood in a tight circle, wishing to high heaven Lailah hadn't called Kat about Dan's Celtic knot pendant. But we needed a focusing object and it was the best fit.

Once Kat found out what we planned, she'd rushed over to the club. She would not stay home wringing her hands with worry. Not with both her best friends' lives on the line. She'd probably follow me into Hell if she got the chance.

I'd tie her up first before I let her do that.

I turned to Pyper. "When we get started, I'm counting on you and Kat to get yourselves out of here. No matter what happens. Got it?"

She downed a shot of rum, slammed the glass down on the bar, and rose from one of the blue, crushed velvet stools. "Got it."

"And take care of Kane," I whispered, hating that I'd lied to him and dragged Pyper into this mess. She'd sent him on a wild goose chase across town to pick up an unneeded part for one of her espresso machines.

I'd promised Kane we'd fight this together, but I didn't see a way to do that without losing him to Meri, and I couldn't let that happen. Pyper would have to pick up the pieces if anything went wrong.

She flung her arms around me, squeezing tight, then pulled back and braced her hands on my shoulders. "Come back to us and take care of him your own damned self."

Unable to speak, I nodded.

"Good." She let go and her tone softened. "'Cause you know I have a life to worry about. I can't be his keeper forever."

I gave her a small smile and led the way across the empty club to join the others at the stage.

"All right then," Lailah said. "Let's get started." She went into full-on sergeant mode, barking orders. "Philip, stand here." She maneuvered him to the exact same spot Bea had sat when she'd opened the portal the first time. The Celtic pendant glimmered under one of the spotlights as she held it out. "Take this."

"Why is she in charge?" Pyper asked.

"Because she's Dan's soul guardian and that's who we're trying to find," I said. "She's going to start the spell and then the circle will team up with her to guide my soul to Dan's."

Lucien turned to me. "Once you do this, you'll no longer be able to call on the coven for power."

"Forever?" An unexpected sense of loss filled me. I hadn't asked to be the coven leader. Didn't even want the job. In fact, I'd tried to give it back to Bea a few times. "Does that mean I'll forfeit my status?"

"No, if…I mean, when you come back, the position will be yours again." He glanced at Rosalee, his posture stiff. Unease flowed from him.

"What?" I asked.

Rosalee raised her eyebrows, waiting for him to respond. When he didn't, she stepped forward. "You'll need to name one of us as leader before you go. Otherwise the entire coven will be vulnerable."

"Oh. Is that all?" I let out a sigh of relief. "Okay, no problem."

Lucien's head snapped up. "You don't understand. Making the transfer drains your power. It takes a few days to regain your strength, but you don't have that kind of time. Which means you'll be in Hell and weak."

"I'm going to have to break into Hell in a weakened state? Why didn't anyone inform me of this all important piece of information?" I balled my hands into fists, fighting to keep my anger in check.

Rosalee held her hands up in defense. "It's really rare for a coven leader to give up their position of power. Most of us have never witnessed it. When Bea did it, she was already weakened. We just found out. Bea warned us."

Pyper shifted to stand in front of me, hands on her hips. "Then she can't go."

I gently pushed her to the side and took a calming breath. "Okay, what do you mean, the coven will be vulnerable? What happens if I don't transfer the leadership?"

"Anything you endure there will affect the members here. In essence, if you die, we die," Rosalee said, her tone flat and clinical. "You can't use the collective because the mystical properties of Hell neutralize the power needed to form coven magic. However, as leader, your connection to us isn't completely severed, and demons will exploit the bond. They feed off physical and emotional pain. Don't think they won't use that."

Son of a … Yes, they did feed off pain.

It's what Kane was experiencing now.

Before anyone said anything else, I grabbed Lucien's hands. My magical spark grew warm in my chest. "I, Jade Calhoun, transfer the leadership of the New Orleans coven to you, Lucien Boulard."

Magic kindled between us until a wave of tiny electric shocks fired from my fingertips. Emptiness blossomed in my gut. The connection I'd never paid attention to was suddenly gone.

"Whoa," Lucien said softly as he took a few steps back. "That's intense."

I watched him, saying nothing. When Bea had named me leader, I'd barely noticed a difference. Had I transferred some of my magic to him? I'd done it before. It's what had created the psychic bond between Lailah and me.

Lucien? I asked.

I studied him carefully as he flexed his fingers, working through the aftershocks of the magic.

Can you hear me?

Nothing.

Lucien!

He finally stopped staring at his hands and backed up, taking a spot on the temporary circle we'd drawn around the stage.

Thank the Goddess. At least I hadn't messed that one up.

"Are you done yelling, Jade?" Lailah asked. "'Cause you're giving me a headache."

I ignored the statement. "Let's get moving. Kane will be here any minute."

Pyper crushed me with another hug. "Be safe."

She let go, handed me a bundle of herbs, and quickly headed for the bar. But not before I saw the tears glistening in her eyes. I met Kat's gaze, silently telling her how much I loved her.

Her lips formed a thin line and she shook her head. The message was clear. I would not fail today. She forbade it.

Her fierce denial filled my heart with courage. I turned to Lailah. "I'm ready."

I stood in the middle of the circle, Dan's pendant in one hand and the earth-magic-infused satchel of herbs in the other.

My only aids for finding Dan and getting out of there as fast as possible. They wouldn't help me break Meri's connection to Kane, though.

Our research showed the only way to do that was either destroy Meri or redirect the connection to someone or something else. Something important to her. Like a prized jewel she kept locked away.

With the map Mom had drawn, my mission was to break into Meri's apartment in Hell and steal a large family ruby she'd once worn as a ring. When I made it back, we'd work on the redirection spell. All I needed to do was find the jewel…and Dan.

No problem. Breaking and entering in Hell was no sweat, right?

A wave of dizziness made me stumble. I took a deep breath, planted my feet, and willed myself to keep it together. In a few moments, Lailah would open the door to Hell. I had to be ready.

Lailah positioned herself on the northern section of the circle, Philip to the south. Lucien and Rosalee filled in the east and west. Lailah raised her hands, and instantly the temporary chalk-drawn circle lit up the club.

I glanced over at the bar. Pyper's face had turned stark white. Fear paralyzed her as no doubt the memory of being tortured by Roy's ghost came rushing back.

"Kat, get her out of here," I called.

Pyper didn't move as Kat tugged at her arm. "I'm fine. We're not leaving."

"Stop being so stubborn. Go. Keep Kane occupied until I get back." I'd tried for confident, but ruined the effect when my voice cracked on Kane's name. I eeked out, "Just go. Please. Be safe."

Kat finally managed to pull Pyper toward the back door. My eyes burned with unshed tears.

Not now, Jade. Not now.

I blinked and faced Lailah. "Let's do this."

She nodded and made eye contact with Philip. "Ready?"

"Remember the incantation?" he asked me.

"Yes." I patted my back pocket. "I have a copy just in case." As soon as I got to the other side, I was to invoke a tracking spell. If done properly, Philip would be able to track me and yank me back home if anything went terribly wrong.

"Make sure you have it engraved in your memory. You don't know what can happen to things when you cross over." His eyes were hard, unyielding.

"Got it," I confirmed, resisting the urge to snap at him. The longer they dragged this out, the harder it would be. My resolve started to wane. I didn't know if it was from nerves or the coven leader transfer to Lucien. Either way, I could feel myself weakening by the second.

"Ready," Philip confirmed.

Lailah started a chant in Latin, soon joined by the other three. *"Portas inferni, portas inferni."*

A black pillar candle started to rise in front of me, and when it was almost eye level, Lailah shouted, *"Flamma!"*

The candle came to life with a sudden spark.

The others continued to chant in soft undertones, *"Portas inferni, portas inferni."*

Lailah stretched her arms up. A shimmery light appeared around her form, making her glow in the dim room. "Goddess of Hell, hear my words. I, Lailah Farmoore, sanctioned angel of New Orleans, command your will."

I stared at the candle still hovering in front of me and prayed Lailah didn't end up possessed. The last time Lailah had called on a Goddess, she'd actually showed up...in Lailah's body.

Talk about freaky. Of course, nothing was freakier than purposely trying to get into Hell. I wrapped my arms around myself and squeezed.

Invisible power exploded from Lailah, pressed in on me, made my limbs twitch with desire to feed the magical stream. I clutched my arms, forcing myself to stay passive. Using my magic now was likely to feed Meri. Even though I'd separated myself from Kane, she could still reach me through our bond. Letting her grab any more of my power wasn't an option.

Philip's deep voice filled the club. "Goddess of darkness, hear my call. I, Philip Pearson, command you to bring forth my son, Dan Toller."

Blue sparks sprung from his fingers, colliding with Lailah's in an impressive display of icy blue fireworks. My body hummed, longing to be part of the circle. I missed the magical connection, the cohesiveness of the coven.

I stared at Lucien, his arms mimicking Philip's, high in the air, containing the circle. The fierce concentration evident in his stance reassured me I'd made the correct choice in granting him the coven. He had the skill and the intelligence to take care of them while I was gone. As much as I'd shunned covens and magic my entire life, I now knew they were part of me. Necessary. A piece of my puzzle I couldn't continue to ignore.

The light danced around me, shifting and winding into unrecognizable shapes. Tendrils of magic split off from the ball of fireworks, snaking their way to the two witches. A crackle ran through the room like lightning and suddenly the threads connected the four magic users around the circle, creating a canopy of magic overhead.

A roar of energy filled my ears like static. Lailah's mouth was moving as she appeared to shout. Lucien's face contorted into something resembling fierce determination, his green eyes glowing with effort. Opposite him, Rosalee, tiny Rosalee, seemed to have grown five or so inches. She balanced on her tiptoes, face raised to the ceiling as she struggled to maintain the overwhelming magic battering her limbs. Only Philip stood calm in his spot, power crackling off him in waves. He stared at me, waiting.

I pushed forward, arms and legs heavy as if moving through water. He nodded, encouraging me as I fought the thick energy.

When I got a few steps from Philip, he mouthed *stop* and held out his hand for Dan's pendant. It dangled from my fist, flashing in the light. I didn't let go, just let the necklace hang from my grasp in front of him.

It was his turn to shout a word I couldn't decipher, and with a stream of magic concentrated around the pair of us, Philip reached out and clasped his hand over mine.

The static vanished. Gasps and shouts of surprise sprouted from my friends and wind kicked up, whipping my hair over my eyes. I pushed it back and gaped.

The icy blue light had formed an unmistakable image of Dan splayed out on a suspended slab, slightly above a roaring fire. Flames licked the sides, making him cringe away.

"Oh, my God. She's going to burn him alive," I cried. The image contorted as the magic folded in on itself, forming a ball. A moment later the ball spread, leaving a medium-sized hole in the club floor. Only this time it glowed fiery orange.

Heat warmed my body as I inched closer.

That was it. My opening into Hell. All I had to do was jump. I took two steps. A tingle of familiar energy brushed my psyche and made me freeze. Trembling, I turned to my left.

There was Kane, a deadly combination of terror and anger consuming every inch of his being. He vibrated with it, setting my already frayed nerves on edge. In one look I tried to portray the jumbled emotions tumbling around inside me—love, regret, guilt.

He acknowledged nothing. Never hesitated. Only moved with dogged determination and purpose, coming straight for me.

I stared into his blazing dark eyes. And jumped.

Everything blurred, heat and light searing my vision. I groped about, uselessly searching for purchase, and seconds later, landed with a thud on a cold hard floor.

"Ugh." Pushing myself up, I squinted. The dim gray room appeared to be empty.

Good. I was alone.

Until a muffled thunk, followed by a groan, echoed behind me. I catapulted to my feet, simultaneously spinning and backing up toward the wall. Mocha eyes stared up at me.

"Damn you, Kane. What the heck are you doing in Hell?"

Chapter 16

Kane pushed himself up, that same determined fury flowing from him. "Coming after you."

I unconsciously took another step back.

"What were you thinking?" he growled as his frame towered over me.

This time I stood firm. He grabbed my shoulders. I stiffened, sure he was going to literally shake some sense into me.

I stared up into his scowling face, waiting.

Instead, he crushed me to him, holding me tight against his pounding heart.

"You shouldn't have followed me," I said into his chest, my words muffled. Unbridled emotion took over, and I started to tremble as more tears filled my eyes.

He stroked my hair, breathing heavily as we both fought for control. Finally, he pulled away and wiped the last of the tears from my cheeks.

"I had to do this," I whispered.

"Dan would not want you to risk your life for his." He traced a finger down my jawline. "No man who loves a woman would want that."

I didn't bother to debate the implication. Maybe Dan did love me. I loved him. How could I not? We'd grown up together.

Been best friends and then lovers. But I wasn't *in love* with him, and Kane knew it. "I didn't come because of Dan. If he was the only reason, we could have tried a summoning spell first." I glanced down at Kane's thigh, appearing so normal covered in the dark denim. "I came for you."

A muscle pulsed in his jaw. "I repeat, a man who loves you doesn't want you to risk your life for him." He tilted my chin up, giving me no choice but to meet his gaze. "Do you really think I could live with myself if anything happened to you because of me?"

A trickle of indignation coursed through my veins. "And if anything happened to you, what do you think I'd feel? Especially knowing I have the tools to fight this." I prayed that was true. Already I couldn't feel the spark of power that usually occupied a place in my chest.

We stared each other down, both of us frustrated.

I raised one defiant eyebrow. "Are we going to stand here all day, arguing, or are we going to go kick some demon ass?"

He shook his head in exasperation. "I'll settle for just getting out in once piece. Please tell me you have a plan."

I smiled as I pulled out Mom's map. "A treasure hunt of sorts."

Kane took the crumpled paper, turned it over a few times, and handed it back. "It's blank."

I swore under my breath, frantically racking my memory for the maze of tunnels Mom had drawn. Green. We needed the green lit one. *Please let us be close.* "Hopefully I can remember the dang thing." I grabbed the invisible map and stuffed it in my pocket. "Follow me."

We crept out of the small barren room through a stone arch. Pale light glowed in the distance. I needed to find the main passageway. The map had shown a web of tunnels that all led back to the core of Hell, where Lucifer himself reigned as king of the underworld.

Unfortunately, Meri's quarters were perilously close to Lucifer's throne. If we were lucky, the locator spell had dropped us in the correct tunnel. If not, we'd have to somehow cross the commons of Hell unnoticed.

I clutched my infused herbs in one hand and held onto Kane for dear life with the other. Philip had armed me with a few powerful earth spells, but if I had to use them before we encountered Meri, we were doomed. She'd drain my natural power through Kane, and I'd be too weak to fight her.

Kane slowed and I glanced back. "What's wrong?"

He rubbed his thigh. "Nothing. Just a twinge."

Fear bloomed in my chest. Did Meri know we were here? All the more reason to hurry. I nodded as Kane fell in step beside me.

The pale light brightened as the stone walls closed in on us, narrowing our path. I stopped. Were we going the right direction? I glanced over my shoulder. Darkness loomed behind us.

No, Mom said to follow the light. We slowed, inching our way along the wall, listening for any movement of nearby demons. Nothing permeated the air except the dank smell of mold and rot. I crinkled my nose and pressed further.

We passed two closed doors, both covered with dust and cobwebs.

Deserted. Good.

The rough stone floor turned smooth, indicating centuries of wear. We rounded a bend in the tunnel and came to an opening in a larger passageway. Bright white orbs of light blinded me.

Shit. We weren't in the right place. According to Mom, each section was color-coded by the magical orbs suspended near the ceilings. Meri lived in the section illuminated with green light. I raised my hand to shield my eyes and was suddenly yanked back into the narrow pathway.

"What the—?" I got out before Kane's hand clamped over my mouth as he pressed me against the wall.

"Shh," he barely whispered.

Seconds ticked by. Then someone grunted and the distinct sound of something being dragged filled the passageway. I stopped breathing. The sound dimmed, and I gently pulled

Kane's hand away from my mouth, took a deep breath, and peered around the corner.

A squat, round man with a head full of thick, black hair walked backwards while dragging a canvas sack. The contents appeared to be heavier and larger than the person hauling it.

I twisted back into the passageway before the man could spot me. Though, judging by his heavy breathing, he didn't appear to be too focused on his surroundings. "Not yet," I whispered.

When the noise faded, we once again ventured into the passageway. All clear. Not hesitating, we took off. Depictions of Bourbon Street buildings, rotting and in various states of disarray, lined the walls. People with deadened eyes filled the brick-lined streets. The illustrations resembled a post-apocalyptic New Orleans. I had to avert my gaze from the disturbing, never-ending mural.

We ducked into each smaller passageway we came to, carefully scoping each section of our journey. Eerie silence grated on my nerves. Besides the one dragging his haul, we hadn't seen or heard anyone.

"Where are we going?" Kane finally asked.

"To Meri's dungeon, where hopefully we'll find Dan and a jewel that we can use to break Meri's connection to you. Then we're out of here." I leaned against the stone wall and took a second to send out my awareness. Kane's heightened sense of worry and unease filled me. I pushed his energy aside and pressed deeper. Only a whisper of emotion reached me. Something close to lustful glee. The dark kind that fed off destruction.

I shuddered, but kept the line open, wanting to sense when we got near to whatever was feeding that emotion.

We pressed on. The air warmed, and the old rotting stench shifted to a rancid plume of burning smoke. I gagged, my eyes watering. "Oh, God."

Kane pulled the collar of his shirt over his nose and mouth. Where were we headed?

One more turn around a bend, and my question was answered. The passageway opened up to a large, enclosed auditorium, the roof at least five stories high. Directly in the middle, a snow-white bonfire of gigantic proportions burned, contained by thick glass walls. An electric spiral staircase wound its way to the top, where the squat man we'd seen stood with his canvas bag.

Kane and I shrunk back into the shadows of the passage opening and watched.

A 360-degree screen flickered to life on the walls of the auditorium. It was broken into four sections, each one showing a different decaying part of the city of New Orleans: A Garden District home overrun with withered vines and rodents; The Mid-City Park, barren of all vegetation and filled with demons; a burning French Quarter; and Uptown, deserted of human life and flooded with blood.

I stifled a cry, unable to tear my gaze from the nightmare before my eyes.

The screens went blank and the images were replaced by a close-up of the man at the top of the bonfire, now reaching into his bag. Directly behind him was an empty red velvet chair, high enough to reside over the entire area. Lucifer's throne. It had to be. Thank the Gods he didn't appear to be in attendance.

Sweat covered man's face and neck. He smiled an evil grin as he slowly pulled the object from the bag.

I gripped Kane's forearm, nails digging into his skin. "What is that?"

His mouth dropped open then he shut it.

"Kane?" I glanced back up at the screen. My stomach rolled. I swallowed, my throat quivering as I forced myself not to vomit.

The demon, now obvious by his saucer-wide black eyes, held a severed arm above his head, turning it in all directions.

A cheer went up from an invisible crowd. Using the limb, the demon saluted his audience and tossed it into the fire.

I gagged, barely holding down the contents of my stomach.

The cylinder of fire raged, bubbled up to the top, and swirled around as if alive. It turned from fiery white to orange, back to white, and so forth through a range of colors as the demon tossed more body parts into the inferno.

The cheers grew louder, filling the auditorium with a bone-chilling evil. My knees started to buckle with the intensity of it all. Kane held me up, locking me to his side, both of us momentarily paralyzed by the scene in front of us.

When the bag was empty, the demon tossed it in and raised his arms, inviting the frenzied crowd's applause. The fiery dance within the glass chamber intensified and snapped together in one last triumphant finale to form an image of a tall, thin man, skeletal even, with distinctive bone structure. Anger and pride defined his facial expression as he stood, feet spread and arms crossed in a defiant stance.

Somehow, I knew the form was of the man the demon had just fed to the fire.

Was this Dan's fate? The vision we'd witnessed back at the club of Dan hovering over a fire flashed in my brain. We had to find him before he was next.

The silhouette of the man in the silo burst apart and the fire returned to its normal blaze, only now the flames burned an iridescent green. Across the chamber, a spotlight shone on a passageway.

From its depths, a tall female demon with an angular face and long black hair stepped up to a small podium. "I accept the honor of the Fire Sacrifice. In two nights forth, you shall have your offering."

Meri!

We were just in time. If we didn't get Dan out, he'd be fire food.

Demons of all shapes and sizes spilled forward from hidden tunnels and passageways. The mobs pushed past us and would have crushed us against the stone wall if Kane hadn't moved and pulled me with him. He yanked me in front of him and steered us along, moving painfully slow toward Meri and the green tunnel.

As the chatter and whoops of celebration filled the chamber, my skin crawled. The instinct to flee was so strong, I started to drag my feet, unable to keep moving forward.

"Stay with me, Jade," Kane said into my ear. "Don't let them take you."

I didn't know exactly what he meant, but I managed to put one foot in front of the other. After a long crawl through the crowd, we found ourselves only one passageway away from where we wanted to be.

Kane pulled me into an empty, darkened tunnel. "Can you do this?"

I struggled to breathe. My limbs were sluggish, and with every beat of my heart, dozens of tiny invisible needles prickled in my chest. I leaned into him, stumbled, and toppled to the side, only saving myself at the last minute when I grabbed onto his waist. My elbow jammed into his thigh. He gasped, biting off an oath.

"Sorry!" I stared up into his pasty-white face. He was suffering more than I'd realized. I pulled out the earth-infused herbs. Mom told me to use them sparingly, but if I didn't stop the drain working over both of us, we'd never get home. I held my hand out, a small mound of dried herbs in my palm. "Here. Swallow this."

He didn't argue. A second later he grimaced and coughed, trying to dislodge the herbs stuck in his throat.

I swallowed my own portion and closed the bag back up. That left one more dose. The pain pulsing in my chest started to dull. I gave Kane a questioning glance. "Did it work?"

He flexed his leg and gritted his teeth, but his color had returned. "I'll be fine."

While my energy wasn't restored, at least I could think and function again. Kane seemed to move a little easier as well. We ducked back out of the tunnel, only to find the crowd was starting to thin.

Not good.

We'd been at an advantage, blurring in the crowded sea. Now we were sitting ducks. A small group of demons started to disperse. I glanced around, desperate for some cover. Nothing. Only the tunnel behind us and Meri's passageway in front of us.

And Meri herself.

The last of the group wandered away. Meri's familiar gray eyes turned almost black as they focused on me.

Instantly, I gathered the earth magic provided to me by Philip's herbs. My chest burned with it, my fingers sparking with foreign power.

Meri's high laugh reached me. "You make this so easy. Where's the challenge, white witch?"

"Bring me Dan and we can call this a truce," I offered, knowing she'd never deal.

Her lips slid into a slow, satisfied smile. "A trade, then?" She gestured to Kane. "One for the other?"

I stared her down with my steely gaze.

"Or I can take both." Meri threw both arms out, magic barely kindling within her.

She hesitated, and in that moment, I sensed a deep internal struggle. Something was holding her back from a full out attack. If I didn't know better, I'd say she was battling her conscience. I stood my ground. "You're not getting Kane. Not today. Not ever."

Meri's dark gray eyes narrowed, and the magic pulsing through me started to slip away. I focused, holding it close, ready to unleash on her at any moment.

Her smile turned evil. "You don't even know what's happening."

"Jade," Kane's voice rasped. I spun, finding him kneeling on one leg, clutching his thigh. He gritted his teeth and forced out, "She's taking my strength. Use your magic to strike while you can."

My magic flared, angry and desperate. I had one shot. Now or never. Without hesitation, I unleashed my fury on the demon. *Destroy. Destroy. Destroy*, I chanted in my head. I didn't need a spell; I only needed intentions.

She held her hands out, accepting my magic. Every ounce of destructive power I sent her way, she ate up, feasted on, and grew stronger with it.

What in the bloody hell?

The earth magic disappeared, and my breathing labored once again as the piercing invisible needles resurfaced in my chest. "Kane?"

He didn't respond.

"We have to go," I mumbled. Reaching down to grab his hand, I finally tore my eyes from Meri and gasped.

Kane lay unconscious, a hole burned right through his jeans. The wound pulsed with ugly gray magic.

Meri moved closer, stalking me like prey. "See that mark? My magic is eating his soul."

It couldn't be. I wouldn't believe it. We had to get out of there. I scrambled to pull the last of the herbs from the satchel. I had enough magic for one more spell. Philip and Lailah could summon us out if I sent up the tracking spell I'd forgotten to perform earlier.

Meri closed in on me. With trembling hands, I dumped the rest of the herbs in my hand and cried, "Nevermore!"

The herbs went up with a whoosh of white smoke and almost instantly disappeared.

Meri paused, eyes narrowed. "My mate taught you that trick." It wasn't a question. She spoke with an air of confidence. Then she laughed. "He's not coming. I would know."

When Meri had still been an angel, she'd been trapped in Hell and waited desperately for Philip to save her. Time passed, Philip hadn't showed, and Meri fell. It was what happened to angels stuck in Hell. She was justified in believing he'd never come for me. What she didn't know was the reason he hadn't shown up the first time—the very reason he would now.

Dan.

I said nothing. She couldn't know Dan was Philip's son. The potential to use Dan for revenge was much too strong.

Beside me, Kane stirred. Thank the Gods. I kneeled down, ready to help him up, but he brushed me off and stood.

Meri raised one crooked finger in his direction. "Come."

And he did. With familiar, jerky movements. The same ones I'd seen in Dan's gait when he'd been victim to Meri's possession.

I stared at Kane, horror filling my heart.

"I told you," Meri said. "He's mine now."

Chapter 17

The closer Kane got to Meri, the more his gait evened out. I steeled myself, frantically searching my memory for some spell, anything to neutralize the obvious possession.

I could make a potion from bluebonnets, but that wasn't a flower I was likely to find in Hell. Binding Meri might work, but with my magic and strength depleted, the thought was useless.

Rage burned through me, mixing with a tiny spark of power. Thank the Goddess I had something left to fight with.

There was no way I was letting her have Kane too. I'd die before she took him from me.

My fingers ached as magic strained to reach the tips.

Meri glided forward, her arms wide. A dark cloud of magical electricity circled her.

"I have plans for you, white witch," she said sweetly. "Together, you and I could be very powerful here in the underworld. You won't even have to give up your lover." Her tone turned flat as her gaze flickered between Kane and me. "Your choice. Join us, or I'll end you right now."

Magic pulsed through my limbs. I held it back. Waiting. "You know I'll never agree to that," I said with a dead serious calm.

An air of impatience flickered over her emotionless features. Electric power crackled around her, and when she moved, I was ready.

Raw magic collided, shooting rays of destruction, cracking stone all around us. My power drained at an alarming rate, and in my weakened state, it was all I could do to hold on, much less overpower her. My magical spark didn't have anything else to give.

She stepped forward, pressing her advantage. I stumbled back. Meri wasn't as weak as we'd thought. Of course not. She'd been draining me through Kane—and still was.

An absolute truth hit me. I was going to die.

Kane shifted into my eye line. He'd followed the demon and stood a few inches from her. His dark chocolate eyes met mine. Everything vanished.

He stared at me, love pouring from his gaze.

He wasn't possessed. He couldn't be. I could see through him, inside of him, and he was still mine.

My body screamed with effort as I moved forward on stiff, lifeless legs. I reached for the last of my power and yanked. Searing energy rippled through me, sending foreign tendrils of power deep into my being. Magic exploded and my insides seemed to rip apart. I fell to my knees, my strength gone.

Meri stopped inches from me, her right arm raised as if to strike me.

I stared up at her, defiance racing through every one of my cells. "Do it!" I demanded.

"With pleasure." She swung.

Kane moved, a small dagger clutched in his hand, and plunged the knife into her left shoulder. She fell to one knee, her face contorted with rage. Her magic vanished, and a weight lifted from my chest.

I scrambled to my feet and rushed to Kane's side.

"Run!" He grabbed my arm and yanked me away from Meri.

The small group of demon spectators, who'd been watching the showdown, seemed frozen with bewilderment. We took off, not waiting for an outcome.

We didn't speak, just headed straight for the green-lighted passageway. Right as we sprinted under the archway, a loud boom rumbled from the auditorium. I skidded to a stop and poked my head out of the opening.

"Oh my God!" I cried. "It's Philip and Lailah."

The pair descended from somewhere high above, landing crouched in a fighting position. The demons instantly formed a circle around them. They'd answered my distress call. Only I'd had no idea that meant they'd show up here. I'd expected them to perform a calling to yank us back to the living world. It was a lot more dangerous for angels in hell. Their souls were extremely vulnerable to black magic corruption.

"Let them be." Kane yanked my arm as he took off running down the tomb-filled passageway.

"But—"

He didn't slow down or even glance back as he yelled, "Now's our chance."

I shoved the fears and doubts out of my mind. He was right. With Meri and her minions fighting off Philip and Lailah, this was going to be our best opportunity.

We passed the crumpled, once ornate ruins of gargoyles, screeching devil-dogs, and statues of humans twisted with torment and despair. I tried my best to not focus on any of them. Even though they were stone, agony poured into my being, tearing at my soul with each step I took.

My breathing labored as my eyes blurred. I blinked. *Focus, Jade.* Almost there. I spotted the rotting archway Mom had pinpointed as a marker. A few more paces, and we'd be at Meri's dungeon. I slowed, senses on hyper-alert for any guards. But I was too overwhelmed with the agony and despair of the stone statues.

A terrible thought came to me. Were lost souls trapped in them? I turned to stare at the one closest to me. With her arms raised and crossed as if to ward off an attack, her big, frantic eyes pleaded for help. I took a step forward, trying not to register the warped, twisted body, shriveled with age. It was only a statue, I reminded myself. A grotesque representation of pain and suffering.

Her eyes seemed to follow my every movement. Another step closer. A trickle of sad misery, lined with a faint trace of hope brushed against my emotional radar.

Shock rooted me to the floor.

A soul resided in that statue.

I reached out, determined to soothe the suffering being. I couldn't do much, but I could send her a little bit of comfort. Just as my hand brushed the icy surface of the statue, Kane jumped back, knocking me sideways.

"Ouch." I cradled my dead-weight arm. He'd hit me hard enough and in just the right spot that I'd been rendered temporarily paralyzed.

"Sorry." He pulled me close. "I think it's a bad idea to touch anything you don't have to."

"But someone's trapped in there."

He turned to inspect the grotesque being, a look of horror transforming over his features. "Oh, no. Not again." He maneuvered me farther from it. "Not only am I not letting you get involved, but we don't have time for this. Meri's chamber is just ahead. Let's go."

I gave the statue one last look and followed Kane. It killed me to not do something for anyone suffering. But what was I going to do? Make it my mission to free everyone trapped in Hell? What if they belonged there? I shook my head, trying to dislodge the thoughts. We had work to do.

As soon as we rounded the corner, I knew we were in the right place. Withered oak trees lined the stone wall in an eerily familiar formation. I squinted, imagining them hearty and full of life. Yes, I recognized these trees; they were the same ones near our coven circle. I touched the wall, and a faint trace of Dan's distinct energy reached me.

I squeezed Kane's hand, hard, and nodded to the stone door. "He's here."

We both stared at the smooth surface. No handle. No lock. No obvious way to open it. Mom had warned us we'd need a spell to get in.

"Can you send energy toward Dan?" Kane asked. "Maybe he'll realize you're out here and open the door himself."

"No. You forget most people can't feel my energy." Kane could, but he was a dreamwalker and, for some reason, had always been able to sense me. Dan didn't have such abilities. "Besides, I think the spell is needed to open the door from either side."

"Right." He ran a frustrated hand through his sweat-soaked dark hair. "Damn it, Jade, the spell is too dangerous. You're too weak after our encounter with Meri. We should find another way."

I sighed. "I'm out of options. Would you prefer I run back to the battle with Meri? Either way, I'm taking a risk. At least if I try this, we have a shot."

A muscle in Kane's jaw twitched as he bit back a reply. Despite his obvious reluctance, he stepped aside, making room for me to cast the spell.

My mother's soft voice rang in my mind. Words she said she'd never forget—Meri's personal signature. The incantation that would open the door if I managed to infuse enough magic into them.

Where freedom's lost and dreams turn to nightmares.
Through this door lies a path to despair.
Hopeless. Destructive. Comfortable.
Open to an existence where disappointment ceases to exist.

I said the words over and over in my head, letting my magic build one layer at a time. The spark was faint, but it was still there. With the mental chant, my body grew hot with the kindled magic, forming a different sensation than I was used to.

Panic shot through me. Was I using black magic? I raised my hands, inspecting my fingers. The last time I'd tapped into darkness, they'd turned black. Here in Hell, I noticed nothing except the extreme change in temperature.

Meri's depressing mantra flashed through my mind one last time. I pressed my palms to the stone. Around my flesh, the door glowed bright orange. The magic spread in a spider web formation across the wide plane. A low rumble sounded from within. The magic popped and crackled as if it were live fire. I stepped back, colliding with Kane. His arms circled my waist steadying me. We both stared.

"Holy shit," I said under my breath.

Kane's grip tightened as the door slowly moved.

The magic faded away, and finally the door stood three-quarters of the way open.

I carefully disentangled myself from Kane's grasp and moved toward the chamber.

My heart hammered, and I barely breathed. *Please let Dan be all right.* Taking one last frightening step, I scooted into the massive room.

The opulence stopped me in my tracks. The space was nothing like the run-down ruins of the tunnels we'd been working our way through. Pale pink silks lined the walls. A lush, thick white carpet lay beneath satin settees and mahogany wood bookcases. I spared one absurd brief thought for the springiness of the carpet. Where exactly did one shop for finer goods in Hell? A silver tea set sat near an armchair, steam streaming from the top of the pot.

The same one I'd dreamed about!

I turned to Kane and let out a gasp of surprise.

Right behind him stood Meri, her eyes pinched in anger. "How dare you defile my space!"

Kane spun and backed up as if to shield me.

"Give us Dan and we'll leave," I bargained and moved to Kane's side, knowing our departure would never be that easy.

She snapped her fingers, and her door started to rumble again. Only this time it closed.

I swallowed the 'no' forming in my throat. Pleading with her would make me appear weak. We couldn't leave anyway. Not without Dan and the ruby.

Meri advanced on us, desperate anger streaming from her.

Desperate? What did she want, Philip? He was her mate.

And what happened to him during their battle? Jesus, we were in deep now.

I moved, dodging Meri's blow.

Another surprise. Instead of following me, she beelined her way toward a narrow door at the end of her chamber. Kane grabbed my arm and tucked me once again beside him.

Getting out in a hurry after we found Dan wasn't going to be easy. I

racked my memory for a banishing spell or some way to magic ourselves back to our reality. Nothing miraculously materialized in my tired brain.

Meri flung the second door open and came face to face with Dan.

His eyebrows shot up as surprise registered over his expression. "That was fast," he said.

She grabbed him, clinging to his frame.

"What happened?" he asked, stroking her hair.

I gasped. Was he possessed again? Had Meri found a way to corrupt him? "Dan?"

He jerked back and stiffened.

Meri released her hold and turned. She stood in front of Dan exactly the same way Kane had earlier while protecting me. She didn't say anything, though. She just eyed me with those deep, almost black eyes.

Dan shifted to stand at her side, pushing his tousled brown hair back with one hand. "Jade, what are you doing here?"

"Saving your ass, you idiot. What are *you* doing?" I gestured to the demon beside him. "Have you lost your mind?"

"Jade," Kane warned under his breath.

I glanced at my boyfriend, sending him a you've-got-to-be-kidding-me look. We risked our lives to save Dan's sorry butt from Hell. Who knows what happened to Philip and Lailah? And he was lounging in Princess Demon's silk-filled dungeon. Drinking tea.

Dan's pale green eyes narrowed. He held his emotions in tight control, but I thought I sensed a faint trace of weariness. "Surviving."

"Not anymore," I said. "Today you're coming home with me."

"No!" Life seemed to come alive in Meri. Flinging her arms out, she reached for more power, but it fizzled after a few short sparks. She stared at her hands for a moment, frustration streaming off her. Odd, she didn't seem at all surprised her magic failed her. Was she still recovering from our battle a week ago? Abandoning Dan, she barreled into me.

I landed hard on my side. My bones screamed in protest, despite the previously believed cushy carpeting. We grappled, each trying our best to get the upper hand. Nails scraped down my arm. I bit back a cry and rammed my elbow into her bicep. She grunted and lunged for me.

"Get what we came for," I yelled at Kane and then choked on a mouthful of Meri's long black hair. Still battling her incredible grip on my arms, I met Kane's eyes. He glanced at Dan and raised his eyebrows.

I quickly shook my head. We needed the ruby first. Then we could figure out how to make a break for it.

While Dan stood, mouth open, staring at us, Kane slipped into the smaller room.

Please, please, please let this stone be easy to find.

I twisted my wrist, trying to dislodge from Meri's grip. Unsuccessful, I tried to yank my arm back, but she was quicker. With a barely detectable thread of magic, Meri slammed me against the floor.

I grunted and swallowed a cry of distress. Kane would never ignore something like that. And I needed him to find that ruby.

"Meri, stop!" Dan demanded and then reached down to pull her away from me.

The demon's eyes lightened to clear gray. A barely contained calm settled over her as she worked hard to let go of what I could have sworn was fear.

Why in the world would she fear any of us? And why was she listening to Dan?

What in the mighty name of the devil was going on here? I opened my mouth, couldn't get the words out, swallowed, and tried again. "Dan? Are you and Meri…?"

The demon glanced up at Dan expectantly.

What the F? Meri was waiting for the answer to my unasked question. The pit in my gut grew heavier.

"We're friends…" His voice trailed off. He stared at Meri, pale green eyes searching hers.

My stomach turned. "Dan! She's a demon."

"You don't understand," he shot back.

"Of course I don't understand. She abducted my mother, possessed you and Lailah, and hurt Kane. She's an evil, energy-sucking, ruthless demon!"

Kane emerged from the other room, slipping unnoticed past Meri and Dan, who'd been staring at me. He pressed against the far wall, leaning as if he'd been present the whole time. He barely tilted his head in a confirmation. He had what he needed.

"Not anymore," Dan said quietly.

Meri gazed at him, something close to adoration streaming off her.

I was going to be sick.

The stone door started to rumble again. Meri sprung into action, pushing Dan back into the adjoining room. She tried to close him in, but she was too late. Philip and Lailah barged into Meri's quarters, covered in soot and demon blood.

Meri bolted forward and then froze, saying and doing nothing.

"We have to find a way out of here," I yelled and ran to Kane's side. "Get Dan," I whispered.

He took two steps, but Dan materialized on his own.

"Got what you need, Jade?" Philip asked, scanning the room until his gaze landed on his son.

"Now we do." I reached for Kane's hand.

Lailah started a chant I recognized as Latin. Her magic quickly built into a small white globe floating in front of her. Philip added a second chant.

His voice snapped Meri out of her trance. "Philip?" she asked, a quaver in her tone.

I thought he might ignore her, but with his sad gaze locked tight on her hers, he gave her the smallest of nods.

Tears rolled down her angular face. "You came," she choked out. "You finally came."

"Yeah," Philip said in a flat voice, void of emotion. "I'm here for my son."

Lailah's orb took off around the room. The iridescent light briefly touched each of our chests before zooming back to Lailah. At the last second, Meri stepped in its path, causing the orb to barely graze her shoulder. She hissed and jumped back.

"Bind us to the earth," Lailah cried. "Take us where death does not live!"

A soft tingle spread through my center, warm and comfortable. Then every nerve ending screamed in agony. My soul stretched and struggled to not shatter beneath the force of whatever was trying to eat me from within.

The world around me spun, making me nauseated. A blur of color, starting with reds and eventually filtering to blue and green, filled my vision. Wind kicked up around me as I twisted, trying to crawl out of my skin. I squeezed my eyes shut and reached for Kane's hand again.

Only it wasn't his. I had someone else's smaller, more delicate hand. I didn't care. I just needed to hold on to someone. Suddenly the nausea and pain vanished, and I found myself lying breathless in a green meadow, bordered with vibrant marigolds.

No, not a meadow. Bea's backyard.

The fingers still clutched in mine twitched. I glanced over and snatched my hand back in horror.

Meri.

Chapter 18

Scrambling to my feet, I glared at the demon in front of me. We had to break her connection to Kane and send her back to Hell.

Now. Before she hurt anyone else.

I took a step and paused. Meri wasn't moving. Her chest barely rose with each shallow breath. Kane and Dan were sprawled on either side of her, and Philip and Lailah were nowhere to be seen.

I fell to my knees beside Kane. He turned his bewildered eyes on me, clearly still addled from the reality jump.

"Don't break the circle!" Lucien's familiar voice commanded my attention.

I spun, finally noticing the whole coven, plus Bea and my mother, surrounding us. Magic sparked between them. I hardly felt a thing.

"Get up!" I demanded and pulled Kane to his feet. He swayed, but managed to stay upright. "Help me with Dan."

Meri sat up and put out a hand as if to stop us, but dropped it and stared at the grass.

What was she up to? Was she too weak? It didn't matter.

I needed to get Dan away from her. He gazed up at me as a small, playful smile crept over his lips. "It's about time," he teased. "I thought you'd never get us out of there."

I frowned. Clearly he wasn't aware of the current situation. "Come on." I extended my hand. "We've got to go."

He didn't move. "Why?"

"Dan, please," I begged, willing him to accept my help.

Finally he grabbed it, but as he sat up, he noticed Meri. "You okay?" he asked her.

Not looking up, she shook her head.

He let go and scooted the few feet to her side.

"No, Dan! It's a trap." My heart jumped to my throat as he wrapped an arm around her. "What the hell are you doing?"

He looked up, eyes wide and eyebrows raised in surprise. "What do you mean? I'm helping her. Just like you do for all your friends."

"You still think she's your friend?" I glanced around, making sure we really were in Bea's backyard. The coven, Bea, and my mother held the circle. Thank goodness—otherwise, Meri would be free. After we broke her connection to Kane, she was headed straight back to Hell.

The group stared at us with a mix of confusion and wonder. Bea's emotions were closed off, as usual, but she carefully studied Meri and Dan. My mother locked eyes with me, fear and distrust written all over her face.

I clutched Kane's arm. "Is this real? I mean, we're not dreaming or something."

"No." He pulled away from the pair still sitting on the grass. "It's as real as it gets."

"But what's that all about?" I gestured to Dan and Meri. "Stockholm syndrome?"

"Maybe." His voice came out strained and with his free hand, he clutched his leg.

Instantly, I went lightheaded. I grabbed on to him and we both teetered over. Kane landed on my left shoulder. "Ouch," I cried.

"Jade." My mom's voice penetrated my dizzy haze.

Kane flopped on his back in the grass, breathing heavy.

My energy came in waves, pulsing through me with each of Kane's ragged breaths. Damn it! Meri was still sucking my energy from him. I placed my hand on his chest. "Do you have the ruby?"

With his eyes closed, he reached into his pocket and pulled the gleaming jewel out.

Dan shot to his feet. "No!" He ran over and dived to tackle me.

I rolled just in time to avoid being crushed. When I sat up, Kane already had his arms wrapped around Dan from behind, holding him in a headlock. Hot, intense anger surged from Kane, no doubt the source of his new found strength.

"What's wrong with you?" Kane seethed. "She put her life in danger to save yours."

"And I gave mine up for her." Dan twisted, trying to escape Kane's grasp.

"Stop," Meri said in a voice so quiet I barely heard her over the struggle in front of me. "Dan, stop fighting them."

We all turned, silent in our astonishment.

Meri had gotten to her feet. Her entire demeanor had changed. Gone was the vindictive, revenge-loving demon, and in her place stood a woman bent forward, hands clasped behind her back, and shoulders hunched. Tired. Beaten. Full of sorrow.

If she wasn't my sworn enemy, I'd feel sorry for her.

Dan stopped struggling, and Kane shoved him away. Rubbing his neck, Dan moved once again to Meri's side.

She lifted her head, tears glistening in her now gray eyes. "Let them do what they have to."

Dan grabbed her by the shoulders, making her straighten up. "If they do, you'll be lost again. And after everything we've worked for—"

She touched his cheek, a gentle, loving caress. "I'm living off stolen energy. It isn't right. None of this is." She waved a hand indicating Kane and me. "They deserve to live their lives. I had my chance. It's time for me to go...back." She choked out the word and glanced away.

I heard their conversation, but nothing made sense.

Meri, a caring individual? A self-sacrificing one? For God's sake, she was a demon.

I turned to Bea. "How is any of this possible?"

My mentor appeared just as shocked as I was. She shook her head, still carefully holding the powerful circle together. She wasn't taking any chances.

And neither was I. It had to be a trick. She'd either possessed Dan again or brainwashed him. Who knew what could happen in Hell?

Centering myself, I breathed deep and sent out my awareness. Usually I made an effort to not invade other people's energy. The intrusion left me drained. But Meri wasn't a person. And if she was acting, we needed to know.

Kane's emotions, on some level, always registered with me. As his frustration came into clearer focus, I squeezed his hand and pushed his energy to the back of my mind. We'd grown so close, I couldn't completely block him anyway.

As Dan's anxiety, impatience, and fear overtook my senses, my blood boiled and adrenaline made me itch for action. But I knew him well. Better than I knew Kane, even. I'd once been able to push his energy to the side. That changed after he'd been victim to Meri's possession a few months ago. Curiously, I didn't have an issue this time. With one sweep, Dan's emotions faded into the recesses of my mind.

I let out a tiny sigh of relief. Maybe he wasn't possessed. Or Meri was too weak to fill him with the vitriol I'd experienced just a week ago, before I'd kicked her ass and banished her to Hell.

I threw my mental energy into Meri. Her sorrow rushed through my limbs, making me shake. My heart weighed heavy with years of her unshed tears. My eyes burned, and I blinked back the intense desire to cry.

Meri turned, probably sensing my intrusion. She locked eyes with Dan, and fearful anticipation engulfed me, along with no small amount of love and loyalty. All of it courtesy of Meri's emotional state. The demon had feelings for Dan. She cared about him. Deeply. But how? What had happened after

I'd broken her last week? You couldn't kill demons, but they could turn into an empty shell of their former selves.

Had she somehow gotten a new soul?

Terror seized me. Was that possible?

Kane reached for me, clasping my hand. A smooth, cold rock pressed into my palm, a small point pinching into my skin. The ruby.

I needed to destroy it to break the connection. I only hoped I had enough power.

Holding my palm up, I met Meri's gaze, her intense eyes searching mine. An overwhelming sense of sorrow rocked me to my core. The sadness poured from her and touched my soul.

I hesitated. Was Meri beyond hope? Bea told me she was, but that was before we'd seen this new side of her. If I didn't destroy the stone, what would happen to Kane? I couldn't put him in danger just because I wasn't sure what was happening with the demon. Whatever it was, she needed to go back to Hell, where she belonged.

"Go on, Jade." Bea urged from behind me. "Say the incantation. We're here to back you up."

In all the confusion, I'd forgotten the coven could feed me power again. Reaching for my magical spark, I frowned. The usual flutter below my breast bone was gone, leaving nothing but an unfamiliar void.

Damn, I'd lost more energy than I thought.

Don't think about it. Just get through this and everything will be all right. I could have a mental breakdown later.

Thank goodness for Bea and the coven. Resisting the urge to close my eyes, I kept a trained eye on Meri and held my hand out. Sun bounced off the ruby.

Meri and Dan froze. Then they exchanged a small glance. I had to cast the spell now.

"Binding stone, hear my call. Sever your hold." A small thread of coven magic pulsed in my chest. It was working. "Break the connection between dreamwalker and demon. Let your magic run cold."

The heat from the stone faded. The coven's power ran currents of magic through my veins. Alive. Powerful. Pure. My body flexed with strength, ready to destroy the stone. Once it turned icy cold, I could unleash the firestorm of destruction built by the coven. I focused on the very center of the ruby, ready to strike.

Dan moved, but I felt, rather than saw, Meri hold him in place. For whatever reason, she didn't want him to interfere. Concern for him? Or did she really mean it was time for her to go back?

A fresh current of power jolted through me with so much force, I stumbled. My knee hit the soft earth and the ruby tumbled to the ground.

My only thought was to retrieve the stone and break Meri's hold on Kane. Now or never. I closed my fingers around the narrow tip. Immediately I let the coven magic go, forcing it into the jewel.

Someone dove in front of me, knocking the stone from my tentative grip, but it was too late. The power I'd unleashed was already doing its job.

Behind me, Kane grunted and muttered obscenities, no doubt suffering a horrific extraction. I turned, expecting to see Dan holding the stone. Instead, he cradled Meri, careful not to let her fall.

If Dan hadn't tried to take the ruby, then who had? I turned and met pale green eyes filled with guilt.

Philip. Where had he been?

"Siste!" he yelled and grabbed the stone. A white light pulsed in his hand.

"Philip?" Meri said in a faint, bewildered voice.

Lailah echoed Meri's call from outside the circle. Her eyes widened with disbelief as she hurried toward him.

Philip concentrated on the ruby until the glow disappeared. A sharp stab of ice ripped through my gut. I doubled over, clenching my stomach with my hands. The pain spread through my core, pulsing. My knees gave out and I fell to the ground, gasping for air.

Philip yelled, "Go!"

Black spots clouded my vision. Who was he yelling at?

I tried to get to my feet, ready to flee, but the spots grew bigger as my head spun. Voices morphed into a dull static of white noise. I clamped my hands to my temples and dropped to my knees once more, rocking back and forth, willing my senses to clear.

"Kane?" I called, but had no idea if he could hear me.

Someone clasped my shoulders, keeping me from falling. The person was talking, but through the static, I couldn't make out any words.

Panic seized me. Blinded and deaf, I groped for the person steadying me. Strong arms came around me and through my haze, the scent of fresh rain reached me.

Kane. His scent. I was safe.

I took deep, steady breaths. Kane's worry started to seep into my awareness. Without thinking, I sent him a tiny dose of calm. His grip around me relaxed, but he didn't let go. I leaned into him, grateful for the familiarity.

He tensed, and before I could react, a zap of magic tingled through me. The static faded, and the bright glare of the late afternoon made me squint.

"Welcome back," Bea said, squatting in front of me on her lawn.

"Um…thanks." I glanced around at the coven, still holding the circle. Only Bea and Kane were with me in the middle. "Where are Dan and Meri?"

"Gone." Bea's face was blank.

"Gone, as in…back to Hell gone?" I clamped a hand over my forehead and rubbed at the headache pulsing above my eyes.

"Oh, no, dear. Once Philip interrupted the unbinding, the three of them took off. In Philip's car."

"What do you mean? Left in his car?" I twisted, spotting Lailah. "What's going on?"

She swallowed, her lips pressed together in a thin line. "It appears Philip has decided to help his mate after all."

The hurt in her bright blue eyes almost made me want to hug her. I pushed the impulse aside. "Does that mean he's on the verge of falling too?"

Lailah shook her head slowly. "No."

"How come? He's helping a demon."

Lailah's eyes locked with Bea's, each of them reading something in the other's gaze.

"What?" I demanded.

"Here's the strange thing." Lailah paced in front of me and paused in thought.

"Yes?" I prompted.

She met my penetrating stare. "Meri isn't a demon anymore."

I shot to my feet, almost toppling over, but Kane caught me. "Thanks," I mumbled and turned back to Lailah. "How is that possible?"

"We don't know for sure," Bea chimed in, her face pinched in confusion.

"Something went wrong when Philip interrupted the unbinding. The spell didn't work correctly," Lailah said, her eyes full of pity.

I spun, grasping Kane's forearms. "What happened? Are you all right?" Hastily, I did a visual inspection and then frowned when I didn't see any obvious damage. "Did she get another mark on you?"

He smiled. "No. In fact, I'm as good as new. See?" He put his full weight on his previously injured leg and grinned. "All better."

"Good. That's good." I let out a sigh of relief and turned back to Lailah. "How is that possible? We were with her the night her soul died. How can she be anything other than a demon without a soul?"

"She has one now. Or part of one."

An ache rippled through my core, settling in my gut. "Part of one? Whose? Dan's?"

"No, dear," Bea said gently. "Not Dan's. For the time being, his is still safe."

"Whose then?"

Lailah took a step forward and rested a light hand on my shoulder. "Whatever Philip did when he broke your unbinding spell caused it to malfunction. Kane was freed from her grasp, but somehow, she managed to siphon part of someone's soul." Compassion radiated from her. "Yours."

"Mine?" I started to tremble, frantically searching for the edges of my soul. I'd touched it once while Bea coached me on finding my inner magic. It had to be there. "Am I...I mean, could I...is it gone?"

Lailah shook her head. "No."

"Thank God." Hell wasn't a place I ever wanted to visit again.

"But it's not one hundred percent here, either."

"What does that mean?"

"You and Meri...well, you're both sharing your soul."

Chapter 19

"How is that even possible?" I asked, lying in Kane's lap. After Lailah had broken the news, I'd lost the ability to stand. I'd still be sharing the lawn with a colony of ladybugs if Kane hadn't carried me to the safety of Bea's living room.

Silence.

I turned my attention to Bea. She held a thick, mystical text open in her lap, one finger tracing the lines as she scanned for information. A few seconds passed before she glanced up, meeting my gaze. Her expression turned sympathetic and she gave me a tiny shake of her head. She didn't have any answers.

Across the room, Lailah paced in a small oval, rapidly typing a message on her iPhone. Somehow she'd managed to rid herself of her blood-soaked clothes and had changed into a coffee-colored blouse and white cotton skirt. Her brow creased and her lips moved, forming a silent curse.

Everyone else was still outside. Gwen, who'd been watching from the porch, and my mother were helping the coven cleanse Bea's yard. They needed to rid the area of any residual evil left behind from our return trip from Hell.

I sat up. "Lailah?"

She whirled, appearing startled, as if realizing for the first time she wasn't alone. Her phone buzzed and, after a quick glance at a message, she let out a cry of frustration and threw the phone into a winged-back chair.

"What's going on?" I squeezed Kane's hand, needing to feel something solid.

She scowled. "The National Order just tasked me with tracking Philip."

"And that's a problem why?" One way or another we'd have to find Meri, because I sure as shit wasn't sharing my soul with anyone…especially an ex-demon.

"If Philip doesn't want to be found, he won't be." She threw her hands up. "No one's that close to him. Not even me." She took a deep breath and mumbled, "Especially not me."

The gut-wrenching ache buried deep inside her made me cringe. Too weak to construct my barriers, I turned to Bea and swallowed my pride. "Can I get one of your healing herbs?"

Bea raised one curious eyebrow and nodded. Under any other circumstance, I would have suffered through my weakened state. But after surviving Hell, I'd be an idiot to reject such a small bit of magical assistance. My choices were to either swallow the damn pill or risk passing out.

With a shaking hand, I took the tea Bea offered me and downed the pill before I could talk myself out of it. Almost instantly, the shaking stopped and the fuzziness in my head cleared. Lailah's pain still pressed on me, but a second later, I raised my imaginary silo.

"Better?" Lailah asked, an edge of irritation in her voice.

"Actually, yes." I set the drink on the table, certain her wrath stemmed from my intrusion on her turbulent emotions.

She locked eyes with me. *I'm entitled to a little privacy.*

I didn't pry on purpose.

She let out a huff and stormed outside, slamming the door hard enough to knock a silver-framed photo right off the wall. It fell, shattering the glass.

Both Kane and Bea turned accusing eyes on me.

"Hey!" I cried in defense. "I tried to block her emotions. Why do you think I asked for the pill? I was just too weak to construct my emotional barriers. I wasn't trying to spy on her."

Kane relaxed beside me and patted my leg. "Sorry."

Bea let out a heavy sigh. "It's been a long day. Everyone's a little on edge."

No kidding. I suppressed the desire to roll my eyes. After all, if the coven hadn't come to the rescue, Kane and I would still be in Hellville. Even though the outcome ended in a clusterfuck, at least Kane wasn't being drained and Dan was back in our reality.

So I was sharing my soul with a demon. There were worse things, right? Like actually being a demon. At least life hadn't gotten that bad...yet.

I grimaced and rose from the couch. "I'm going to find Lailah."

Kane got to his feet and followed me.

When I reached the door, I turned. "I think it's better if I talk to her alone. Do you mind?"

A tinge of his anxiety touched me.

I rose to my tiptoes and kissed his cheek. "I'll be fine. A bunch of witches are out there. What do you think is going to happen?"

Skepticism rolled off him as he raised an eyebrow.

"Okay, so anything could happen, but you being present probably isn't going to change anything. And right now, I need to have a one-on-one with her." I gave him an apologetic look. "With the questions I need to ask, your presence will make our chat awkward at best."

He took a step back, and he nodded as my words sunk in. "I see."

"Thanks." I hugged him and then headed out the door.

Before it closed, I heard Bea say, "They need to work through their differences on their own. The sooner they figure out how to work together, the better. If not—"

Click.

Damn it. If not, what? I paused and contemplated reopening the door. No. There would be time to question Bea later. I moved to the railing of the porch and scanned the grounds.

The coven members were still gathered in a circle. My mother and Gwen were inside, smudging away with sage bundles. I almost laughed. I highly doubted sage would ward off any evil from Hell, but I'm sure the process put Mom at ease. Smudging used to be one of her specialties. In her mind, a space was never quite right until it got a good dose of smudging.

Lucien caught my eye and trotted over. "Feeling better?"

"A little. Bea hooked me up with a healing herb."

"This should help, too." He grabbed my hands. "I, Lucien Boulard, transfer the leadership of the New Orleans coven to you, Jade Calhoun."

A small zing of power sparked into my fingers, traveling to my chest. The coven magic filled the vacancy I hadn't quite gotten used to. I sighed in relief. "Thank you. That does help."

He gave me an awkward hug. "Glad you made it back safe."

With a short nod, he rejoined the coven as I made my way down the steps, scanning for Lailah. After a quick, unsuccessful peek at the back porch, I headed down the driveway past the main house. Bea lived in the carriage home on an old plantation property in the middle of the Garden District. Rich violet and pink flowers lined the immaculate, manicured lawns. She'd told us her cousins lived in the family home, but I'd yet to see any of them. Did Lailah know them? Maybe that's where she'd escaped to.

A narrow stone path veered off into lush gardens on the side of the driveway. On impulse, I followed it. No harm in checking before I bothered people I'd never met. Deep red wine-colored rose bushes framed the walkway until I got to a curve, where a large, thick orange tree to the left blocked my view of the rest of the garden.

Before I made the corner, I already knew I'd found the angel. Her inner turmoil, a murky mix of guilt and trepidation, came through loud and clear.

I didn't bother to slow my steps. Just as I sensed her, she no doubt heard my thoughts. What a pair.

"Did you miss the part where I stormed out?" she asked as soon as I spotted her on a green-painted wrought iron bench. "Or are you too clueless to realize I wanted to be alone?"

"I noticed." The chill of cold metal seeped through my jeans as I took a seat next to her. I sagged in relief, grateful for the break in exertion. Bea's vitamin hadn't helped as much as I'd hoped.

Lailah stared straight ahead, watching a chirping red bird sitting at the base of the orange tree. "Spit it out."

Normally I'd take my time assessing someone's emotional state before asking such a personal question, but Lailah had to know what I was thinking. This was her way of making me squirm. I hated to pry, but my soul was on the line.

There was no use beating around the orange tree. "What exactly is your relationship with Philip?"

She made a small noise in the back of her throat.

"Oh, come on. You already knew I was going to ask. I'm sorry, but considering the circumstances, I think it's a fair question."

Her pale face flushed pink. "We're…friends."

"And?"

She turned to me, her eyes narrowed and angry. "That's all. He's definitely not my boyfriend, if that's what you're getting at."

That's exactly what I'd been asking. Hadn't he slept in her bed with her? I wasn't convinced their relationship was entirely platonic. Judging by the blush deepening on her cheeks, I was right on target. "So you're friends, but you're sleeping together. Right?"

She pursed her lips and bit the side of her cheek. Then she gave me a short nod.

"Goddess, Lailah. Was that so hard? It's not like I was going to call you a slut or anything."

She plucked at an invisible thread on her white cotton skirt. "He has a mate," she said quietly.

"A demon one. What's he supposed to do, stay celibate for the rest of his life?"

She shook her head. "He's free to do whatever he wishes. But there's something you don't understand about angels."

I waited for her to enlighten me. When she didn't continue, I prompted, "And that would be?"

She met my gaze with her intense one. "Once angels lose their mate to Hell, they are incapable of truly loving another. Something crucial is lost. A piece of them dies." A single tear glistened in her right eye. She lifted a finger and wiped it away.

"You're in love with him." It wasn't a question, but a statement.

She didn't respond. She didn't have to. The vice seizing her heart said it all.

A long moment went by as we both stared at nothing. Finally I turned to her. "Then why were you so fixated on Kane?"

She barked out a laugh. "Philip has a bad habit of popping in and out of my life. I never know if or when he'll be around. The last time he left, I promised myself I wasn't going to wait for him anymore. That's when I started dating Kane."

She got up and paced again. "Our relationship didn't last long. How could it? I mean, I was always dreaming of Philip. And since Kane dreamwalks…well, it wasn't long before we broke up."

A dose of guilt shot up my spine. All this time I'd been jealous of their relationship, and Kane never said a word about Lailah's feelings for someone else. Of course, he'd never betray her trust, but still. The information would have defused quite a bit of tension.

She smiled wistfully. "Maybe knowing about Philip would've saved us some tension, but not likely."

"Why not?"

She ran a hand through her long mane. "The thing is, I did like Kane. It was easier to pine for him than it was Philip."

I frowned, not following.

She sat next to me again, turning so her knees almost brushed mine. "You see, my heart was safer pining for Kane. I knew we'd never get back together. But if I devoted my energy to him, I wouldn't have to think about Philip, and at the same time I'd be free if Philip ever came to town again."

Her heartache started to fade with her confession. Suddenly compassion for her overtook all my other emotions. How awful to be in love with someone who could never love you back.

"Exactly." She rose and offered me her hand. "I owe you an apology. If I'd faced my reality sooner, there never would have been a strong enough connection between Kane and me for Meri to get her hooks into. He'd never have been marked and you wouldn't be in this mess."

"You don't know that." I shook my head as I grabbed her hand and stood. "Besides, none of this is your fault. We can blame Meri, but it's not her fault either. She didn't want to fall and lose her soul. It just happened, and now we need to deal with the consequences."

She nodded and started to walk back toward Bea's house. "You're right. The question is, where do we start?"

"You know Philip better than any of us," I said, following her. "If anyone can find him, you can."

"Goddess, I hope so." She stopped and picked up a fallen rose petal. She held it out on her palm and blew. As it glided on the mild wind, she whispered, "I really, really hope so."

Chapter 20

I followed Lailah down the narrow path toward the driveway. Her sandals slapped against the stones, filling the silence between us. I stared at my dirty Skechers, racking my brain on how to locate Dan.

Could Kane dreamwalk me to him? A tiny shudder ran through me. The last thing I wanted to do was ask Kane to invade Dan's dreams.

Lailah snorted. "Good luck with that."

"Get out of my head." I kicked a tiny rock in her direction. The pebble missed and landed in the dirt.

She stopped at the edge of the driveway, holding her hands up in defeat. "Sorry. I can't help it."

I rolled my eyes and swept past her.

"You know…" She fell in step beside me and let out an exaggerated sigh. "There is one way to smoke them out, but it's pretty drastic."

I sent her a sideways glance and raised my eyebrows.

She massaged her temple before answering. "I could get them on Goodwin's 'save' list. Then all of his followers would be on the hunt."

I froze. "Are you serious?"

"Well, sure. It's not like we can put an APB out on them or anything. This is the next best thing."

My stomach turned at the thought of unleashing hundreds of 'saviors' on anyone. It was too damn bad the idea had merit. I closed my eyes and took a deep breath. "Let's check with Bea and Lucien first. If they don't have any suggestions, I guess we can try."

"Great," she said her tone flat.

"You don't think they can help?"

She shook her head. "No, that's not...look, I'm just not crazy about working with Goodwin."

"I'm not crazy about the idea either, but it was your suggestion."

"I know." She plucked a leaf from a nearby tree. "Just because it's the only suggestion I have doesn't mean I want to do it."

Watching her, I narrowed my eyes. Exactly what was their relationship? Were they mates or not? Hard to believe if Lailah had feelings for Philip.

She spun. "Goodwin is most definitely not my mate. No matter how delusional he may be about the subject."

Her indignation made me smile. "So why would the good Reverend think such a thing if it's out of the realm of possibility?"

All the fight seemed to drain out of her as her shoulders sagged and the irritation vanished from her face. "We dated as teenagers."

"Really?" I had trouble reconciling the conservative religious evangelist and the bohemian free spirit actually dating. "For how long?"

She swallowed. "Three years."

"Holy smokes!" I gaped. "No wonder he thinks you're mates."

"You dated Dan for years. Do you think you're destined to spend the rest of eternity with him?"

"Of course not, but I'm not an angel."

She shook her head in exasperation. "Angels are only mates once they claim each other in a formal ceremony." The tone of her voice softened as she continued, "I never claimed Jonathon."

I'd never heard her so vulnerable before. I took a step closer and gently touched her arm. "But he claimed you."

Tears filled her bright blue eyes and she nodded.

"What happened?"

She brushed a hand across her eyes and pasted a forced smile on her face. "The classic runaway-bride scenario. I made it all the way to the binding ceremony, but when it was my turn, I ran. By the time I found the nerve to face him again, he'd joined the church and turned into someone I didn't recognize."

Oh, God. How awful. "How much time went by?"

"Six months."

"Poor Jonathon." I let the words slip before I had the time to bite them back. Yikes. "Sorry."

She shook her head. "You're right. It was an awful thing to do, but I was young and I panicked. Afterwards, I didn't know how to approach him. Since then…well, we are two very different people. But I wish he'd come to terms with the fact that we are no longer meant to be."

"And Philip's the right angel?"

She shrugged. "Probably not. Especially since he's helping Meri now." Sadness flashed in her eyes, but she pulled her hand away and held her head high. "Let's get going. We have an ex-demon to find."

I followed Lailah back to Bea's. We were climbing the porch steps when a red VW Bug roared up the drive and skidded to a stop behind Bea's silver Prius. Kat jumped out and ran over, grasping me in a fierce hug. "Thank God you're okay."

"Whoa." I laughed and gently pushed her away. "Did Gwen call you?"

"Lucien." She nodded to Lailah. "Thanks for taking care of her."

"All in a day's work." Lailah smiled and moved onto the porch.

Kat turned to me. "Where's Dan?"

"Lucien didn't tell you?" I mentally cursed him. I hated to be the bearer of bad news…again.

She shook her head.

"He's—" A crippling flash of anger rippled through me. The weirdly familiar yet foreign energy made my knees buckle, and I grabbed Kat's arm for support. Uncontrollable rage took over my senses. I dug my fingers into Kat's flesh until she cried out.

"Jade, stop!"

Her cry sliced through the unwanted mental energy, bringing me back to myself. I let go. "Oh my God. I'm so sorry."

Kat cradled her arm against her chest. "What was that?"

I took a step back as the rage tried to overtake me again. Quickly I raised my mental silo, the one that never failed to give me peace. But this time, the anger only grew stronger. And worse, I couldn't get a read on Kat at all. She was usually the one person I could count on to lend me strength when I needed some. I grabbed my head with both hands, trying to curb the intense pounding caused by the turbulent rage.

"Jade!" Kat cried again and shook me. "What's going on?"

My barriers disappeared, and Kat's panic started to edge out the foreign energy. "It's okay," I said, letting out a long breath. "I'm okay."

I sought out Lailah, now holding Kane back on the porch. When had he come outside? I gave him a weak smile. He tried to brush her off, but she moved in front of him. "She needs to work this out herself."

I met her worried eyes. "Meri's causing this?"

She nodded. "I'm afraid so. The sooner you learn to control the connection, the stronger you'll be."

Ugh. My trusty silo wasn't going to do the trick this time. How did one block out emotions connected to her own soul?

I leaned against the counter at The Grind, the café I worked at, and popped my sixth magically enhanced vitamin of the day. My chai tea scalded the roof of my mouth as I choked the concoction down.

"Again?" Pyper asked, packing grinds into the espresso machine.

"Yes. I can't seem to get through a few hours without needing one."

She made a face. "Your *condition* is getting worse."

I twisted, stretching my back. "I know, but until we find Meri, there isn't much else I can do."

Five days had passed since our trip into Hell. After hours of research, neither Bea nor Lucien had found any practical way of locating the trio. Bea tried a finding spell, but as suspected, Philip had the group shielded by a specialized spell only angels could wield. Lailah knew the counter-spell, but couldn't reverse it unless she was near them.

We also tried the same locator spell we'd used the night we transported Philip and Jonathon to the coven circle. It actually backfired and Bea produced a mirror image of herself. That was weird. Especially since Bea number two didn't fade for twelve hours. It was like having a doppelganger following her around.

"Has the good reverend and his merry band of proselytizers had any luck?" Pyper handed me a chocolate cinnamon danish. "You look like you need a pick me up."

I took it and jammed a piece in my mouth, barely chewing before I swallowed. I'd been having sugar cravings all week. Serious cravings. Like, get up at two in the morning and run to the neighborhood Quick Mart for some ice cream cravings.

Afterwards I always felt a little more energetic. I was sure I was only contributing to a future hypoglycemic crash, but damn. I was sharing my soul with a demon. There couldn't possibly be any other better excuse for overindulging on the sweets.

Reluctantly, I set the danish down. Caving to chocolate and cinnamon was one thing. Inhaling my food was another.

I turned back to Pyper. "No luck yet from Goodwin or his followers. This morning he released pictures of each of them on his television show. We're hoping his TV audience can help with the hunt."

Her eyes went wide. "Goodwin put out a religious Amber Alert on them?"

I made a face. "Sort of. I mean, for our purposes he did. But his followers think the three of them voluntarily sent in pictures asking for prayers. He didn't say they were missing, only that if anyone spotted them, to please offer them prayers and assistance. Then he added a hotline number asking the three of them to call him directly so he could be their personal savior. Knowing Goodwin's zealots, if Philip, Dan, or Meri are spotted, someone will call."

Pyper shook her head. "Remind me to never get on the wrong side of Goodwin. I can think of nothing worse than being hunted down by a bunch of religious fanatics."

"I know it's extreme, but we're out of options. Lailah's on the phone constantly with her angel connections, but she wasn't kidding when she said if Philip doesn't want to be found, he won't be."

The bell chimed, and in walked Charlie, the manager of the strip club next door. "Hey, pretty ladies. Lookin' sexy as usual."

I laughed, and Pyper rolled her eyes. "You need new contacts," Pyper said, scanning the milk-stained apron she wore. She tilted her head toward the carafe of premade Columbian. "Coffee?"

"No, thanks. I'm here on a mission." She walked behind the counter and grabbed a metal pitcher then rummaged through the refrigerator.

I stepped up. "Need help?"

"I've got this." She reached out and untied my apron. "You look like you could use a break. Take a load off. I can cover you."

I retied my apron. "That's sweet, but no. I need to help Pyper. We close in an hour and there's still a lot of cleaning to be done."

Charlie put on a no-nonsense manager face I'd never seen before. "It's not a request. The boss sent me to check up on you." She scanned the length of my body. "I'm sorry to say, despite finding you hotter than a fried green tomato, I'm going to have to insist you call it a day. If Kane walks in and sees you dead on your feet, I'm gonna be the one who has to deal with his cranky ass all night." She poured soymilk and some chai tea concentrate into a cup, filled it with ice, and handed it to me. "Now go. I'll help Pyper clean up."

I sent Pyper a questioning glance.

She shook her head. "I don't want to deal with his cranky ass either. Go on up to your apartment. We can manage from here."

With my chai in one hand and my danish in the other, I took off through the back door and headed up the first of the three flights of stairs leading to my studio apartment. At each landing I had to pause, taking bites of my snack to regain some energy. Stupid soul-stealing angel-demon. I couldn't even get up to my apartment without a major sugar injection.

When I finally stopped in front of my door, I frowned at the tiny sliver left of my danish. Darn it. I should have taken another one for later. Deciding it was too hard to hold the pastry and unlock my door at the same time, I stuffed it in my mouth.

I jiggled my key, forcing the sticky lock that had been acting up for over two weeks. Since I hadn't been home much, I hadn't gotten around to telling Kane, who also happened to be my landlord. I made a mental note. He needed something else to focus on other than me.

Inside my apartment, I didn't stop to change out of my café clothes. All I cared about was my bed.

Five steps later, and I flopped on the goose down comforter. Ah, the soft pillow top was better than heaven. Better even than the chocolate cinnamon danish. The bed shifted. I squinted at Duke, my golden retriever ghost dog, now lying next to me, his head on the second pillow. "Enjoy yourself while you can, buddy. Once Kane shows up, you're back to the couch."

The dog let out a muffled snort and in seconds was snoring.

I closed my eyes, more than ready to follow him into dreamland.

My reality faded and a moment later I found myself in a rustic shack with white paint peeling off the wood plank walls.

The floors were constructed of the same thick wood planks, but no one had bothered to ever paint them. Swollen with years of humidity, the grain was rough against my bare feet as I moved to the only window in the old structure.

Unfortunately, the glass was completely obscured with layers of caked on dirt. I paced with my hands laced behind my back. A heavy dose of anxiety rippled through me, but I didn't know why.

Female voices carried from the hall into the small room. Nervous energy made me bite my nails, but I quickly dropped my fingers from my mouth as the door creaked open.

I stood stock-still, terror and hope fighting for my dominating response.

My shoulders hunched with disappointment when Dan filled the doorway. I didn't mind seeing him. I just expected someone else.

He smiled reassuringly. "Don't worry so much. Everything's going to be fine."

I grimaced. Easy for him to say. He wasn't the one sharing his soul.

"You'll see." He stepped into the room, leaving the door wide open, and gestured to me. "Ladies, Meri's waiting."

Meri?

Holy shit! He meant me. In my dream I was Meri. Was this happening right now, and I was witnessing it? My excitement was squashed by the turmoil churning inside her.

A second later, a woman with long, pale blond hair and striking Caribbean blue eyes hesitated in the threshold. Meri held her breath. The last time she'd seen her sister, she'd been wielding enough magic to bring down half the state of Louisiana.

An incredible amount of relief rushed through Meri. Felicia was safe.

"Where's Priscilla?" Meri asked, her voice quiet and strained.

A slow smile crossed Felicia's face, and she headed straight toward Meri.

"Felicia!" A fierce voice carried in from the hallway, followed closely by its owner. Priscilla stomped into the room, hands on her hips, eyes narrowed. "Don't go any closer."

"I can assure you she's safe," Dan said mildly.

Priscilla shot him a skeptical look and then dismissed him with a cut of her eyes back to Felicia. "If what he says is true, her soul is still compromised."

Felicia sighed, and Meri could almost hear her praying for patience. "Yes, but she isn't tainted."

"Not yet," Priscilla said.

Felicia moved closer, carefully studying Meri from head to toe. She squinted. "Your posture is different."

"What?" She straightened, pulling her shoulders back.

"You're carrying yourself differently." Felicia walked around her in a circle, nodding. "Yes, that's it. You're less confident, and it shows."

"You're right." Meri's shoulder slumped in defeat. "This can't last. Two people weren't meant to share the same soul. One of us will eventually overtake the other. Then what happens? I want a normal life, but not at the expense of someone else."

Dan's face clouded. "What do you mean, one of you will take over the other?"

Meri stared at him for a minute, sadness squeezing her heart.

"She means two people cannot share the same soul forever." Philip leaned against the door frame. How long had he been standing there? Meri's heart started to hammer with excitement, quickly replaced by disappointment and rejection.

He uncrossed his ankles and stood straight with his hands shoved in his pockets. "They can for a little while, but when one becomes too weak, the soul will migrate to the stronger individual."

"Do you think Meri's stronger?" Dan asked.

Philip nodded. "She's an angel."

"No, I'm not," Meri said.

"You're not a demon anymore. What else would you be?" Philip countered.

"What about Jade?" Dan frowned, worry creasing his brow. "What will happen to her?"

"That's for the council to decide." Philip moved to stand in front of Meri, his eyes filled with longing, regret, and something tortured.

Meri's two sisters retreated from the room. Dan hovered near the door, uncertainty clear in his expression.

With Philip's gaze so intently locked on her, Meri asked, "Why didn't you come for me?"

"I…" He swallowed. "I wanted to, but I had Dan to watch over. By the time I formed a plan, it was too late." He closed his eyes. "I can't begin to imagine what all you—"

"No, you can't. So don't even try!" She curled her hands into fists, nails biting into her palms as unbridled anger rippled through her. Meri's mind filled with dozens of unwanted memories, all shared and stolen moments with Philip. The pair of them sitting on a porch swing holding hands. Their first kiss. Their first…

"You're not my mate," she spat. "Whatever the witch did to me dissolved our connection. Including the mating bond everyone says is unbreakable. Lucky you. Now you can go off with your airhead hippy girlfriend and forget about me. Like you've been trying to do for the last twelve years."

Philip moved closer.

She bristled. "Leave me alone, Philip. Go take care of your witch's soul. There's nothing left for you here."

He took a long time before answering. When he did, he raised his chin and met her haunted gaze. "I gave up on you once. I won't do it again."

Chapter 21

My eyes flew open and my survival instinct kicked in, adrenaline racing through my veins.

No way was Meri keeping my soul. It was mine, damn it. *Mine.*

So what if I'd been the one to destroy what was left of hers? She'd been a demon at the time. It was justified. She'd tried to corrupt Bea with black magic. It's what demons did. What they were conditioned to do, once they fell from angel status.

My breathing returned to normal, and after a while, a tiny bit of guilt touched my heart. Hadn't I said Meri was a victim too?

Sure, she took my mom from me, entrapped Dan in Hell, and stole half my soul, but should she be held accountable for those things? She wasn't a demon anymore. Maybe she was responsible for the soul-stealing thing, except I wasn't sure she had control over the connection.

Until I had the chance to talk to her, I had more questions than answers.

My newest mission was to find Meri so we could share information.

Of course, all my friends thought I'd lost my mind, but they hadn't had the benefit of sharing Meri's emotions in the dream like I had. I'd witnessed firsthand her aversion to keeping my soul. Why she still held on to it, I didn't know. Maybe she didn't have a choice. What would happen to her if she didn't?

"Somebody has to know how to fix this," I whined to Lailah, Bea, and Kat. The four of us had met at Bea's to discuss my dream.

Some sort of silent communication traveled between Lailah and Bea before they both shook their heads.

"Don't think I didn't see that." I waved an accusatory hand. "What about the angel council? Or whoever you take orders from?" I asked Lailah.

"That's not a good idea," she said slowly.

"For who?" I stabbed my fork into a baked potato. "You or me?"

"Now, Jade," Bea said. "There is no need—"

Lailah held up her hand. "It's okay. She has every right to be frustrated." She turned to me. "The council is unpredictable. Asking them for help might result in…an undesirable outcome."

I made a face. "Undesirable outcome? What does that mean?"

"An earth-bound angel's job has always been to do everything in her power to save an individual's soul." Lailah paused for a moment, apparently organizing her thoughts. "There's rarely a debate about who a soul belongs to, because everyone has one of their own. As far as the high council is concerned, the person isn't important. They don't care about the vessel. The battle for souls is about ridding the world of evil. The betterment of the greater good. Not for protecting any one person."

Kat's hand tightened around my arm. A thick film of outrage circled her. "You mean, they could give Jade's soul to Meri?"

Lailah pressed her lips together in a flat line. She took a deep breath, staring me in the eye. "Since Meri is a former angel…"

She didn't need to say anything else. The reality of my situation stripped all my bravado and left my heart raw. Angels were rare. If the council had a chance to save one of their own, they would.

Kat stood, her hands on her hips, anger rippling off her. "Why do they have to give Meri Jade's soul? Why can't they give her someone else's if Meri's so important? Not that I think they should be ripping people's souls out, but it's hardly fair they'd just take Jade's."

Lailah took a deep frustrated breath and turned to Kat. "Because Meri is already sharing her soul. The council doesn't have the power to completely rip souls from people. But since Jade's is compromised, they can help bind it to one or the other."

All the fight drained out of Kat as her anger turned to fear. Then she put into words what I didn't have the courage to ask. "If they give Meri Jade's soul, what happens to Jade?"

My vision turned myopic as everything faded but Lailah's pained face. Our eyes locked and silence filled the room.

Demon. I'd be a slave to the twisted underworld.

"No." Lailah's harsh voice punched through the static filling my ears. "You wouldn't be a demon. You'd fall into a coma and your body would start to shut down. Life support could sustain you, but eventually your heart would give out." Her tone turned soft and almost apologetic. "The only part of you that will remain are our memories."

Eyes still on Lailah, I stayed seated, too shocked to speak.

"Don't be ridiculous." Kat stalked across the room before abruptly moving to stand behind my chair, hovering protectively. "Meri lost her soul and she didn't die."

Frowning, I wondered why that even mattered. Without my soul, I wouldn't want to live anyway.

Lailah slumped and cast a weary glance at Bea.

My mentor patted her hand and gave Kat her full attention. "Only angels turn demon. Human souls can be corrupted by black magic, but their essence prevents them from turning. Without both an essence and soul, a human cannot live."

"And Priscilla and Felicia? How come they didn't die when their souls and essences were taken?" I asked.

Bea's eyes turned cold with quiet unease. "Meri preserved them in Purgatory. If they'd been here, in our world, they would have."

I nodded numbly. So much for sharing information with Meri. If I wanted to survive, I had to find a way to rip my soul from her before the angel council could intervene.

Kat steamed from behind me. Righteous indignation exploded from her chest, making the room temperature rise a few degrees. "You're just telling us this now? It's been five days. I can't believe you've been holding this information back. Jade had a right to know. You should have—"

I pressed my fingers to my pounding temples and did my best to block my friend out as she continued to rage. I supposed if I were in her shoes, I'd be just as angry, if not more. Although, I had no idea how things would have been any different had they told me.

Kat started to pace again, still verbally berating our friends. They kept still, appearing appropriately chastised.

During one of her trips through the living room, I slipped out the front door and stood at the porch railing. I breathed in the cool air and wished I could will it to cleanse away all that ailed my weakening body.

After a few moments, I dug a bag of M&Ms out of my pocket and proceeded to chump down my chocolate energy treats. I was going to need a whole new, slightly larger wardrobe if I kept up the sugar craze.

The front door creaked open, and somehow, even though I couldn't feel her energy, I knew it was Lailah.

"Your headache's better?" She took a place beside me on the porch.

I nodded. Studying Bea's marigolds, I asked, "What would you do?"

She leaned over the railing and in a quiet voice said, "I'd spend every spare second with those I love and put my affairs in order. Then I'd fight like hell to keep my soul."

I tore my gaze from the flower garden and turned to her in surprise. I'd gotten so used to her reading my thoughts I hadn't felt the need to clarify my question. "I meant, if you were Philip."

"Oh." She gave me a half-smile. "I told you the connection would start to fade. I'm only getting snippets now."

Finally. At least something was going in the right direction. "So, if I'd been your assignment and you had to choose between an angel and a human, what would you do?"

Her smile faded and her shoulders hunched. "It isn't that simple."

"I know. Meri is his mate. It complicates things. But try anyway." I wasn't going to let this go. Would all angels sacrifice a human for one of their own? When it came time to fight, I needed to know who to trust.

She fidgeted, taking her time before she answered. "Field angels are very different from council angels. They live in a reality separate from our world. In a sense, people are interchangeable to them. For those of us living among humans, it's not so cut and dry. We live and love just like everyone else. I can't look at you and only see a soul. I see Jade, who is made up of her own unique soul and spirit. You aren't you without both."

"So you're saying if Meri ends up with my soul, her spirit takes over and mine dies. Like you said before, I cease to exist."

"Yes, but that isn't what I meant. I'm saying you're my friend. No matter how rough the journey we've had in our rocky relationship, I'm not willing to let you go."

The conviction in her voice made me stand taller. She mimicked my movement, and I flung my arms around her. She stiffened momentarily and then returned my hug.

"Thank you," I whispered in her ear. "You have no idea how much that means to me."

"I think I have an inkling."

I stepped back and grinned. "Psychic connections do have their uses every once in a while."

She laughed and shook her head. "I wouldn't go that far."

We were still laughing when the front door banged open. Kat stood in the threshold, excitement streaming off her. "He's been spotted."

The laughter died on my lips. "Dan?"

"Philip?" Lailah asked at the same time.

"Philip," she said. "He's in Cajun Cove."

Having spent less than a year in Louisiana, and most of that time within a ten-mile radius, the name of the town meant nothing to me. "Where's that?"

Lailah whipped out her phone and tapped in a number. "South of here, in the middle of the bayou."

I stepped into the house and snatched my purse. As I turned to leave, Lailah strode back in and took a seat at the table. "What are you doing?" I asked.

She grabbed a piece of paper and a pen. "Making a list of supplies so we'll be ready in the morning."

I hitched my purse higher on my shoulder and tightened my grip on the handle. "In the morning? We need to go now."

"We can't go in the dark," Lailah said. "Cajun Cove is an island in the middle of the bayou. We'll need an airboat, a guide, and supplies. Philip isn't staying there. Too many people. He'll be holed up at a camp somewhere and only going to town for food and stuff."

Slowly, I relaxed my grip on my purse and set it back down. Despite every nerve screaming to hunt down my guardian angel, I took a seat at the table. "What can I do?"

She stopped writing and softened her voice. "Nothing we can't take care of. Go home, Jade. Get some rest. Spend a quiet evening with Kane. Tomorrow we'll start early. With any luck, you'll be able to pinpoint the camp you've been seeing through Meri's eyes."

I didn't move. How could I leave them when we finally had a lead? I glanced at Kat.

She stood. "Come on. I'll drive you."

After all the days of worrying about Dan, she wasn't staying to help either? "What are you going to do?"

"Take you home and then call Lucien to study some maps."
I nodded. "Sounds like a great plan. I'll help."

She shook her head, and Lailah chimed in once more.
"Remember what I said earlier? What I'd do in your shoes?"

My stomach dropped. Once I found Meri, one of us
wasn't walking away from the encounter. How long could a
soul stay separated? Judging by my weakening state, I was the
underdog. I crossed the room to stand behind Bea, placed
my hands on her shoulders, and bent to whisper in her ear,
"Whatever happens, take care of them." My voice came out
low and strained.

She placed her right hand over mine and squeezed. "If
anyone can survive this, it's you."

Tears burned my eyes, but I blinked them back. I straightened and rejoined Kat. "Let's go."

We crossed Canal Street, heading into the French Quarter.
"Can you drop me at my studio?" I asked.

"You're going to work tonight? What about Kane? Isn't he
waiting for you?"

"He is, but I need to take care of some things first. I won't
be long."

She quirked a skeptical eyebrow, but dutifully made the
turn to the glass shop. A few minutes later she put the car in
park. "Want me to wait?"

"No, thanks. I can walk from here." I pushed the door open.

Kat reached over and grabbed my arm. "I'm going with
you tomorrow."

"I know." Nothing I said would stop her. The two people
she loved most in the world were in the middle of this mess.
Besides, as selfish as it was, I wanted her there.

"Good. Now do whatever you have to do and then get
home. You need rest."

"Yes, Mama Kat." I smiled and scooted out of the car.

"And Jade?"

I leaned back down and peered at her. "Yeah?"

She tossed me a new package of Junior Mints. "Don't let that man of yours wear you out."

Laughing, I slammed the door shut and watched as she sped off. The humor faded as I wondered if she'd ever get a chance to tease me again. I bit my lip and hurried into my sanctuary, popping a handful of minty chocolate. It would be enough to get me through at least a few hours of studio time.

I hit Kane's number on my phone. After filling him in on the Philip sighting, I let him know I needed a few hours to myself.

"Sure, love," he said. "But don't be too late. I'm making dinner."

"I won't." I smiled at the idea of him slaving away in his kitchen. "And, Kane?"

"Yeah?"

"I love you."

"Love you, too, pretty witch."

The line went dead, and I sat at my work bench. For years, glass had been my escape from my empath gift. Imagine going through life not only knowing everyone's emotions, but experiencing them right alongside them. Sure, joy and happiness were a bonus. Who didn't want that little boost? Unfortunately, just like a sugar high, a few hours later I'd come crashing down. And don't get me started on those who were suffering their own demons. I had enough of my own to deal with. The world was filled with far too many unhappy and deeply wounded people.

To block everything out, I'd turned to glass. Alone in my studio, the lure of the flame called to me. The perfect thing to calm my nerves.

After two weeks of neglecting the studio, I first checked the pressure on my oxygen tanks and then the gas line. Mollified everything was in working order, I flipped the switch to turn my kiln on and lit my torch.

The tight pinpoint flame flickered to life, strong and steady. I dipped the end of a glass rod into the two-thousand-degree heat and as it melted into a molten ball, the tension drained from my temples, and the last of my headache vanished.

Chapter 22

A few hours later, a dozen steel rods adorned with glass beads poked out of my kiln. I set the digital controller to run and sat back down to pull a bunch of spaghetti-thin glass stringers. It was a ritual I'd gotten in the habit of doing over the years. I loved being ready for my next torching session.

The simple act of preparing for a future settled me. Growing up, my mother always told me the best way to accomplish what you wanted was to look in the direction you wanted to go.

Well, I wanted a future. One with my mother, Aunt Gwen, Kat, and the rest of my friends. And most especially, I wanted one in New Orleans with Kane.

Kane. Tonight could be my last night with him. My heart squeezed. What was I doing? Abruptly, I put the glass rod down and turned off my torch. I'd made a dozen beads. The act of crafting product for future sales was enough affirmation of a future. Now it was time to do what Lailah said. Cherish my loved ones.

I stopped at the front desk to say goodnight to Dave, the shop manager, and squashed the unwelcome thoughts of possibly never seeing him again. Instead, I waved and said, "See you in a few days."

"Have a great night," he called as I left the building.

I turned back to wave and forced a smile. One thing was for sure; I planned on making it a night to remember.

Ten minutes later, I let myself into Kane's house. Despite the copious amounts of Junior Mints I'd downed during the short walk, my mouth watered at the delicious scent of garlic and heady Cajun spices. I headed straight to the kitchen and paused in the open doorway, admiring his profile while he stirred with one hand and sampled a sauce with another.

"Hey, pioneer man. Whatcha making?"

His lips turned up in a slow smile. "Something guaranteed to inspire you to thank me in a variety of inventive ways."

"Really?" I sauntered over and peered into the pot, wrinkling my nose. "Spaghetti sauce?"

"Spaghetti sauce?" He turned, mock horror on his face. "Tell me you did not just say that."

I wrapped my arms around him and gave him a half-shrug. "Oops, guess I was wrong."

He narrowed his eyes. "If mamaw ever caught you disparaging her *etouffee* recipe in such a way…"

I grinned. "*Etouffee*, you say?"

"You know damn well it's *etouffee*." He closed the distance and pressed his lips to mine, cutting off my bubble of laughter.

All the playfulness faded away as he pulled me closer. A small shiver tingled down my spine. I pressed my body against his, wanting to feel every part of him. He trailed kisses along my jawline until he reached the soft spot on my neck just below my ear.

I sighed and melted into him.

"Jade," he whispered and tightened his grip as if he might never let go.

"I'm right here," I whispered back.

"And that's where you'll stay. Here. With me. Always." He buried his head in my neck, his big hands splayed across my back.

"Always," I agreed, running my fingers through his short, dark hair.

We held each other for a long time until footsteps on the hardwood broke us apart. A few seconds later, Mom and Aunt Gwen appeared. Gwen sent me an apologetic smile. "Sorry, but your mother is finally hungry."

"No need to be sorry, Ms. Calhoun. Have a seat." Kane gestured to the table. "I made plenty for everyone."

"Call me Gwen. Family shouldn't be so formal."

Kane glanced at me, pleasure clear in his eyes. I moved to Gwen's side, squeezed her hand, and mouthed 'thank you.'

She shrugged, but a knowing smile tugged at her lips.

What exactly was she thinking about? I didn't have time to ask before Kane set a large bowl of rice and the *etouffee* pot on the table.

He picked up a bottle of wine and announced, "Dinner's ready."

I took a seat and sat back, watching while Kane served everyone.

"This smells delicious, Kane," Mom said.

"Yum," Gwen murmured after her first bite.

"Thank you." Kane poured the wine and settled next to me. He glanced over, worry clouding his eyes. He leaned in. "Everything all right?"

With damp eyes, I nodded. In this moment, life was perfect.

He nodded in understanding and placed a soft kiss on my temple. "The first of many nights to come."

Mom and Gwen raised their glasses and repeated his words in unison.

Love warmed my insides, and I joined them in the toast. Whatever tomorrow had in store for me, tonight I was surrounded by those I loved best. Nothing could take that away from me.

For the next hour, Gwen and Kane monopolized most of the conversation. Gwen spoke of her farm, and Kane of his life in New Orleans as a child. My mother interjected with a few nostalgic moments of my youth. I sat quietly and soaked all their words in.

Finally, after the plates were scraped clean, I rose and started clearing the dishes.

"Excuse me," Kane said and joined me at the sink. "You've been quiet."

I picked up a plate, smiling. "I was just enjoying the atmosphere."

He took the dish from me then placed it in the dishwasher. His warm hand slipped into mine, tugging as he guided me back to the table. "The evening isn't quite finished." He pulled my chair out. "Take a seat."

I eyed him. "What are you up to?"

He raised one eyebrow and nodded toward the chair.

"Hmm." I sat, turning my attention to Mom and Gwen. "Are you in on the secret?"

Mom smiled, and Gwen shook her head innocently.

"Yeah, you're definitely up to something." I accused Kane. "Well?"

"Give us just a minute."

Each of them scattered into the kitchen, gathering various items. Mom returned with four pillar candles, Gwen with two wine glasses and a bottle of Riesling. She placed one glass in front of me and one in Kane's spot.

"Are you and Mom converting to teetotalers this evening?"

She laughed. "Hardly."

"We've got plans to meet your friend Pyper for a night cap," Mom said.

I raised an eyebrow. "Night cap?"

"Pyper and Ian are taking them to a jazz club," Kane called from behind the refrigerator door.

"Tonight?" I stood up and wedged myself between Mom and Gwen, linking arms with both of them. "But we're supposed to be spending the evening together."

"We did, shortcake." Mom cupped my cheek. "We'll be back soon. Right now, you and Kane need some privacy."

I stiffened. Was my mother actually leaving so my boyfriend could seduce me?

"Relax, Jade. This is a good thing." Gwen gently removed herself from my grip and gestured to Mom. "Ready?"

Mom gave me a small hug and instead of turning to leave, retreated back to the table and repositioned the candles to stand in the middle of each place setting. "Jade, honey, would you light them please?"

"Sure." I reached over and grabbed a box of matches from the counter.

"No." Mom held up a hand. "I meant magically."

"Oh. I'll try." With how weak I'd been the last few days, I hadn't worked any spells. My magic was draining. I was conserving as much as I could, but because Mom asked, I couldn't say no. Especially since she seemed to be behaving so normally.

I turned my focus inward, searching for my spark. To my surprise, it instantly flared to life. A huge grin tugged at my lips as I whispered, "*Illuminate.*"

Four blue-tinged yellow flames did exactly what I asked. Gwen reached over and dimmed the lighting. The white pillars glowed.

"What's going on?" I asked again.

"That's for you and Kane to discuss. Now stand behind your chair." She glanced over her shoulder. "Gwen, Kane, you too."

Everyone did as they were told, each of us staring at Mom expectantly. I got the distinct impression I was the only one in the dark about what was to come next.

Mom stood across from me. Her gaze met mine as she held a hand out to both Kane and Gwen. They each clasped her hand, and I reached out to each of them, forming a circle. A lump clogged in my throat as I recognized the blessing. It was the one to strengthen family bonds.

Mom had recited the incantation at every solstice and every important event throughout my childhood. But no one other than Gwen had ever been invited to participate. It had either been just Mom and me or the three of us.

I glanced at Kane. Did he have any idea how much meaning the ritual held? The pride and nervousness radiating from him suggested he did. I squeezed his hand and stared at the candle dancing with life in front of me.

"Four souls, four flames. Tonight we cast a circle of strength. One bound by trust and love."

One by one, each of the flames doubled in size and brightened, burning almost white.

"We stand together as one unit, one family."

The flames turned electric blue, much brighter than the usual ice blue produced by Mom's words. A surge of excitement ran through me. Mom's magic was powerful, but I'd never seen her perform this ritual with such strength. Maybe it was because I'd finally embraced my own magic. I didn't care about the cause. A strong family bond would only help me in my quest to save my soul.

"Goddess Hera, join us in our blessing. Honor us with your gifts. Two flames, two souls joined and supported by two flames, two souls."

I jerked my head up, my eyes boring into my mother's.

She smiled and said, "Two flames, two souls."

Kane and Gwen repeated her words in unison.

I stood still, my mouth open, unable to form words.

My mother's smile widened. "Jade, you need to say the words to complete the blessing."

I swallowed, not daring to look at Kane. If I wasn't mistaken, Mom had just performed a very specialized blessing. One I'd read about, but never witnessed.

"Jade?" Kane said softly.

I met his concerned gaze. His lips turned up in a small hopeful smile, love pouring out of him as if he held his heart in his hand.

My own heart swelled and my breath hitched. Everything stopped, and I whispered the words they were all waiting for. "Two flames, two souls."

A short blast of air came out of nowhere, extinguishing the candles. Then everything was still as Kane and I stared at each other.

Gwen dropped my hand, and I vaguely heard her say good-bye as she and my mother slipped out of the house.

When the door clicked closed, Kane grabbed my other hand, turned both over, and kissed each of my palms. "Don't say anything yet. I have something for you."

Totally speechless, I nodded and let him guide me back into the chair. It wasn't until I picked up my water glass that I noticed the shaking. Before I drenched the tablecloth, I set the drink down and clasped my hands together in my lap.

Kane returned bearing a small round cheesecake adorned with chocolate-covered strawberries and what appeared to be homemade whipped cream. He'd combined all my favorite desserts into one mouth-watering piece of perfection. But that wasn't what caught my eye.

Right in the middle, surrounded by the chocolate-covered strawberries, sat a red embossed jewelry box.

This was it. I'd known it as soon as Mom had called upon the Goddess Hera—the goddess of marriage—in her blessing. Suddenly my lungs didn't want to inflate.

Kane placed the plate in front of me and pulled his chair over so we sat almost touching. I continued to stare at the cheesecake, afraid to look at him.

"Jade?"

"Hmm?" Light from the chandelier bounced off the shiny red sections of the jewelry box.

He dipped the fork into the dessert and offered it to me. "Take a bite."

I pressed my lips together, somehow convinced if I didn't open my mouth, we'd stay frozen in this moment forever. I would never hear what he said next, and I wouldn't have to answer.

Tears burned my eyes. Despite my best efforts, I had no hope of blinking them back.

Slowly, Kane put the fork down and ever so gently wrapped his arms around me. "Shh, it's okay, love."

I snuggled into his shoulder, grateful he didn't ask me what was wrong. He already knew. How could I let him ask me to marry him? At any moment, my life could be stolen from me. As he held me, my despair quickly turned to anger. This wasn't fair. Life wasn't fair. I'd been proposed to once before by a man I loved deeply, but that time I had secrets to deal with. And when I'd come clean, Dan hadn't been able to deal with them.

This time, Kane knew everything about me. I wanted this. I hadn't realized it, but now that the moment was here, I wanted this more than anything.

Damn Meri and her soul-sucking curse. She couldn't have mine. It already belonged to someone else.

I pulled back and wiped the remaining tears out of my eyes. Then I leaned in. "I think you have something to ask me."

His lips quirked up in a half-smile. "You sure you want to hear it?"

"More than anything."

He reached over and grabbed the fork he'd discarded. "Take a bite first."

Chuckling, I opened my mouth. The sweet, creamy goodness made me sigh in pleasure. "Oh my Goddess, that's good," I said after I licked the fork clean.

"Better?"

I nodded, acutely aware of the sugar jolt reviving my energy.

"Good." He plucked the tiny red box from the center of the gorgeous cheesecake. In one smooth movement he pushed his chair back and dropped to one knee.

My heart picked up pace, and I couldn't tear my eyes from his.

"Before I ask, I should tell you I purchased this ring not long after you woke up from your Roy-induced coma."

"You're kidding." He had to be. We'd only been dating a few weeks when Roy, the previous owner of Wicked and all-around evil ghost, had trapped me in an alternate reality. "We barely knew each other."

He lifted a shoulder, indicating the fact wasn't significant. "I knew then you were the one for me. And I know it now. I'll be damned if I'm going to let you go. No matter what happens, I'm ready to commit a lifetime to you. A long lifetime. I'm aware deep down you doubt your strength, but I don't. You can fight this. We can fight this together. As one."

A swarm of butterflies took flight in my stomach.

He opened the tiny box. The most gorgeous round emerald, surrounded by a circle of diamonds, twinkled up at me. "Jade, my pretty witch, I love you more than words can express. I'm on one knee, offering you all that I have. Body, soul, and spirit." He freed the ring from its velvet bed. "Will you marry me?"

All my reservations disappeared. Even if we were only happy for one day, it would be worth it. Besides, he knew the risks. He'd been living this crazy life right along side of me the last few months. I didn't hesitate. "Yes."

He slid the ring onto my left hand and studied it, as if admiring how it looked on my finger. His joy sent sparks through my arm, and my heart fluttered as I felt him treasuring the moment.

Kane stood, wrapped me in his arms, and swung me around. I laughed, hugging him fiercely. He was right about one thing: I would fight this. With everything I had, because I wasn't letting him go, either.

He cradled me against his chest and headed toward the hall. "Come on, pretty witch. It's time to show you just how much I need you."

"Wait," I said.

He paused, but didn't turn back.

"I want my cheesecake."

"Of course you do." He returned to the table, and I grabbed it and a fork. "Save at least a bite or two for me," he said.

I sent him a wicked grin. "Don't worry, pioneer man. By the time we're finished with this, you won't be unsatisfied."

Chapter 23

With the help of the cheesecake's sugary goodness, my energy level managed to sustain itself through the night while I found plenty of inventive ways to express exactly how much I adored my fiancé.

Fiancé. Just the word sent my heart into my throat.

The bathroom door creaked. Kane walked out, his hair wet, a green towel hung low on his hips. "Good morning."

I took my time admiring his well-defined chest, narrow waist, and the dark trail disappearing beneath the towel. God, he was gorgeous. And he was all mine. Meri could have ripped the rest of my soul from me right then, and I'd have been happy to fade away on my cloud of supreme contentment.

"Morning." The bed shifted as Kane sat next me. I laced my hands around his neck, tugging him down for a gentle kiss. I barely brushed my lips over his and murmured, "I could stay right here with you forever."

He nuzzled my neck, his feather-light kisses producing chills over my naked body. Those magic lips made their way to mine, and the kiss turned heated until he pulled back. He gave me a rueful smile. "Tempting. Especially since you look thoroughly ravished and sexy as hell."

"So what's stopping you?" I brushed a strand of wet hair

back off his brow. A bead of water ran from his neck, down to his shoulder. Gently, I traced a finger over the trail.

He sucked in a shaky breath and closed his hand over mine. "The people waiting for you in the living room might get a tad bit impatient."

I groaned. A glance at the window confirmed the weak morning sun was starting to peek through the blinds. Damn it. My perfect night with Kane had come to an end, and it was time to scour the bayou. Lifting myself up on my elbows, I gave him one last kiss before climbing out of the bed. I paused before disappearing into the bathroom.

Kane watched me, his eyebrows pinched and faint worry lines crinkled around his eyes.

A strange sense of finality settled over me, as if we'd come to the end of something. The end of us as we knew it. A sharp arrow tore through my heart, leaving a small ragged hole right where all the warmth of the night before had been.

Grabbing the door frame, I steadied myself.

"Jade?"

"I'm fine." My answer sounded timid and unsure even to my own ears. I cleared my throat. "Nothing a little breakfast won't cure."

I closed the bathroom door and leaned against the frame, listening to Kane move around in his room. Cripes, what was that? Some sort of premonition? Or my fear manifesting itself? I wasn't a psychic. Never once had I even come close to seeing the future. Empaths weren't usually gifted with such abilities.

Stress. That's all it was. Time to finish this. Ten minutes later, clean, but slightly weak from the exertion of standing up, I stepped out of the shower. On the counter sat a mug of what I would bet anything was chai tea, a chocolate muffin, and a note.

Breakfast is ready when you are, but here's a morning pick-me-up. Love, K

I was going to marry the perfect man. Great sex, love, and chocolate all rolled into one. After I inhaled the muffin, I threw on a T-shirt, jeans, and sneakers. Boots would be better, but

I didn't own any without heels, and I wasn't sacrificing any to the bayou.

I opened Kane's bedroom door. Undistinguishable chatter spilled into the hallway, combined with the clattering of silverware against plates.

I glanced at the clock—6:25 am. Holy ghosts! It sounded like a dinner party in Kane's kitchen. Not at all sure I was up to speaking to anyone, I poked my head around the corner.

Eight people sat crammed together at the six-person table: Kane, Mom, Gwen, Ian, Pyper, Lucien, Lailah, and Kat. What were they doing here? No way was I taking all of them to deal with Meri and Philip.

"There she is!" Pyper jumped up, ran over, and dragged me back into the hallway. She wrapped her arms around me and squeezed until I couldn't breathe.

"Morning," I forced out with a half-laugh.

"Oh my God, he did it." She released me and stepped back, dabbing at the tears glistening in her deep blue eyes. "We're going to be sisters now."

I grinned. "As if we weren't before."

She nodded. "Right, but now it'll be official."

Pyper and Kane weren't related, but they were as tight as brother and sister. Pleasure warmed my heart. A few short months ago, I'd had only two people in the world I'd been close to: Kat and Gwen. Now I had a whole new family, and Pyper was a very important part of it. This time I hugged her. We clutched each other for a long moment and then broke apart laughing.

Kat rounded the corner, stopped, and planted her fists on her hips. "What's going on back here?"

I glanced at Pyper. "No one else knows?"

"Umm, I told Ian, but only because we took Gwen and Hope out last night."

Of course Mom and Gwen knew. Kane had asked their permission before he'd asked me. The formality was totally old-fashioned, but made me love him even more for making my family feel so important.

"I hope you don't mind." Pyper scrunched her face up in mild trepidation as her guilt crept into my awareness.

"No, it's fine." I turned to Kat and grabbed her hands, making sure my ring was front and center as I gestured to it with a short nod. "Kane gave me this last night. We're engaged."

She averted her gaze, and a jolt of her shock shot through me as if it were my own. The exact same reaction I'd had when he'd asked me. Only her shock wasn't followed by joy. An emotion that felt suspiciously like anger simmered around her.

I dropped her hands and stepped back. All the excitement of sharing my news drained right out of me. "Something wrong?"

"Huh? Oh, no." She shook her head. "Just surprised. You know, with everything going on."

Pyper shifted to meet Kat's gaze. "Seems like the perfect time to me."

"Really?" Kat and I said in unison. As happy as I was, I kind of agreed with Kat. We didn't even have time for this conversation right now. I should have been getting on the road with Lucien to sniff out Philip and Meri.

"Well, yeah." Pyper faced me. "With Meri playing tug of war with your soul, doesn't a deeper connection to Kane keep you grounded? Give you more strength to fight? Besides, Hope told me planning for the future helps solidify tomorrow's existence."

She was right. About everything. The connections and the affirmation of tomorrow. Hadn't I been operating under the same principles the night before, when I'd made beads and prepped for my next torch session?

"When did Mom say that?" Had Kane only asked me as a way of saving my soul and not because he actually wanted to get married?

"Last night at the club. Why?"

I quickly shook my head, dislodging the thought. He wouldn't have been able to hide his intentions from me. I was an empath, after all. Even though I was weakened, my gift hadn't suffered one bit. Not once did I feel anything but pure love and hopefulness during the proposal. "No reason."

"Jade?" Kane called. "Ready?"

I sent Kat a troubled glance and retreated to the kitchen.

The fresh scent of coffee, waffles, and maple syrup filled the air, making my mouth water. I took a seat between Mom and Gwen. They both looked at me with questioning eyes. Casually I rested my left hand on the table, letting the shining emerald speak for itself.

Gwen grinned, giving me a half-hug and whispered, "Congratulations."

Mom tried to smile, but it came off as more of a grimace. The last of my happiness vanished.

"Hope?" Gwen's concern wrapped around me.

"Sorry," Mom said in a quiet voice meant for the two of us. "I'm having trouble dealing with my baby being engaged. I still see her as a young girl. I'll adjust."

I wanted to lean into Gwen, protect myself from Mom and Kat's unwarranted negativity. After everything we'd all been through, couldn't those closest to me just be happy? Not willing to allow anything or anyone to spoil my mood, I got up and moved to the bar. Mom frowned. A tiny thread of guilt streamed off her, but she didn't say anything more. No one else seemed to notice my departure. Thank goodness. The last thing I needed was one more person to bring me down.

I made my way through half a waffle before Lailah appeared by my side. Her khaki cargo pants and beige T-shirt were in classic Lailah colors. What I wouldn't give to put her in pastels.

"It's time to go," she said.

"Okay." I dropped my napkin on my plate and followed her to the front of the house. All the chatter stopped, chairs scraped against the tile floor, and footsteps clattered behind us. "Where are they headed?" I asked Lailah.

"With you, apparently."

My eyes widened as I gaped at them. "How in the world are we going to go on a recon mission with an entourage?"

She shrugged. "I tried to tell them."

I stepped back and almost collided with Kane.

He grabbed my shoulders, steadying me, and bent to whisper in my ear. "Did you think even for one second I wouldn't be going with you?"

"No. But why everyone else?" I whispered back. "I barely have enough strength to take care of myself, much less a half-dozen others."

Pyper and Kat appeared, boxing me between them and Kane. Their collective determination penetrated the air.

I'd fully expected a lecture from Pyper, as that was her usual M.O., but Kat beat her to the punch and shook a finger at me. "Why can't you get it through your thick skull that you need us? Didn't Pyper help you destroy Meri the first time, when her love helped you work through the black magic? And aren't I always there to lend you my energy when you're weak? You're not the only one who has something to offer in a crisis, you know."

Gently, I closed my hand over her finger. "I do know. You're right, I'm sorry."

"Where Pyper goes, I go," Ian chimed in. "Not to mention I have extensive knowledge of the bayou. The last thing you want to do is get lost."

I raised my hands in defeat. "Okay, okay."

Lucien was our official bayou guide. At this rate, we'd need two airboats. Ian could man one, while Lucien manned the other. That left Gwen and my mom.

I met Gwen's hazel eyes and tilted my head in question. She shook her head and cut her gaze to Mom.

That one look made everything clear. Mom wasn't ready to face the upcoming battle, and Gwen wasn't going to let her leave. No matter what.

"Give me a sec. I'll be right back," I said to Kane. I crossed the room and wrapped my arms around Gwen in a massive hug. "Take care of her, okay?"

"Don't you worry about us. Just make sure you bring yourself home. Whole."

"Yes, ma'am."

She laughed then sobered as Mom moved to join us.

Gwen pulled me in another hug, and brought her lips close to my ear. "Tell her you need her to stay here and work on spells or blessings or something. She can't go with you, Jade. She's too fragile."

"Of course." We broke apart, and I proceeded to do just that. Only Mom wasn't having any of it. "Jade, I have more knowledge about demons and angels than anyone here—well, except the angels themselves. But my experience in Hell trumps that. I am going. If you try to stop me, I'll only conjure a summoning and you'll be right back where you started."

After arguing for five minutes, I finally caved. "Fine. Come with us." I gave Lailah a what-can-you-do? look and turned to Gwen. "I have a favor to ask you."

"What?" Concern clouded her eyes.

"Go to Bea's and keep her informed with anything you might see."

"Jade—"

"Please, Gwen? We have so few tools right now. I know you don't like to voice your visions, but if you see anything go terribly wrong…well, Bea might be able to help."

Gwen took her time before answering and finally she nodded. "I can do that." She retreated then turned and walked back to me with purpose. "I've already seen something."

My mouth popped open. Gwen almost never talked about her visions. She said the consequences were too high. Choices made due to knowing the future ahead of time often led a person down the wrong path.

She nervously licked her lips. "The details are vague, but the feeling is strong. Remember this, okay?"

I nodded. The likelihood of me forgetting this conversation was about as likely as me willfully giving up my soul and everyone I loved in the process.

Her fingers gripped my wrist in earnest. "When the moment comes, a choice will be made. And not an easy one. Someone close will betray you. Another will sacrifice everything…but it will be for naught." She let go and headed toward the guest room.

"Gwen?"

She paused in the doorway. "If you pay attention, his true colors will shine through."

His colors will shine through. My only clue, *his*. I clenched my hands into fists and tried not to scream. Damn it all to Hell and back. She could mean anyone. I eyed the men around me one by one. My speculative gaze landed on Ian, then Lucien, and finally on Kane.

My heart twinged. Nothing like a cryptic piece of advice to make you start doubting and worrying about your friends. I leaned into Kane, one arm around his waist and put the conversation out of my mind. "Ready?"

"Ready."

"Bayou…here we come," I said. "'Cause I have a soul to save and this time it's mine."

Chapter 24

Within a half hour, our caravan pulled into a small parking lot next to a metal-sided building. A faded green sign with a man straddling an alligator read, *Jean's Alligator Tours. Don't be afraid of shallow waters.*

Kane followed me. I tried to peer through the dirt-crusted glass door. No lights shone from within, and I couldn't sense any foreign human emotions.

"I don't think Jean's in," I said.

"He's here." Lucien typed a message on his phone. A second later it buzzed with a reply. He jerked his head toward the back. "This way."

Everyone was relatively quiet as we followed Lucien to a metal chain-link gate. He pressed a button resembling a door-bell, and an annoying buzzer went off. Lucien pushed the gate open, leading the way to the mysterious Jean.

Hidden behind the building was an old weather-worn dock with another sign that read, *Swim with the gators. $5 a head. No refunds.*

"Funny guy," Pyper said with a smirk.

A loud motor rumbled to life. I spun, searching for a vehicle.

"It's out there." Kane pointed to the river lapping against the dock.

Sure enough, the rumble grew louder as a dented gray airboat came into view, backing up into the narrow slip to the right of the dock. The entire left side appeared to have been crushed and then smoothed out as best as possible. The crinkled metal caused the rig to list slightly to the left while floating.

I blanched. "He's not taking us out on that, is he?"

"No." Lucien chuckled.

"Oh, good." I sighed in relief.

"We're going by ourselves."

I turned to Kane, giving him a look of despair. He sent me a sympathetic smile and draped his arm around my shoulder, tucking me close.

"Geez, Lucien. Could you have found a bigger piece of floating garbage?" Pyper yelled over the growing noise.

Another airboat glided into view. Remnants of blue paint peeked through the cancerous rust claiming its hull. If possible, the second one appeared even more unseaworthy. I imagined one tiny collision would crumple the decaying metal.

Lucien turned his back on the boats and glared at us. "Save your snark for later. Unless you want an angry Cajun tossing you in the bayou."

Pyper raised a skeptical eyebrow, but kept silent.

The engines died with a rough sputter and a middle-aged, paunchy, dark-haired man with crooked teeth jumped onto the dock. He lumbered his way over and held a hand out to Lucien. "My boy! Ah haven' seen ya since dat crawfish ball at Nannak's."

Lucien smiled and pumped his hand. "It's been too long."

"Yous been hiden up in da city. You come to my ohm de next Friday for shrimps. Ya?"

"I'd love to. Thanks for the invite." Lucien waved in our direction. "Uncle Pete, I'd like to introduce you to my friends."

Each of us shook Uncle Pete's unnervingly strong grip, thanking him for his help.

"De boats, dey are ready." He handed Lucien two sets of keys. "Take care of dem." Uncle Pete said a few more words to Lucien and then he and his helper disappeared into the metal building.

"That sweet man would throw me in the bayou?" Pyper laughed. "Right."

Lucien handed a set of keys to Ian before focusing on Pyper. "I've heard rumors Pete has connections with the Family. Don't make the mistake of underestimating him. He's a hard-core Cajun, been living off the bayou since he was a boy. You don't survive that kind of existence without some notoriety."

"The Family?" Pyper lowered her voice. "As in, the mob?"

Lucien ignored her and climbed onto the dented gray boat.

"Shit." Pyper glanced back at the building.

Lucien's lips twitched as if he was trying not to laugh.

I rolled my eyes. "Can we get started now?"

"Hold on." Mom pulled me to the side. "I want you to wear this." She unclasped the bead I'd given her and secured it around my neck. "You need this more than I do."

I fingered the smooth glass and opened my mouth to protest, but she cut me off.

"I added my own form of protection. Do your mom a favor and don't argue." She clasped my hands, warming them with her touch.

My eyes misted. I nodded. "Okay."

"That's my girl." She gave me a kiss on the cheek and followed Ian, Pyper, and Kat onto the rusted boat. Kane, Lucien, Lailah, and I took the gray one.

Ian tossed me a two-way radio. "This way we can keep in touch with any sightings and our whereabouts."

"Are you sure you're up for this?" Lucien asked him. "The bayou can be a dangerous place. And I don't just mean the terrain and the wildlife. A lot of the land is privately owned, and people around here don't take well to trespassers."

"I'm aware. My grandfather had a place out here."

Lucien saluted him and fired up the airboat.

I nearly jumped out of my seat. The vibration, along with the ear-splitting noise, set my teeth on edge. How could we sneak up on a cabin with all this commotion?

After a few false starts, Ian finally got his rust trap going. Before he glided out into the open river, Lucien gestured for him to wait and climbed back onto the dock. Lailah joined him. Kane and I cast Lucien questioning glances, but we were ignored.

The pair walked in a tight circle, their lips moving in what appeared to be a chant, but I couldn't hear anything over the roar of the engines. Power started to build, and through my connection to Lucien as his coven leader, a small ball of magic pulsed inside me, making me itch with anticipation.

Lailah threw her head back, arms stretched wide. A white light materialized around her. Lucien mimicked her movements. The light spread to encompass him. I gasped as power exploded from my center. My head spun, and I clung to Kane to keep from falling out of my chair. Holy shit balls. They could have warned me.

The magic around them shot straight up and covered both boats in a dome formation. The engine noise faded to a low rumble. Lucien and Lailah stepped back on the boat.

Lailah smiled. "Better?"

"Sure. If I didn't feel like you stole every last bit of my energy," I grumbled.

She frowned. "What?"

"I'm the coven leader, remember? You two just worked some sort of powerful spell and now I need another pill, or a chocolate bar."

Lucien stopped fiddling with the dock ropes. "Jade, the spell was a simple one. With Lailah and me casting it, you shouldn't have felt anything."

"Well, something went wrong then, 'cause the spell used a big portion of the magic I'd been storing up." I leaned against Kane for support, fighting the panic growing in my belly. "I'm going to barely have a spark left when we find them."

Lailah moved to my side. She placed a hand on my arm and frowned. "Your defenses are too weak." She turned to Lucien.

"She shouldn't be going with us. In this state Meri will have no problem claiming her soul."

"No!" I stood on wobbly legs. "It'll only get worse if we wait. I'm not backing out now. Lucien, get this boat in the open water and follow Ian before he disappears."

Since I was the coven leader, Lucien had little choice but to follow my orders. A moment later the boat glided away from the slip, rolling with the gentle waters of the river. The cool morning air carried the aroma of cypress trees and dense moss.

"At least let me transfer some energy to you." Lailah's face pinched in worry.

"Uh…" It was something I was prepared to do with Kat, my best friend, the one who was always there for me in such situations. But Lailah? I clamped my jaw together and sucked air through my teeth. "I don't know."

"Relax." She grabbed both of my arms and, even though I'm certain she was not at all authorized to do such a thing, she started pushing her clean energy into my being.

Pure bliss. I closed my eyes and soaked the energy in as every last nerve ending came to life. *Good Goddess, is this what angels felt like all the time?* I'd trade places with her in a heartbeat if I could and ask God to strike me down if I ever complained about anything. I was ready to take on the world.

Lailah tried to let go, but I clamped a hand on her arm. "Not yet." The sensation was too good to abandon.

"Jade!" She shook me off. "You greedy witch! You'll drain me. Then where will we be?"

I sat up straight in my chair and pushed my wind whipped hair out of my eyes. I blinked. Everyone stared at me with concern and shock radiating from them.

Kane put an arm around my shoulder. "You okay?"

I nodded. Holy Jesus. I'd been drunk on Lailah's energy. Is that what people felt when I sent an energy boost?

"No, it isn't," Lailah said, reading my mind. When had our mental connection come back? With the energy transfer? "They only get a trickle from you. They don't know how to seize your energy and suck you dry." She scowled. "Like you just did."

Oh, shit. I grimaced. "Sorry, I didn't mean to."

"Next time have better manners." She dug around in her pack, pulled out an energy-enhanced pill, and washed it down with water from a plastic bottle.

I leaned back in my seat, guilt eating away at my restored strength. I had to get myself together. Time to focus. A deteriorating white camp house was out there somewhere, with an angel and an ex-demon who had some explaining to do.

"How long until we get to Cajun Cove?" I asked Lucien.

"About thirty minutes."

"Okay." I pulled a notebook out of my backpack and paid attention to the surroundings. The trees had started to lose their leaves. Stumps from long-dead Cypress trees lined the edges of the bayou. Large dragonflies buzzed overhead, and a hawk screeched and flew off in the opposite direction.

An ominous sense of loss settled over me. The river became quiet except for the faint hum of the airboat, and I had the eerie sensation we were all alone.

But that wasn't right. No one was ever alone in these parts. Landowners and fisherman never left the waters for long. Not to mention the abundance of wildlife.

Lucien slowed the boat and turned into a narrow opening. Bare tree limbs threatened to scrape the hull on both sides. The air started to warm, bringing a blanket of moisture from the humidity. Though I hadn't touched the water once, I suddenly felt damp all over.

Ian waved from ahead as they continued up the main channel.

"They're not following?" I asked.

"No." Lailah pulled out a hand drawn map and pointed to a section highlighted in blue. "They're covering this area." She pulled out an identical map, this one with a section outlined in yellow. "And we're taking this one. Keep an eye out for the camp."

"Got it." I hoped my hastily drawn description was enough for Kat. She was scouting the house from the other boat. I wasn't a two-dimensional artist, so combined with vague details and my lack of talent, she had her work cut out for her.

I prayed she didn't identify the wrong camp. I could just see the four of them barging in on some family. One of two things would happen: Either they'd scare the occupants to death, or the owners would shoot and ask questions later.

The algae floating on the surface became dense, and Lucien slowed to maneuver his way through the thick vegetation. Something moved, startling me as it splashed into the river on the right. Gator. It left a sizeable wake as it glided toward the airboat.

My muscles tensed, and I clutched Kane's leg.

"Don't worry. He isn't going to climb into the boat," he said, chuckling.

"You're sure?" I couldn't tear my eyes away from the massive thing. "How sturdy is this contraption?"

"Sturdy enough to haul us through the bayou," Lucien said.

I glanced at the left side and gasped as the gator rose up in the water and snapped at the side of the boat. "Go faster!" I cried, clinging to Kane.

Kane wrapped his arms around me and tried to hide a smile. I grimaced and turned my attention to Lucien.

"We can't." Lucien appeared unfazed by the five-hundred-pound monster trying to eat the airboat.

"But—"

"Stay away from the edge," Lailah said. "He can't jump into the boat."

"You sure?" I stared at the still water, wondering where the beast had gone.

"Positive. During tourist season they're trained to come up to the boats. As long as you don't feed him your hand, you'll be fine."

I bit my lip and moved over one seat so I was sitting right in the middle of the boat. For the remainder of the trip, I planned to stay as still as I could, frozen in my spot.

"I'm sure you'll be much safer there," Kane teased.

I shot him my best death glare, but he only laughed.

The morning sunlight bounced off the trees, casting long shadows and dark corners. At every turn, I was convinced the gator or, worse, a water moccasin, would find its way into the listing airboat. Honestly, the way the hull was crumpled, it wouldn't take much. I was shocked the boat glided along the top of the water as well as it did.

The radio crackled with an update from Ian. They were a few miles downriver, circling the town of Cajun Cove. We were trolling the small waterways around the island. So far, we'd worked our way past a dozen or so deserted camps, none of them even closely resembling the one I'd dreamed of.

Lailah and Lucien sat together making notes on the map. Kane moved to my side, resting one hand on my knee. He grabbed the binoculars and scanned the banks for any sign of activity. Despite Lailah's energy transfer, my body became heavy with fatigue. Even the hard candy I'd brought along didn't help perk me up. My eyes became heavy, and I swear I started to drift off right there in the middle of the bayou. No one bothered me, even though I was supposed to be searching for Philip's hideout. I'd been still for so long they'd stop paying attention to me.

A tingling sensation washed through me, and I shot up in my seat. Standing, I faced west and stared into the trees and vegetation. Something just beyond the bend called to me.

"Lucien." I pointed to a small opening between the over-grown grass. "Turn here."

He let up on the throttle and the boat cruised to a stop. "You sure?"

"Yes." I turned to Lailah. "I feel it. The rest of my soul is there. With Meri."

Chapter 25

The warped, wood-sided house sat buried in the overgrown marshland. With most of the windows boarded up, the camp appeared deserted. There wasn't a boat, or even a footpath cut through the thick brush from the dock to the front door. No light, no movement, no life.

I knew better. My emotional radar went into overdrive. I couldn't sense Philip, but a tiny thread of Dan's energy reached me. He was inside. Antsy, but not nervous. More like he had cabin fever. Who could blame him?

Most importantly, Meri waited inside with the rest of my soul. My fatigue instantly vanished, and I felt *whole* for the first time in days. Did Meri feel it too? Would she know I was nearby? It didn't matter. We were already here. I stepped onto the rickety dock. "Let's do this."

"Hold on." Lucien radioed our location to Ian and stashed the device under a seat.

I eyed the radio and then raised my eyebrows in question.

"The silence charm only works while we're on the boat. The last thing we need is Ian trying to reach us before we secure them in the building," Lailah said.

"Secure them?" What was this—a sting operation? All I wanted to do was confront Meri. Surely if we duked it out, my soul would find a home with one of us. And that one of us was going to be me, if I had anything to say about it.

"Yeah." Lailah gestured to the house. "So Philip can't transport them anywhere."

"He can do that?"

She sighed. "Yes. He's an extremely powerful angel."

More powerful than her. The thought popped in my head before I could stop it. I winced and glanced at her, but either she ignored me or our mental connection was on the fritz. "You better hurry. My soul feels whole again. If Meri is paying attention, she might already know I'm here."

Lailah nodded and split from Lucien as the pair crept along the bank in opposite directions. Their magic collective barely brushed against my skin in a feathery caress. Magic filtered in a silver stream toward the house, split apart, and circled around until the two threads met again, sealing together. Another transparent bubble covered the shack. It was the same type of spell they'd used back when we'd gotten on the airboats. Though, this time the magic hadn't affected me at all. My soul had to be the difference.

Lailah nodded. "They aren't going anywhere now."

With her statement, I strode straight up the front door, not caring who saw me. I didn't even knock. What was the point?

I threw the door open, surprised they hadn't even bothered to lock it. Not that a deadbolt would've stopped me. I had my strength back. Or so I thought.

My eyes met Meri's determined gray ones and an internal battle began. My newly won strength faded just as quickly as it had appeared.

Meri seemed to stand taller, more confident with each passing moment. My eyelids grew heavy, and my legs ached with fatigue. All I wanted to do was sink to the floor. A hollow sensation grew inside my gut, and that's when it hit me. Meri was sucking me dry.

I had to do something. Anything.

I lunged.

Surprise flickered over her face and she side-stepped me, but she was too late. I tackled her, and we crashed down on the rough wood floor. My right elbow throbbed. I grunted and clutched Meri's arm. Her energy and my soul started to fill the empty crevices of my being. Everything hummed with possibilities. I'd never felt so…powerful.

"Give it up," I growled, grasping the raw, tingling edges of my soul. I gripped tighter, ready to suck the last strands from the former demon.

Her sad gray eyes stared straight into me as if she were searching my hidden depths. Then she spoke, her voice broken, defeated. "Take care of him for me."

"No!" Dan sprinted from another room and pounced.

I lost my grip, and a sliver of heat slashed through my gut, causing a vague sense of loss. My strength wavered slightly then stabilized. I searched the rough edges of my soul, and I realized a small section had snapped back into Meri.

A small gasp of surprise escaped her lips, echoing my own.

"Dan, move," I grumbled, scrambling to get out from beneath him as Kane grabbed his arms.

"Don't touch her again, Toller." Kane's voice was low and dangerous, matching his hard face. I shuddered a tiny bit. I'd seen him mad before, but never like this. "Next time I'll put a permanent dent in that straight nose of yours."

I sprung to my feet, rubbing my battered knee. "Dan! What are you doing? She forced you into Hell."

"You don't understand." Dan tried to struggle out of Kane's grip. Kane tightened his hold, forcing Dan's arms behind his back. "Ouch. Damn it, let go. I'm not going to hurt anyone."

I stalked up to him. "I've been trying to save you from the moment you sacrificed yourself, and this is how I get repaid?"

"It's not his fault," Meri said, keeping her distance.

"Oh, I know," I spat at her. "A demon is to blame."

She winced and a bone-deep shame filled her, echoing in my being.

I closed my eyes for a moment and heaved a heavy sigh. "Kane, you can let Dan go. She's right, it isn't his fault."

"Are you sure?" he asked.

I nodded.

"If you say so." He jerked back on Dan's arms one more time for good measure and leaned in to speak into his ear. "Touch her again, and I won't hesitate to break you in half."

Dan nodded, grimacing.

Kane released him, pushing him forward. Dan stumbled. He caught himself on the back of a wooden chair and glared at Kane.

"What's wrong with you?" I demanded, pointing a finger at Dan. "Why are you helping her?"

Dan's eyes darkened. "She isn't a demon anymore."

"But she stole my soul!" I cried.

Meri winced. Dan frowned in sympathy then turned back to me. "She didn't do that on purpose. She can't control what's happening. Don't you understand? She's a human now, possibly even an angel. You can't just...she doesn't deserve this."

I shook my head and eyed Meri. She still had a piece of my soul, but she wasn't trying to drain me anymore. What was I supposed to do, give up my life for hers? She leaned against the rough wall, her burgundy button down shirt askew and her tattered jeans ripped at the knees. She gazed through an open door a few feet from her.

Muffled voices filtered into the common room, one of them Lailah's. Keeping a wary eye on Meri, I inched toward the door. Inside the small, pea-green kitchen, Lucien stood slightly behind Lailah with his arms folded over his chest, while she proceeded to chew someone out. I couldn't see the person in question, but it didn't take a psychic to figure out who.

"I can't believe you." Her normally pale face was covered in angry red splotches. "You have no right to mess with Jade's life this way."

"You know it's not that simple." Philip's voice was quiet, but steady.

I moved closer to the door, hyperaware of Kane at my back and Dan hovering protectively over Meri a few feet away. Lailah gripped the edge of the sink until her knuckles turned white. "She was a demon, Philip. Now you're trying to save her by sacrificing someone else."

"The council won't see it that way."

I tensed. Was he planning to invite them to this party?

"I didn't know it was happening," Meri said, her tone almost apologetic. "The sharing of your soul, I mean." She slid down against the wall, as if her legs couldn't possibly hold her up any longer.

I took a slow step toward her, taking in the purple smudges under her eyes and the way her hand slightly shook as she smoothed her rumpled shirt. She was weak. Exhausted. Barely holding on. Exactly how I'd been when she had the majority of my soul. In the other room, Lailah continued to argue with Philip, while he patiently tried to reason with her.

I ignored them and focused on Meri. "How did it happen?"

She stared at the rotting floor. After a moment, she glanced at Dan. He nodded. "After you destroyed me..."

I winced. She'd been a demon. My choice had been her or Bea. Holy ghost on a cracker, why did that statement make me feel so guilty?

She cleared her throat. "I was just a shell, a nothing, trapped in my gilded rooms in Hell. Not a demon, but not an angel either. Just a void wrapped up in human-like packaging."

"You weren't nothing," Dan interjected.

I glared at him. "You do know if she succeeds in stealing my soul, *I* will cease to exist, right?"

"No. Philip said that wouldn't happen." He spun and stared through the open door, where Lucien was holding Lailah back.

Jesus Christ. Had they come to blows already?

Dan let out a huff of frustration and turned to me. "Philip said the council would do what was best for everyone."

"They won't." Meri raised her head. "They'll do what's best for them."

"And more angels are what's best in their eyes, right?"

She shrugged. "I've been away a long time. Maybe things have changed."

"Jade." Kane wrapped his large hand around my wrist and tugged me backwards to his side. "I think you should end this now. Do what you have to."

With Lailah monopolizing Philip, I wouldn't get a better opportunity. Kane was right. Meri was weak; this was my best shot.

In three large steps, I leaped to Meri's side and kneeled on the floor beside her.

She flinched, trying to move away from me, but I caught hold of her arm, keeping her in place.

Immediately, the last remnants of my soul started to flow toward me, a cool salve on my battered insides. Slow at first, then faster, sensing its rightful place.

Whole. I'd be whole again. All me, ready for my new life with Kane. I'd get to know my mother again. Dan would be free. My body tingled with anticipation, welcoming what Meri had stolen from me.

Through my giddy haze, my focus narrowed on her pale, slumping body. I snatched my hands back, horrified to realize I was draining every last bit of life out of her.

I was killing her.

"Meri!" Dan cried as he ran over and scooped her in his arms. She lay motionless, her body limp.

"I...I was only trying to get my soul back." Angry tears sprung to my eyes. Mom was right. Nothing was black and white. Meri didn't deserve to become a demon and now that she wasn't one, she didn't deserve to die, either. Even though I knew it was a her-or-me situation, I couldn't do it.

Kane slid to the floor beside me and pulled me close. "It's okay."

"Kane, I..."

"I know, pretty witch. I know."

We sat against the wall with my head on his shoulder. I stared at the emerald stone on my left hand, trying only to think positive thoughts for the future. Though the exercise was useless if I couldn't bring myself to claim my soul. But would I be able to live with myself if I did? I'd never considered I might not be able to go through with it. I hadn't let myself think of Meri as a real person.

Dan picked Meri's lifeless form up and carried her toward the single bedroom. As they passed me, a sliver of my soul slipped from me to her. Her eyes fluttered open. "What happened?"

"Shh." Dan smiled down at her. "You fainted."

Philip came storming into the small living room with Lailah at his heels.

She ran around him, begging, "Don't do this. It's not fair."

"None of this is fair." The despair in his voice was unmistakable. "I lost my mate. Do you understand what that means? My mate! It was my fault for not going after her. I can't sit by and let her slip away again. I won't."

"But Philip." Lailah took a small step, edging slightly closer to him. "She isn't your mate anymore. The bond is broken. You know as well as I do it's highly unlikely to form again."

Hot fury exploded from him, noticeably raising the temperature in the old shack. "This is not about that, Lailah. Are you so self-centered—"

Lailah swung. The loud smack of her open palm against Philip's face rang through the room.

He stepped back in stunned silence.

Everyone else froze, too.

"How dare you?" she seethed. "Do you think me so shallow I'd be worried about whatever *arrangement* we have? The one where you decide to come into town for a night every four to six months and expect me to drop everything to keep you company in my bed? Fuck you, Philip." She waved an angry hand in my direction. "I'm worried about my friend and what's going to happen to her. Not your goddamned ex-demon mate. It's not Jade's fault Meri got stuck in Hell and her soul corrupted. It's yours. And here you are, using a witch to right your wrongs. You should be ashamed of yourself."

His eyes had gone progressively wider during Lailah's rant. I had a feeling my own expression mirrored his. I'd never heard her speak like that before, and I was willing to bet neither had he.

His lips turned down in a sad, almost hopeless frown. He reached for her hand, but pulled back when she flinched. A ray of sun spilled in the window and over his face, illuminating the deep sadness burning in his eyes. "You're right. I am ashamed." His troubled gaze flickered to me. "I'm so sorry, Jade. You don't deserve this."

"Damn right, she doesn't," Kane said, not bothering to hide the anger coursing through him.

"You have no idea how much this pains me," Philip said.

I started to nod. But when Philip raised his hands and an ice blue circle sprang up around me, I jerked, trying to scramble out of it. No witch ever wants to be caught in an unsanctioned circle. Anything could happen. My shoulder slammed into what might as well have been a concrete block. I let out a cry of pain.

Clutching my arm, I realized Kane was no longer pressed against me. He was sitting outside my circle, pounding on the invisible wall. There was no sound, only an eerie cone of silence while I watched his mouth move, frantically trying to communicate with me.

Jade! He mouthed and then turned in the direction of Philip.

The angel stood in the middle of the room, bright light shining down on him like a sunbeam from Heaven. The anguish shone clear on his face as his pale green eyes bore through me.

Almost as if in slow motion, the front door swung open behind him and our friends appeared: Ian. Pyper. Kat.

And just behind them, my mother.

Her jade green gaze was the last thing I saw before I was blinded by Philip's brilliant sunlight.

Chapter 26

The blinding light faded and I blinked, clearing the moisture from my burning eyes. One thing became immediately clear— I was no longer in the shack out in the bayou. Lailah and Lucien's anti-transportation spell had failed. The cold, hard floor gleamed in the sunlight. Its gold and white checkerboard pattern stretched out in front of me, leading to white marble steps. I squinted.

Lined up on what looked to be a dais sat six robed individuals, all of them staring in my direction with stern frowns.

I scrambled to my feet and stifled a cry when someone rested a hand on my shoulder.

"It's me, Jade," Dan whispered.

"Where the hell are we?"

A collective gasp echoed through the room. Slowly I turned and focused on the surroundings. Rows of gorgeous, perfectly groomed, flawless faces stared back at me from the spectators seated behind us in what were unmistakably pews. They were all dressed alike, in white robes, adorned with intricate embroidered gold ruins.

Who were these people, and why were we in a church? I glanced around, desperate for a clue as to where we'd ended up.

Please, God, let us still be in Louisiana.

I gazed upward to the arched ceiling and the familiar murals. Instantly, recognition dawned on me. I should have known right away when I saw the tiled floor, but the colors were off. In fact, there weren't any colors at all except shades of white and gold in the entire building. Even the paintings had been white-washed.

I covered my mouth with my hand, horrified. What had happened to New Orleans' most notable landmark—Saint Louis Cathedral? And who were the drones filling the pews?

"What's going on?" I demanded.

"Jade." Lailah, who for some crazy reason wore one of the gold-thread-embroidered robes, rose from the front row and joined Dan and me. "We've been summoned to the angel council."

Philip, who'd been sitting next to her, stood, revealing his matching robe. Meri, still in her burgundy shirt and ripped jeans, followed his movement and faced the dais.

Holy cherubs. We weren't in the French Quarter Saint Louis Cathedral. We were in an alternate angel realm, just like we'd been in an alternate New Orleans underworld when we were in Hell. Was this Heaven?

An ominous bell chimed, and everyone stood. Dan took a few steps toward Philip and Meri and then looked back at me, indecision clear in his eyes. His inner conflict made me queasy.

I glanced away, unable to deal with his turmoil. What was he doing here, anyway? Had the council summoned him, too? If so, why?

A tall, white-haired angel stepped forward, ethereal in her graceful movements. Her undeniable beauty triggered an intense desire to weep. I'd be happy to bask in her presence forever. Then her cold blue eyes locked on mine, sending a startling ripple of fear through me. I shivered and took an involuntary step backward. How could someone be so beautiful and scary at the same time?

Lailah pushed me forward and whispered in a harsh tone, "Do not show weakness."

"Jade Calhoun," the woman said, her face void of all expression. Her emotions were hidden from me as well, though most angels' were. "How exactly has the ex-demon, Meri, obtained a piece of your soul?"

I wasn't sure what to say. Couldn't someone have prepped me on the correct way to answer? I glanced at Lailah, but she stared straight ahead, just as blank as my inquisitor. Fine. What was the worst they could do to me? My soul was already compromised.

I raised my chin. "She stole it."

The ice blue stare didn't falter or soften. "Speak truthfully, or you'll suffer the consequences."

Was she calling me a liar? I narrowed my eyes, too irritated to temper my reaction. "I am speaking the truth. When Meri was a demon, she stabbed my fiancé in the thigh. Even though the wound healed, somehow she maintained a connection to him. Through him, she began slowly sucking away at my soul. We managed to sever his connection to her, but mine remained. Earlier today, she almost succeeded in killing me as she tried to claim the last of my soul. I demand you put a stop to it."

"Jade!" Dan and Lailah gasped at the same time. While Lailah reprimanded me, Dan's tone was one of shocked surprise.

I ignored both of them and took a step forward.

"Plus, Philip over there—" I waved a disgusted hand in his direction, "—the one you put in charge of my soul?"

The woman glanced at Philip.

"Yeah, him. He bailed on me, opting instead to worry about his ex-mate. Seems kind of unethical, doesn't it?"

One of the other council members joined the ice queen angel. He had long hair that hung perfectly straight in a sheet of the palest blond I'd ever seen. His mane barely moved, not one strand out of place as he stepped up to the microphone. "Ms. Calhoun," his voice boomed. "You will address the council with respect, or you will not address us at all."

I opened my mouth to speak, but Dan strode over and put a hand up in a wait-a-moment gesture. "What do you mean, she almost killed you?"

"Exactly how it sounds, Dan. She's been surviving off me. We can't share my soul forever. One of us will die. And today when I burst into the cabin, Meri almost won the battle."

His face paled, matching the council members' stark white robes. Fear and an overwhelming burst of anger shot through him. The sharp stab of his emotions pierced deep inside me. I clutched my chest, trying to dull the pain as he whirled on Philip.

"Is that true?" Dan took three steps, his fists clenched.

Philip met his eyes, staring him down, unapologetic. "Yes. That's why we're here, to let the council decide the best course of action."

"You son of a bitch." Dan's right fist flew, followed by a sickening crunch as he broke Philip's nose. Philip recovered quickly, trying to stem the blood flow with one hand and raising the other in defense as Dan came at him again. "This whole time you were aware Jade's life was at risk and you never said anything?"

Lailah inserted herself between Dan and Philip. Meri stood to the side, staring at me. I met her gaze, trying my damnedest to sense her emotions. But I got nothing. You'd think with our connection, she'd be the one person I could read.

"Fucking bastard," Dan spat, reaching around Lailah.

"Dan!" she cried. "Now isn't the time."

"It's the perfect time." Dan reached out and grabbed Lailah by the waist and lifted her off the ground.

"Stop it. Put me down." Her arms and legs flailed as she tried to dislodge herself.

He set her off to the side. "Stay out of this, Lailah. This is between me and my father."

"It's angel business," she reasoned with him, but he'd already turned his back on her.

"You used me," Dan accused, advancing on his father once more. "You abandoned me and my mother and only connected with me when you thought I could help you get your lover back."

"That's not how it happened," Philip said in a calm, steady voice, despite the blood trickling from his nose. "I've never been more than a phone call away."

Dan's anger ratcheted up to fury, making my stomach turn. "This isn't about my daddy issues," he said with disgust. "It's about Jade. A friend of mine. Someone I care about very deeply. How dare you use her? Use me to get to her?"

This time, when Dan pulled his arm back for another blow, Philip countered it with a block and sucker-punched him in the stomach. Dan staggered then found his feet. After a small moment to catch his breath, he launched himself on Philip, and the pair went down in a heap, brawling right in the middle of the church, with the angel council looking on.

Meri stomped over to them and yelled, "Stop it. Both of you."

Neither of them listened. They were too far gone, duking out whatever personal battle they needed to wage. Sure, for Dan it was partly about me, but not all of it. I suspected not even most of it.

My shoulders sagged as a bone-wary exhaustion settled over me. Would anyone care or notice if I sank to the floor?

Lailah moved forward, giving the brawling men a wide berth. "Members of the council, please, I beg of you to put a stop to this unproductive display of male aggression. Before you stand two women with one soul. Your wisdom and assistance is humbly requested for a resolution in this unusual circumstance."

The pale, long-haired councilman gestured off to the side and nodded to Philip and Dan, who were grunting and rolling around on the tile, steadfastly trying to kill one another. Or at least Dan appeared to want to kill his father. Philip was doing his best to hold Dan off as long as possible and to avoid any more bone-crushing strikes.

Two large bouncers, both resembling some sort of angel giants, emerged from the wings. In no time they had Dan and Philip restrained. Dan did his level best to break free from his captor. Philip relaxed, despite the guard securing his arms behind his back.

"Take them below," the councilman said.

Dan twisted and called to me, "I didn't know."

I nodded, a piece of my heart mending. Even though Dan had been helping Meri, he hadn't chosen her over me. My turbulent emotions overwhelmed me. I longed for a quiet place to curl up in the fetal position.

The bouncers guided the duo out of the room.

Lailah seemed to sense my weariness because she stepped up beside me and linked her arm through mine. "Lean on me if you have to."

"Ms. Farmoore," the ice queen angel on the dais said. "Wasn't Mr. Toller's soul assigned to you?"

"Yes."

"Then I suggest you join him." She waved a hand toward the hall leading out of the sanctuary.

Lailah tightened her grip on my arm. "I don't think so. Philip was assigned to Ms. Calhoun, but he's abandoned her. At this time, Ms. Calhoun is in far more danger than Mr. Toller. She deserves an angel in her corner."

She stared down at Lailah as an eerie silence filled the church. None of the parishioners spoke or even moved. Finally, she murmured something to the councilman to her left. He nodded and headed for the pair of us. He stopped on the other side of Lailah and whispered in her ear.

Lailah didn't make any indication she heard him. The ice queen's cold gaze passed over me and then she said, "Though we don't agree that Mr. Pearson has neglected his duty to guard Ms. Calhoun's soul—part of it does reside within the ex-angel Meri—we find your request acceptable."

"Thank you," Lailah said.

"You have been granted permission to guard Ms. Calhoun's soul," the councilman confirmed. "Do you understand since you claimed her, her fate is yours?"

Lailah nodded solemnly. "I understand."

Her fate was mine? Holy shit balls, what did she just agree to? I clutched her arm tighter. "Lailah?"

"Not now, Jade." My new angel guardian moved to stand in front of Meri. She stood with her feet shoulder-width apart, hands settled on her hips. "You know what that means, right?"

Meri raised her head and gave Lailah a grim smile. "Yes, I know what that means."

"Good. Then you know I won't be giving up."

Meri gazed at the floor and mumbled, "I never expected you to."

The lead councilwoman stepped up to a mic. "In light of recent events, the council will recess until further notice. Ms. Farmoore, you and your associates will be shown to guest quarters. We'll summon you when your presence is required."

A short, redheaded angel materialized from behind us. She held a hand out in the direction of the hallway and nodded, indicating we should follow her. We did as instructed, and I fell into step beside Lailah. "Want to tell me what that meant? My fate is yours?"

She sighed. "When an angel abandons an assignment for another, she is then forced to suffer the trials of her new charge. That means anything that happens to you, I will be forced to experience it with you."

I froze in horror. "You mean if I lose my soul, you will too?"

"Keep up, please," the redhead called over her shoulder, not slowing down.

Lailah grabbed my arm, propelling me forward. "No, I will remain unaltered, but I will experience the extraction as if it were my own."

Oh, Jesus. What had she done? "So you will feel all my emotional and physical pain?"

She gave me one curt nod. "It is what it is."

I gaped. It was worse than being an empath. "But why would they do that to you? You're only trying to help me."

"Angels are preprogrammed to want to help troubled souls, but we can't possibly help everyone. The council sends us our assignments based on importance. The bonding is sort of like a punishment for redirecting our focus away from our regular clients. It's to discourage us from going rogue and helping every poor soul that crosses our paths."

"But Dan is here and Bea's not in any danger." Especially since the whole reason Bea had an angel guardian was because of me. While I was here, she should be safe.

Lailah shot me a confused look. "You didn't think they were my only assignments, did you?"

"Well...yeah. I mean, you didn't say anything about anyone else."

"It's confidential, remember?"

That's right. Angels didn't reveal themselves to their assignments. And they certainly didn't go around telling other people about them. I wondered how many souls Lailah was ignoring right now. I opened my mouth to ask more questions, but she cut me off.

"Let it go. Please, Jade?" She stuffed her hands in hidden pockets in her robe. "While things might get unpleasant, my life isn't in danger. Yours is. I'd like to focus on keeping you around, if that's okay with you?"

I nodded and let her go ahead of me. My footsteps slowed and my limbs started to go numb. I was in shock mentally and it was affecting me physically.

The white halls we traveled down were bare except for the gold gilded sconces and soft yellow flames that flickered within them. Hallway after hallway, it was all the same golden-splashed whiteness. My vision narrowed to our escort's feet. Just when I thought I couldn't take one more step, she stopped and produced a gold key.

She unlocked our room and pulled open the gold door. Inside was a lush suite, filled with elegant, white, overstuffed couches and chairs. A mountain of gold silk pillows rested on the plush gold and white checkerboard carpet, and four separate bedrooms circled the common living room and kitchen area. The only colors in the entire place were from the plates of fresh fruit piled on the dining table. I wandered in, collapsed on one of the couches, and sighed in relief.

Meri and Lailah hesitated in the hallway.

I raised my eyebrows in question.

"Not everything is as it seems," Lailah said and then confronted our guide. "How long will we be held here?"

The guide said nothing, not even acknowledging Lailah spoke. She held the door open, waiting for her to enter.

Lailah's face turned dark. "Speak, young one."

This time the guide flinched and looked up at her with wide, pleading hazel eyes as she shook her head.

"She's fulfilling her vow of silence," Meri said, pointing to a thin gold ring on the angel's hand. "She can't answer you. Besides, she likely doesn't have the answer."

Lailah took another step away from the room. "Even so, she knows."

I sat up. "What's going on?"

"Those committed to silence know everything," Lailah continued as if I hadn't spoken. "They run the council's errands and serve their every whim."

"We just got here. She can't know," Meri argued. "What does it matter anyway?"

Lailah turned on Meri, her face contorted in disgust. "Did you not learn anything in angel training? That room is a time warp. We could think we're in there five minutes and a whole year could go by."

"Oh, shit." Meri started to back up. "I'd heard of the time warp rooms, but I didn't think they put angels in them."

"Didn't they tell you? Technically your angel status is pending until after the hearing, and I'm tied to Jade's fate," Lailah said in exasperation.

Meri shook her head. "No one told me anything."

I flew off the couch, ready to join the group in the hall. I would not get stuck in a place where time stood still. I had a life to lead, damn it. But when I tried to cross the threshold, I couldn't. An invisible wall kept me trapped inside. Frantically I banged on the barrier, yelling profanity at the small guide.

Her lips turned up in a sad, twisted smile as she started to grow right before my eyes. She shot up three feet and her body morphed into a transparent image of her former self. When she flickered back into solid form, there was two of her.

The twins moved fast, each crowding Lailah and Meri. Horrified, they both started to move forward, though their stiff movements made it obvious they were being forced. What were the twins doing to them?

They had to be using some sort of angel magic. Slowly, painfully, Lailah and then Meri made tiny, reluctant steps. They both put up a tremendous mental fight. Their fierce determination filtered through their angel defenses and pulsed around me. But the key master was too strong for either of them. With one final push, the twins propelled the two angels into the suite and placed one palm on the invisible barrier. It flashed solid white and instantly became a seamless part of the interior wall.

The gold door was gone. The three of us were trapped in a gilded cage.

Chapter 27

Silence filled the room as we stared at the seamless wall. I took in the surroundings, realizing for the first time the lack of windows. We might as well have been in a dungeon. For all I knew, we were.

"Shit!" Lailah turned and headed for one of the bedrooms, mumbling, "Freakin' power-hungry, no-good pieces of council slime."

I walked to where the missing door should be and placed my palms on the wall, fingers searching for any sign of an opening. Nothing. Not even one minor bump grazed the perfectly constructed wall. Damn angel magic. Methodically, I worked my way from top to bottom and then proceeded to the right, intent on checking every last inch of the surface.

"You're wasting your time," Meri said, her voice flat.

"I have to do something." I eyed her lounging on the snow-white couch, her feet tucked under the shiny gold pillows. "Living the life of a trapped princess isn't my idea of happiness."

She snorted. "Happiness. Yeah, that's what I'm worried about."

I swallowed, realizing I'd put both feet in my mouth. Fifteen years in Hell with no soul would certainly color someone's perspective. "Right. Sorry."

She shrugged and picked up a gold, leather-bound book from the table.

Shaking my head, I sat next to her. "Can you answer a question?"

She gazed over the top of the book, her eyebrows raised.

"I'm pretty sure Philip transported me here, but what about the rest of you? Did you come willingly? What about Dan?"

"Philip brought me too. Lailah and Jonathon were summoned and because Dan comes from angel blood, he was able to tag along with me. He wasn't invited, but now that he's here, the council will listen to what he has to say." She went back to her book, clearly dismissing me.

Jonathon had been at the council meeting? Where had he been hiding?

I fidgeted, acutely aware I didn't have my tight circle of friends at my side. What I wouldn't do for Pyper's sarcasm and Bea's wisdom right now. Not to mention Kane's solid presence.

I put the wistful thoughts out of my mind and focused on finding a way out of the plush cell. After what seemed like hours, I'd touched every inch of the walls in the main room. How much time had gone by in the real world? Hours? Days? Months?

The thought of Kane giving up on waiting for me made my heart sink to my stomach. How long was too long to wait? He'd have to move on eventually.

No. We were getting out of here. I stormed into Lailah's room. She lay face-down on the luxurious white pinstriped down comforter. "Get up!"

She rolled slightly to peek at me with one eye. "For what?"

"We need a plan to break out of here."

She sat up, her shoulders slumped in a clear display of dejection. "The room is sealed. No magic can free us—not mine and certainly not yours. We're stuck here until the council deems fit. Any planning we do is useless. Trust me. It's never been done."

Stubborn irritation crawled up my spine. "I'm a white witch. No one knows what I'm capable of. Not even me."

"And that's what we intend to find out," an unfamiliar deep voice said from behind me.

I jumped and raised my hands in defense.

A black-haired man about my height held his hand out in invitation. He wore a red and gold robe—yay for color!—and had a long sword strapped across his body.

I took two steps back. "Where'd you come from?"

"Devon." Lailah moved to stand just slightly in front of me. "I'm surprised to see you here."

"Ah, sweet Lailah, I very much doubt that." His thin lips curved up in a sardonic smile.

She crossed her arms over her chest. "I guess you're right, but I am surprised the council deemed it necessary to start their interrogation off on such a combative note."

He inclined his head in acknowledgment. "Your witch appears to be highly valuable. Not to mention the prospect of an angel returning to the fold."

"That's what I was afraid of." Lailah turned to me and wrapped me in a tight hug.

Surprised, I bristled and tried to step out of her grasp. "What are you doing?"

"It's okay, Jade. Don't be scared," she cooed and then whispered harshly in my ear. "Whatever happens, don't fight him. Cooperate no matter what he asks. The consequences are too dire."

I stopped struggling and tried to process her warning.

"Everything will work out fine," she continued in her motherly farce. "Go with Devon. I'll be right behind you." She released me, glaring at the angel warrior. "If anything happens to her, you'll have to answer to me."

He laughed, a low and seductive sound. "Don't tempt me."

I shivered, ready to crawl out of my skin.

With one last slow smile in Lailah's direction, he snapped his fingers, making my world shift from the pale white reality to a stark gray one. Rows of reclining chairs were lined up in front of me. Behind them, computers with dangling electrode wires filled the walls. My field of vision narrowed in on a tray of hypodermic needles.

Oh, God. A test lab.

I whirled around and ran smack into Meri.

"Ouch," she grunted as our skulls banged together.

White spots filled my vision and my head swam. "You're here too?"

"Obviously." She held her forehead with one hand and scowled at me. "Better to be here than our guest quarters."

"Because being a lab rat is much more preferable to the soft beds and mountains of food we had available," I scoffed.

Another red and gold-robed angel materialized and guided Meri to one of the chairs.

"What are you doing?" I whispered urgently when she didn't even protest.

She sent me an impatient look. "Getting this over with. They'll get what they want one way or another. The longer you fight them, the longer we'll end up locked in the time warp chamber."

"So? We have to try." I grabbed for the restraint the angel was trying to clasp around her wrist.

He lifted his head, a stern scowl on his face.

Meri slapped my hand away with her free one. "For God's sake, Jade. Don't you understand? The time warp room is called that for a reason. To us it may seem like five minutes, but it could be five years. Years—not months, not weeks, not days. Years."

I froze, the reality of what she said finally sinking in. "But why?"

"Angels don't *want* to hurt humans or cause pain. Their main concern is souls. You know that. The room is to make you as comfortable as possible. But they will leave you there until they make a decision, and that could be instantaneous or it could be indefinitely. It all depends on how the council votes. We have no way of knowing how much time has passed."

Panic took over and I started to tremble. "You mean, years could have passed already?"

She met my terrified gaze and nodded. "Yes. That's why as much as I don't want to be prodded, I'm willing to endure this to get on with whatever life I may or may not have. I advise you do the same. The longer you fight it, the longer they'll keep you here."

Kane's image flashed in my mind. I stared at the emerald secured to my finger and my stomach ached with a sick emptiness.

Meri lay back in her chair and closed her eyes.

I barely noticed as Devon guided me to the one next to her. They were angels. They might take my soul, but they wouldn't torture me. Right?

I had to get home. To Kane and my family. Gwen would be heartsick. A pinprick in my arm brought me back to reality and I flinched, but the restraints kept me in place. Magic flared in my chest as the urge to escape seized me. The machine to the right started flashing and a high-pitched alarm filled the room.

"Good. It's working." Devon adjusted the volume to something slightly lower than deafening levels.

I glared at him, holding on to the magic, not afraid to use it if I had to.

He winked and pressed a button.

Hot fire burned through my veins. "Argh!"

Beside me, Meri grunted. I tried to turn and look at her, but my vision blurred and my whole body felt heavy. One last thought flashed in my mind: I'd been drugged.

I came to in a cozy farmhouse. A sense of familiarity put me at ease, except I didn't recognize the furnishings, and I was certain I'd never set foot in the place. I found myself at the old white porcelain sink, hand-washing a stock pot. Clean dishes were lined up on a rack beside me, drying in the warm summer air.

The back door banged open, and Philip strode in, his face breaking into a wide grin. "There you are. Get back out here. Everyone's waiting."

"Just a sec, I'm almost done."

"The dishes can wait." He grabbed my hand and tugged. The pot slipped from my hands, clanging loudly in the sink. I laughed and tucked a dark strand of hair out of my eyes. "All right, but if I forget, you're in charge of cleaning the dried-on food in the morning."

"Meri, hurry up!" a female voice called. "It's time for cake."

Somewhere in the depths of my consciousness, I realized this was Meri's memory, not mine, but there was nothing I could do to block it.

Philip laughed and kissed Meri on the temple. "Come on, birthday girl. Someone else can worry about the dishes."

She smiled and let him lead her to the backyard, where her friends and family were gathered.

A few minutes later, Meri had a piece of cake in her hand as she sat by a pool, taking a moment to observe Philip from afar. He was interacting with her sisters, Felicia and Priscilla, laughing and describing a spell Meri had botched a few days before. She smiled, warmth and love filling her heart.

A fierce protectiveness settled over her and she knew she'd do anything for her family. Anything at all.

The scene shifted, and panic flooded Meri's chest as she ran down a darkened street, desperate to catch up with Philip. He was in danger. Life-threatening, game-changing danger.

Her lungs screamed in protest as she pushed herself harder, ignoring the cramp in her side. A demon was loose in the city. And Philip had been sent to meet with him, but he wasn't prepared. He thought he was meeting a witch. His directive had been mistaken.

She rounded the corner and came to a dead stop at the mouth of an alley. In front of her, Philip kneeled, using every last bit of his magic to fend off not one, but two demons. They had him trapped between them, each throwing ropes of invasive black magic.

Time had run out. The demons had succeeded in binding him. His strength would be depleted in mere seconds.

"No!" she cried and leaped forward, unleashing all the power and love she harbored. White met black in an impressive monochromatic starburst.

Philip collapsed at her feet. Anger and fear bubbled up, mixing with her powerful love. A cloud of black fog circled her and when it cleared, Meri's magic had turned black.

The knowledge came to her immediately and despite Philip's moan, she lowered her arms and stepped back. Even through her rage, she knew Philip would never want her to turn to black magic. She'd sooner die first.

"Meri." Philip opened his eyes and stared at her.

"I'm here," she got out before the demons advanced on her.

"Run!" Philip rolled over and a lightning bolt of power shot from his fingers, straight into the closest demon.

The agent of Hell staggered and then froze right before he toppled over.

"And miss the excitement?" Meri laughed as her magic turned white again. She hurled a ball of power toward the remaining demon.

But he was ready for her and somehow sucked it in, using it as an energy source. "You're mine now, angel. Here I thought today wasn't going to be any fun. Looks like it's two for the price of one."

The demon redirected Meri's magic and attacked Philip, but she jumped in the way just before it hit him. Her body convulsed. She fell, her limbs paralyzed. Fully conscious, she couldn't do anything but pray Philip got them out of this mess.

Philip let out a roar, his magic crackling, and lunged at the demon.

The demon's eyes went wide and then he vanished, barely avoiding the attack. He reappeared inches from Meri.

She stared up at him, fear churning through her veins.

In one motion, the demon scooped Meri up and vanished into the earth.

Into Hell, where Meri waited for Philip to come rescue her. For months.

Only he never did, and Hell claimed her soul.

The scene faded. Familiar energy reached me before my vision cleared. Stale lust and desperate excitement. There was only one place I connected with those particular feelings.

Kane's club.

It was just like any other night—dancers working the pole as men threw dollar bills at them, Charlie mixing drinks with one hand and popping bottle caps with the other, and music reverberating through the entire place.

Except I floated in the air over a glass box, and Kane was across the room trying to beat up a ghost. We were floating because Kane had dreamwalked us there. Below me, Pyper was trapped in the glass case, her hands and feet nailed to the bottom.

My heart thundered as I relived the terrible night I'd switched places with Pyper and become a prisoner of the resident ghost. The vivid memory of being held captive and mentally battling with Roy to keep him from torturing me seared my insides and made me tremble. By the time the scene faded away, all I wanted to do was curl up in a ball and cry.

Only I couldn't because I was once again forced into another of Meri's memories.

Chapter 28

I pried my heavy tongue off the roof of my mouth and tried to swallow. "Water?" I croaked.

One of the lab techs brought a cup with a straw up to my lips. Not caring if the liquid was tainted with some other sort of drug, I sucked it down until the straw gurgled with air.

"Better?" Meri asked.

She was already sitting up, her restraints shed. Someone had given her fresh clothes, a white cotton shirt and white linen pants. I glanced down at myself and scowled. Mud caked my sneakers and dirt stained my jeans. Not to mention I was still a prisoner in the lab chair.

"How'd you end up with the spa treatment?" I asked.

She smiled. "The dream-inducing drug wears off faster for angels...or former angels. I'm sure they'll let you shower before the hearing."

I tried to sit up and groaned in defeat. "The what?"

"They're going to make a decision today." The smile vanished from her face and her voice became barely a whisper. "We'll find out which one of us gets to keep your soul."

Instead of panicking, my whole body went numb. The drugs had taken us through another round of Meri's memories and one of my own. Both focused on the same theme: Each of us sacrificing ourselves for someone else.

After experiencing her fear for her loved ones and her unwavering courage, even I couldn't say who was more deserving. If Meri was saved and restored to being an angel, wouldn't she be in a better position to help people? I didn't speak for a while. Finally I turned to her. "At least we don't have to go back to the time warp room."

She gave a noncommittal shrug. "I guess."

Sadness blossomed in my chest. Room or no room, either way I had a fifty-fifty shot I'd never see Kane again. Wrap my arms around him. Feel the gentle caress of his lips. I slammed my fist down on the counter. A metal tray clamored to the floor, the noise echoing off the walls.

Meri didn't even flinch.

I clenched my teeth, my jaw aching with the effort. Screw the council. I wasn't going down without a fight.

I did indeed get my spa hour. Not long after I woke up, two young angels came and led me to a room where I was given a bath, some food, and then dressed in the most beautiful green-silk dress. My grungy clothes were taken away and my meager possessions tucked in the hidden pocket of my skirt.

They curled and styled my hair, and when they were finished, they guided me to a full-length mirror. I gasped at the reflection staring back at me. I'd never looked so radiant. My skin glowed and my eyes illuminated the deepest jade green I'd ever seen.

A sad, ironic smile barely turned my lips up. If this was my last night of existence, at least I'd go out in style.

I didn't see Meri again until I was led back into the sanctuary. She sat at one of two throne-like chairs, both positioned in front of the two sections of pews. Every last seat was occupied with white and gold-robed angels. A nervous excitement filled the room.

My pair of angels guided me to the straight-back chair opposite Meri. I sat, resting my hands on the wooden armrests, staring straight ahead, afraid I'd throw up at any minute.

The council filed in, one by one, onto the dais. A tiny angel, no more than five feet tall, scrambled from the wings up to the microphone. She pulled on a long velvet rope, causing bells to clang at near-deafening levels. "Court is now in session. Angel Drake Davidson will preside over the proceedings."

She scurried off to the side, stumbling over her too-long robe. Her high, tinkling laugh echoed through the room.

Davidson, the angel with the long white hair, cast the announcer an impatient glance before moving to his seat at the council table. Five more angels followed, taking their positions beside him.

The bells gonged again, only this time no one pulled the ropes.

Silence fell inside the sanctuary. An ominous monotone voice came out of nowhere, saying, "This trial is now in session."

Davidson rapped a gavel and turned to his fellow council members. "We have balance today. Two character witnesses for each of the ladies on trial. Madeline, please call the first witness."

Madeline, an elder angel with age lines gracing her eyes stood and shuffled to the podium. "I call the Angel Philip to the stand."

The air shimmered next to the dais, and a golden chair appeared out of thin air. Philip strode in through a thick golden door behind the dais and settled gracefully in the chair.

"You understand that by voluntarily taking the stand, you'll have no choice but to answer truthfully?" Davidson asked.

Philip glanced once in Meri's direction. "I understand."

The head councilman nodded toward Madeline. "You may proceed."

The older woman produced a pair of spectacles and slid them on her nose. She shuffled through a few papers and finally settled on one. "Angel Philip, please state your relationship to both the women on trial."

He cleared his throat. "I met Jade Calhoun a few weeks ago after I was assigned to be her soul guardian. Angel Meri is my ex-mate."

"I understand you are a witness for the ex-demon?"

"Yes."

"And she has lost her own soul? She survives by sharing Ms. Calhoun's?"

Philip nodded. "That is correct."

Madeline peeked over her glasses, eyeing Meri and then me. "Tell me, why would you witness for an ex-demon over the witch? Is it because Meri used to be your mate? In other words, are you basing your decisions on emotions or logic?"

He took a second before answering and then looked at Madeline, pain written all over his face. "It's no secret I take responsibility for Meri's original fall to demonism. I suppose on some level I feel it's my duty to help her as much as possible, but that isn't why I'm here today. The council put me in charge of protecting Ms. Calhoun's soul, and that is ultimately what I am trying to do." He took a deep breath. "Right now, Meri is half a being. Somewhere between angel and human. By an odd twist of luck, somehow she ended up sharing Ms. Calhoun's soul."

Some odd twist of *luck*? When Meri was a demon, she'd done everything in her power to steal souls. She'd have gotten Kane's, Lailah's, Dan's, and my mother's if I hadn't stopped her. The only reason she had part of mine now was because she'd marred Kane. Odd twist of luck, my ass! The demon Meri had left an opening when she'd staked Kane. The twist was that I'd been able to almost destroy her. Now as a pseudo angel, she was going to destroy me.

Philip swallowed and continued with his testimony, "This happened without Meri's knowledge, and she didn't seek it in her current non-demon state. If she's given the chance, I'm confident she will once again return to the mighty angel who saved countless others. As much as it troubles me to condemn Ms. Calhoun's existence, I believe Meri should be the vessel who carries this shared soul."

Madeline made a few notes and then stared pointedly at Philip. "You're saying you do not believe the white witch deserves to keep her own soul?"

Philip cast a sad glance in my direction. "No, I didn't say that at all. I'm being forced to make a decision. Given all the facts, I believe Meri can help the world more effectively."

I curled my fists, restraining myself from an outburst. I'd get my chance. Wouldn't I?

"You may be seated, Philip. Angel Lailah, will you please take your place on the stand?"

Lailah appeared from the gold door and as they passed each other, Philip tried to rest a reassuring hand on her shoulder, but she skirted his reach. She stared at him with narrowed eyes as he took a seat behind Meri. I caught a faint trace of her thoughts. *His fault. He orchestrated this.*

Lailah sat and was placed under oath. It was declared she was a witness for me. That I'd expected. It had to be her and... Dan? I wished with all my heart that wasn't a question. But who else would witness for me?

A different council angel came forward. He was a handsome, clean-cut blond man who appeared to be in his early twenties, though age was notoriously hard to judge when it came to angels. Just like witches, they had ways of slowing down the biological clock.

He inclined his head. "It's good to see you again, Lailah."

"Peter." She gave him a skeptical nod.

His lips quirked in a knowing smile, as if he knew exactly what she was thinking. I guessed something along the lines of, *I'd rather eat live crawfish than be in the same room with you.* But she kept a neutral expression on her face and waited for his questions.

"You're friends with Ms. Calhoun?" Peter asked with a fair amount of accusation in his tone.

"Yes, you could say that."

"And you have a romantic relationship with Philip, Meri's ex-mate?" He lifted a smug eyebrow.

Lailah glared at him. "Yes."

Peter's expression turned serious and almost angry. "Is that why you neglected your assignment of watching over Mr.

Toller's soul and, instead, decided to do everything in your power to get rid of the ex-angel Meri?"

Fury, so strong it filled the courtroom, sprang from Lailah. "No! That isn't what happened at all."

"So Mr. Toller didn't end up in Hell with Meri?"

"Well…uh," she sputtered. "Yes, he did, but only because he sacrificed himself."

Peter pursed his lips. "So, not only did you not do your job, but your assignment showed braver courage than you did."

Lailah stood and faced the rest of the council. "He is introducing conjecture that has no bearing on this case. I respectfully request a new inquisitor."

Davidson stood to address her. "I'm afraid that's not possible. The urgency of this situation has required us to task each interrogation to one council member. Peter is yours. The council is capable of weeding out unnecessary information." He nodded to Peter. "Proceed, please."

Peter went on to interrogate Lailah on how she'd handled herself over the last few months, even going so far as to accuse her of being the cause of Dan's possession by Meri. She did her best to answer his questions, all the while trying to interject opinion on what was happening at the moment.

"I don't see what any of this has to do with Jade keeping her soul. It's hers. It isn't right for us to decide to take it away because a demon managed to form a connection to her." Lailah waved an impatient hand toward the angels seated in front of her. "Isn't that what we're here for? To protect souls from this sort of thing?"

"That isn't what I asked you, Lailah," Peter said patiently.

"Well, that's the answer you got," she snapped.

"One last time. Did you or did you not end up in Purgatory with Ms. Calhoun's significant other?"

She took a deep breath and let it out slowly, clearly trying to get a grip on her frustration. "Yes," she hissed.

He turned to the council. "I declare the angel Lailah unfit as a character witness. Her ties to Ms. Calhoun and the other people involved in this inquiry have clearly clouded her judgment."

I gasped. My main spokesperson was being dismissed.

"Noted," Davidson said then turned to Lailah. "You may step down."

"But—"

"Now, Lailah. Take your seat."

If a bucket of water had landed on her right then, steam would have clouded the dais. She sat where she was, obvious outrage keeping her glued in place. Two guards finally stepped up. She shot them one last glance of disdain and then escaped to a seat behind me.

Jonathon took the stand next.

I closed my eyes, praying he'd be gone when I opened them. No such luck. There he was, sitting in the witness chair, staring down at me with tight eyes. God. Could this get any worse? If this good-for-nothing charlatan said anything to contribute to my eminent demise, I'd come back from the beyond and haunt his ass until the end of time.

A few moments later, he was sworn in, and the first question was asked by yet another woman of the council. Endora. It suited her perfectly, blue eye shadow and all.

"Jonathon, please tell us your relationship to the ones on trial."

"I don't have one with Meri. Ms. Calhoun is one of my parishioners."

Say what? I whipped around, staring at Lailah. *Make him stop*, I screamed in my mind. *Make him stop*. She didn't seem to hear me. Damned psychic connection. Never worked when you actually needed it. I absolutely did not want to be associated with Goodwin's brand of crazy.

"Are you saying you are here as a character witness for Ms. Calhoun?"

"That is correct." Jonathon smiled down at me.

I bit my lip to keep from yelling at him. This couldn't end well. Snippets of my life flashed through my mind: Stolen moments with Kane, laughing with Kat, dancing with Pyper, making strawberry shortcake with Mom. Fun, special memories. They all started to slip away. The beginning of the end.

Endora asked Goodwin's opinion, and he went on and on about God's plan and how taking my soul to give to someone else wasn't an angel's job. God had the sole power to make such decisions. We served him, and all of us should get on our knees and pray for forgiveness. He actually gave quite the strong argument, albeit he did use the God card too many times.

Every time he brought up the Supreme Being, Endora became more and more agitated. "Your religious fanaticism is not welcome here, Jonathon. Please stick to the facts as you see them."

I had to admit, her statement left me baffled. They were angels, for…well, God's sake, were they not?

Jonathon fixed her with a disbelieving stare. "I was asked for my opinion. I'm giving it to you."

"I assure you, your beliefs will be discussed among the council." Endora grimaced. "All of them. Before I release you, I'll leave you with this piece of advice. If you wish to continue to be in good standing with the angel community, you'll find a new form of employment among the humans."

The color drained from Jonathon's face. "Why?"

"Angels are soul protectors, Mr. Goodwin."

"That is exactly what I'm trying to do."

She fixed him with a disgusted look. "No, *Reverend* Goodwin, you are sitting in judgment over those you swore to protect. True men and women of the cloth are called to serve because they love mankind. You serve out of anger. Find a new career or your days as an agent of this organization are numbered."

Jonathon's face froze in a stunned expression.

Endora stalked back to her chair, keeping her stare straight ahead at the spectators.

Ouch. I guess he hit a nerve.

"You may step down now," Davidson said, dismissing him.

Goodwin opened his mouth to speak, but the elder angel's warning glance silenced him. He let out a frustrated sigh and moved to sit next to Lailah.

"Dan Pearson Toller?"

What? My two witnesses had already testified.

Realization dawned.

Dan was there for Meri.

Hot, angry tears burned my eyes. After everything we'd been through, he was willing to let my soul be given to someone else? What happened? Last time we'd been in front of the council, he'd defended me when he'd realized my soul was in danger.

I brushed the tears away and focused on Davidson.

He glanced at my ex and frowned. "You're not an angel."

Dan stood near the podium. "No, sir, I'm not."

The head councilman turned to his underlings. "How did this mortal end up as a witness?"

A gaunt, pale angel on the very end stood. She pulled her mass of curly black hair back and tied it into a haphazard bun. "Mr. Toller is Philip's biological son. He's intimately connected to both the women on trial today."

Intimately connected? What kind of relationship did he and Meri share? *Please, Goddess, don't tell me Dan and Meri are involved.* Talk about twisted.

"I see. Will you be questioning him, Selma?"

"Yes, sir."

"Fine. Mr. Toller, please take a seat." Davidson dropped back and sat with the council.

After Selma swore Dan in, she asked, "State for the record your relationship to Meri and Ms. Calhoun."

He glanced at me, eyes full of sorrow. "Jade and I were childhood friends until we started dating. We were together for over four years and almost got engaged before our relationship fell apart." He took a deep breath. "Meri possessed me as a demon and entrapped me in Hell as her minion. Jade managed to break her, almost destroy her completely, but somehow Meri survived and was no longer a demon. We took care of each other in Hell until Philip came for us."

"My notes indicate you're a witness for Meri, correct?"

Dan swallowed. Opened his mouth. Then shut it. Finally he nodded. "Yes."

My heart seized and threatened to crack into a million pieces. I stared down at my white-knuckled hands, knowing if I looked at him, I'd either scream or burst into tears. Neither seemed an effective strategy at the moment.

"Tell us why you'd advocate for an ex-demon over someone who was obviously important in your life," Selma said.

Dan cleared his throat. "That's just it. Meri isn't a demon anymore, is she? I want to make it clear I'm not advocating for Meri's life over Jade's. I just think Meri needs someone to speak for her."

Frustration filled me to the point I was almost shaking.

"And why is it you've taken on this role?"

Dan's voice turned hard, angry. "Meri sacrificed herself for my father, and he left her in Hell. She. Saved. His. Life. And he left her there."

Something close to hatred streamed from Dan. I glanced up, watching him try to calm himself.

He met my gaze and when he spoke, his words were for me. "Meri deserves a second chance. She paid the ultimate sacrifice. I hope the council can spare them both."

I couldn't help myself. It wasn't that I didn't agree with him. Meri did deserve a chance at life, but I didn't see how his plea was possible. I stood, my chair scraping loudly on the tile floor.

The pressure of the hearing, and my ultimate fate, made me snap. "But there's only one soul! Mine. What do you propose they do? Take someone else's? Condemn some poor innocent? You can't have it both ways. Damn it, Dan, you have to choose. Meri or me?"

A tiny burst of magic collected at my fingertips with my emotional outburst. The entire room let out a collective gasp. I tamped the magic down instantly, but I was too late. Davidson gave a command, and two guards closed in on me. Lailah jumped to my side. Jonathon followed, sliding to a stop right in front of her.

Dan stood in the witness box, his face contorted with a mix of confusion and horror. "Of course not. I don't want to condemn anyone." He turned to the dais. "You're angels. Surely you can do *something* to save them both." Apparently he hadn't been filled in on the rules of this particular game.

No one answered him.

"Stop right there," Lailah ordered the guards.

They ignored her and closed in tighter.

Jonathon took a step toward them. "There's no need for this. I'm sure Jade will calm down."

"Seize her," Davidson demanded.

The guards grabbed Lailah and Jonathon, bodily removing them.

I held my hands up. "Now, wait a minute. I just lost my cool with Dan. Not the entire council. Let's all take a moment to calm down."

"Ms. Calhoun, outbursts are not permitted in the sanctuary from anyone. Especially not a witch. You'll be taken to your room to await our decision."

"The time warp room?" I gasped. "No—"

Dan appeared just behind the guards. "That isn't necessary. Jade would never hurt anyone."

Meri pushed her way through the small crowd and nudged Dan to the side. "I humbly request Ms. Calhoun stay for the remainder of the inquiry. I'm sure she'll give her word she won't wield any magic during this trial." She turned to me. "Right, Jade?"

"Yeah, yeah. Of course. It isn't my wish to harm anyone."

The sixth member of the council stepped forward. She was so beautiful, light seemed to radiate from within her. Her skin glowed, and the only thing I felt from her was love, an oddity in the room full of seemingly emotionless and political angels. She placed a soft hand on Davidson's arm. "Ms. Calhoun may stay."

A hush fell over the crowd. This angel must be important. And while I was grateful, the command she had of all the other angels made me uneasy. I fought the urge to wrap my arms around myself in a protective nature.

"Please, everyone be seated," the beautiful one said, and everyone except Lailah returned to their seats.

"If it pleases the council, I'd like to chaperone Ms. Calhoun for the remainder of the proceedings," she said.

Davidson sent her a look of exasperation. "Fine. We've heard from Ms. Calhoun. It's time to hear from Meri."

I opened my mouth to protest, but Lailah nudged me with an elbow and gave me a slight shake of her head.

Meri stood. "Thank you."

"Former Angel Meri, please tell us why we should award you Ms. Calhoun's soul."

She stared right into Davidson's eyes and with a strong voice said, "You shouldn't."

Chapter 29

I gaped at Meri. Her words hit me hard, leaving an aching guilt in the pit of my stomach. She'd sacrificed herself for my sake. Something she didn't have to do.

The gorgeous angel of light held her hand up to stop Davidson's response and stepped back up to the podium. "Would you care to elaborate, Meri?"

"If you wish."

The angel nodded. "Please."

"It's clear to me after the memory extraction that Ms. Calhoun is a good person. She loves those around her and regularly puts herself on the line for those in need. Angels aren't the only ones who can save souls. I've had my chance. It's not fair to take hers away."

The air vanished from my lungs. She'd forfeited her last chance at having her life back because she wasn't willing to take mine. A raw ache of grief overwhelmed me. I wished with every inch of my heart I could find a way to spare us both.

"I see." The angel of light turned and said something to Davidson.

A second later, he announced, "The council will now convene in chambers to make our decision."

Together, the six of them disappeared through the golden door behind the dais.

The place erupted with chatter.

Philip scowled and strode over to Meri, clearly upset with her statement.

Dan ran up to me, grabbed my arm, and yanked me to him in a possessive hug.

"Let go." I twisted, trying to get out of his grasp.

He did as I asked, visibly shaken. "What just happened?"

"You didn't take my side." Hot tears pricked my eyes. "Now the council has to choose between Meri and me. One of us will…die."

"No! I…" He took a step back and glared at Philip, anger dominating his surface emotions. Slowly, he walked over to his father and tapped him on the shoulder.

Philip turned, his face pinched with guilt. "Dan, I—"

Dan tensed, his body poised for another fight.

Philip took a step back, holding his hands up in surrender.

I glanced around for the guards, but they were nowhere to be seen. They must have left right after the council members.

Dan advanced once more. "You son of a bitch. You lied and told me the council could save both of them. How could you ask me to throw Jade under the bus? She's been part of my family since I was fifteen years old!"

"Stop it." Meri interjected herself between them. "Fighting isn't going to solve anything."

"No, but I'll feel better." Dan clenched his fists again, but stayed put.

"Dan," Philip said. "This isn't about one person—"

"The hell it isn't!" Dan shouted. "This is about you trying to make up for your mistakes. Damn you! All this time you've been telling me you stayed away to protect me, that you didn't save your mate because you needed to keep an eye on me." He side-stepped Meri and took a small step forward. "But you didn't. You weren't around when I needed you. Not the day I was almost beat to death when I was fifteen. Not when I was possessed by a demon, and certainly not today when you convinced me to stand for Meri. I'd never have done that if

I'd known the consequences. No, Dad, this is all about you and what you want. Not about the greater good. You and your conscience can go fuck yourself."

Dan spun and marched back over to me. Still fuming, he jammed his hands in his pockets and visibly tried to contain himself. "I'm so sorry. I would never...well, if I'd known, I would have made different choices."

"And what choice would that be?" I asked quietly.

"Give me a break, Jade. You know me." The frustration he'd tried to bury rushed out, swirling around us. "You know I would have—"

"Sacrificed your soul for mine?" Relief eased the resentment and betrayal I'd been clinging to. His actions over the years had already proved to me the kind of man he was. My Dan, the one I'd grown up with, was back.

He raised his gaze to mine and nodded.

I cupped his cheek gently. "I know."

With that one touch, he pulled me to him and hugged me, desperation and sorrow filtering through his defenses.

"It's all right," I whispered. "Whatever happens..." I choked back a sob. "Just take care of Kat for me."

He pulled away, his eyes intense and full of determination. "The three of us will take care of each other."

I struggled to breathe and forced out, "There's a very real chance they'll choose Meri."

"Promise me, no matter what happens, you won't give up. I'll be here fighting with you. Every step of the way."

He'd demonstrated this form of determination once before, a long time ago, back in Idaho on the fourth of July. He'd possessed an inner strength I'd never witnessed in anyone before or after. I stared into his pale green eyes and knew he wouldn't give up on me. If the council willed my soul to Meri, Dan would do whatever it took to save me, including risk himself. I couldn't ask that of him again. I had to convince him I could save myself this time. "Okay. No matter what, I won't give up."

"Promise me."

"I promise," I said with a firm voice.

We stood together, Dan hugging me and me holding on, trying to muster up some much-needed courage.

The chatter reached deafening levels as the chaos ensued. Through it all, I heard Lailah berating Philip. I squeezed my eyes shut and willed everyone to disappear. A pit of despair settled in my stomach. Would I get my happy ending with Kane, or…disappear as if I'd never existed? A picture of Kane and me standing together on our wedding day flashed through my mind. A small spark of determination fluttered to life inside me. I concentrated on the vague beacon of hope and waited.

A few seconds later, a hush settled over the crowd. I was almost afraid to open my eyes. As much as I feared I'd magically quieted the crowd, I knew better. Magic pulsed in my chest, contained as I'd promised.

The bells clanged, signaling the council was back.

Dan released me. I stared at the council members, my body shaking with fear and anticipation.

The angel of light stepped forward. "Will everyone please return to their seats?"

There was a fair amount of shuffling as the audience settled themselves. Dan stood on one side of me and Lailah and Jonathon on the other. Meri remained at her table, Philip only a half-step away from her.

The angel stared down at us, and she repressed a sigh as she blinked twice. "Very well. A verdict has been reached."

I stuffed my hands in the hidden pockets of my skirt to keep from fidgeting. My right hand closed over something hard and cool. A bead. The one I'd given my mother. I pulled it out and rubbed my fingers over the smooth surface like a worry stone. The action calmed me and even though my heart still raced, I no longer felt like jumping out of my skin.

The angel of light produced a parchment scroll.

She cleared her throat and started to read. "Case number eight seventy-four D. Angel versus white witch. A decision has been reached. After careful analysis of our internal testing and the testimony heard here today, it is of the opinion of this council that the soul in question shall reside within the one who has shown the most dedication to protecting the souls and loved ones she's come in contact with. This was not an easy decision. Both parties have an admirable history of self-sacrifice. However, one speech in particular by the ex-angel Meri resonated with the council."

Oh my Goddess. Did that mean they listened to her? Were they really going to restore my soul? I glanced over to Meri and held her gaze. I sent out a wave of gratitude and hoped she sensed my mental thank-you.

"Meri's heartfelt words and reasoned argument made it clear what path we should follow. Although Meri—in her current state—did not ask for the burden of sharing someone's soul, she has handled herself with grace and compassion. She has gone so far as to once again sacrifice herself for a fellow being. This is why the council has decided to award the soul in question to Meri."

"*What?*" Lailah, Dan, and Meri all said at the same time.

The blood seemed to drain right out of my body, my limbs growing heavy and numb. Shock was the only explanation. I clutched the bead in my hand and my fingers tingled with sensation. Trying for feeling in the other hand, I turned my engagement ring around and around. Warmth spread through my forearms.

I focused on my breathing, anything to keep from passing out. Then all at once, my life energy started to drain. I cried out and fell to one knee, staring up at Lailah. They were forcing my soul out of me already.

My friend's face contorted with pain. She raised her arms and threw a silver film of magic over me. I didn't even have the strength to flinch. But as soon as it hit me, my body responded to her magic. No, not magic. Energy. She'd given me the one thing I needed to fight for my soul.

The guards closed in on Lailah as she collapsed in a heap in front of them. Oh God. She was tied to me. Her energy had been drained and she'd given me the last of hers. One of the men picked up her limp body and started carting her off. *Lailah!?* I screamed in my mind. *Wake up. You can't do this now. You can't die.*

No response. *Fuck!* She wouldn't actually die, would she? They had to save her. They were angels for Christ's sake.

Dan stood over me, shouting, but I couldn't hear what he was saying. I couldn't hear anything actually and, despite Lailah's help, my soul continued to rush into Meri. Every last bit.

Focusing on Lailah's energy, I absorbed her powerful gift, but it was immediately sucked right out of me. I grew cold, uncaring, ready to let go.

I clutched the emerald ring and the bead mom had given me, trying desperately to hold on to the last pieces of my loved ones. Both were achingly heavy in my hands.

Life was so cruel. I'd just gotten Mom back and now all I had left was a stupid bead. I focused on the solid weight. An old sense of home washed over me. Comfort. In my last moments, Mom had found a way to soothe me.

I sobbed and turned my thoughts to Kane. The man who'd loved me unconditionally these last few months. The man I'd given my heart to. The man I'd never see again. My heart squeezed, and I pressed his ring to my chest. I would've probably given up right then, but someone yanked me up off the floor.

My eyes flew open, and Dan stared at me. Emotions ranging from fear to fury flashed over his features. He clutched my shoulders, and his face scrunched as he yelled in frustration. I tried to shake my head, to let him know I didn't understand what he was saying. Nothing happened. I was too weak.

Dan shifted, pulled me closer, his eyes pleading. *Don't give up,* he mouthed.

I'd promised. No matter what, I'd fight.

Something triggered inside me. I didn't have any energy to battle the soul transfer. Instead, I focused on the objects clutched in my hands. They represented what was most important to me in this life. Love. Family. Home. With my heart full, I searched deep within myself for the remnants of my soul.

I'd touched it a few times before. I could find it again. And I did. Almost instantly. Right below my heart, where my magic usually hovered.

I grabbed and held on for dear life as it tugged and stretched and fought to leave my body. The remaining pieces were worn thin, but as I mentally clutched tighter, my soul settled firmly beneath my breast.

I squeezed my fists, as if the action could help me physically hold on to what I had left. The tug of war stalled, my battered soul immobilized in place.

Angel magic crushed my ribs. The air whooshed out of my lungs from the beating. The angel of light stepped forward, held her hand out in a clawing motion, and invisible tenterhooks embedded themselves into my chest and yanked.

I let out a cry and stumbled forward. Miraculously, the portion of my soul I'd managed to grasp onto didn't budge. No way was I letting go. They'd have to pry my soul from my cold, dead grip if they wanted it.

As I steeled my resolve, a massive wave of power hit me, so strong it all but paralyzed me. Instinctively I knew this was the end. I'd tried. Done what Dan had asked, but I was only one white witch up against a full council of angels.

My chest seized and my core seemed to rip in two. Fire erupted in my bones as I convulsed on the floor. They'd done it. I'd lost. My soul belonged to Meri.

Screaming, I curled up in the fetal position and rocked back and forth until my world turned to nothing.

Chapter 30

I woke to the sound of hushed voices and someone stroking my head. I blinked, trying to clear my hazy vision. "Meri?" My voice came out wobbly.

"Jade! Thank the Goddess. You survived."

"No," I mumbled. "I died. Angels killed me." A small, hysterical gasp escaped from my lips.

"Jade?" Someone blond and faceless hovered over me.

"Lailah?" A vague memory of her being carried off by bad angels surfaced in my mind. Had she died, too? Poor thing.

"Yes, I'm here."

"I'm sorry." I closed my eyes, more exhausted than I'd ever been in my entire life. Static hummed in my ears, and my mind started to fade into the abyss.

"Jade!" a familiar male voice cried out.

Kane. He'd found me. I frowned.

How could he find me among the angels? That's when I knew for sure I'd lost. He had to be a figment of my imagination.

"Where are you?" I asked, hopeful I'd glimpse his mocha-colored gaze one last time.

"Saint Louis Cathedral," he said.

I opened my eyes and tried to glance around, but I couldn't lift my head. The black and white tile floor stretched out in front of me. Odd. I thought it was gold and white.

Strong arms lifted me. A sense of something peaceful settled into my being, and blackness overtook me again.

Someone clutched my hand, and I flinched. The tiny movement sent an ache through my core. "Ow."

"Jade?"

I squinted as my eyes adjusted to the light in the strange room. "Kane?"

He gripped my hand tighter and let out a long, relieved sigh. "Thank God." He smiled. "Welcome back."

Frowning, I glanced at his hand in mine. It sure felt real. "Are you really here?"

"Huh?" His brow crinkled in confusion. "Of course I'm here. I've been here the entire time."

"Okay." I closed my eyes to give them a rest. Focusing hurt.

The bed shifted as Kane sat next to me, running his fingers lightly over my cheek. "Rest, love. We can talk later."

The suggestion was so welcoming, I almost drifted off into unconsciousness. But irrational panic forced my eyes open. "Don't leave."

"I won't. Promise." He smoothed my hair and placed a gentle kiss on my lips as I drifted off again.

The third time I woke, two people were arguing. I couldn't quite comprehend what they were saying, but the urgent tone jolted me awake.

"Hey," I said through dry lips. "Any water?"

The arguing stopped immediately.

"Oh my God, Jade, of course." Even though I couldn't see her yet, I knew the voice. Kat. My best friend. She rushed over and held out a cup.

I took a sip. "Thank you."

"Need more?"

I shook my head, eyeing her outfit. She wore her favorite faded jeans and a wool sweater she'd had since our freshmen year in college. If she was a figment of my imagination, at least I'd dressed her comfortably. "So, does this mean I'm not dead?"

She snorted. "Hardly. You're recovering."

"And Lailah?" My heart sped up waiting for the answer.

Kat frowned. "She's okay. Still a little weak. Whatever they did to her left her pretty banged up. She could barely stay awake for the first twenty-four hours. Bea made her stay here for a few days, but let her go home yesterday after a massive infusion of energy pills."

"Thank the Goddess." I tried to sit up, but my chest hurt too much for me to move. I grunted.

"Here." Kat handed me a large yellow pill. "This will help."

I frowned. "Don't tell me it's enhanced."

She gave me a stern look. "You know darn well it's one of Bea's healing pills. Swallow it. Unless you want to be laid up here for the next month or two."

A month or two. Her words triggered a memory. "How long have I been gone?"

She sat next to me. "You've been in and out of consciousness for about four days now."

"No. How long was I *gone*?"

She stared at her hands and didn't say anything.

"Kat, tell me."

She bit her lip. "Four weeks."

Four weeks. Only a month. I blew out a sigh of relief. That was far better than a year or more.

Her eyebrows raised in question. "You're okay with that?"

"Not exactly, but I was expecting much worse." I glanced around at the tasteful, eighteenth-century nightstand and the sunflower quilt and recognized Bea's guest room. "Anything happen while I was gone that I should know about?"

She let out a strangled laugh. "I'll fill you in later. Now take your pill or I'll—"

"Tell on me?"

She laughed. "Well, yeah."

I did as I was told, but only because the weight on my chest made it tough to breathe. Seconds after swallowing the pill, the ache began to ease. I'd need to remember to thank Bea. This time when I tried to sit up, I managed to get the pillow under my shoulders enough to see the rest of the room. "Who were you arguing with?"

"Don't worry about that now. We'll talk about it later."

"Kat," I said. "What's going on? Why am I still alive?"

She fidgeted. "Maybe Bea should answer your questions."

I reached and squeezed her hand softly. "Please, Kat, I'd rather you told me."

She pulled her knee up, making herself more comfortable. "Okay, the official word is your soul split. As in, you have a portion and Meri has a portion."

Dan appeared right behind her. "But what we don't know is if the two parts of your soul will try to rejoin if you and Meri are in a close enough proximity."

"Dan!" Kat jumped up. "I told you, now is not the time."

I lifted a weak hand. "It's okay. I want to know." In truth, I was too tired to care. I was alive, and that was enough for now.

"Kane's going to kill me," she mumbled as she moved toward the door and peeked out.

My heart pounded, and I craned my neck hoping to see him. "Is he here?"

"No, he went home to shower and change, but he'll be right back. Dan is supposed to be waiting downstairs." She sent him a glare.

I chuckled. It was almost like old times. I stared at Dan, so grateful to see him. Smiling, I held out my hand.

He grasped my palm lightly. "I'm so sorry. I never intended—"

I cut him off. "I know, Dan. It's over. Can we move on? Try to be friends again?"

He stood still, silent in his thoughts. I'd give anything to know how he was feeling right then. But he didn't project even one tiny emotion. Not even through our hands. Usually when

I touched someone, it was incredibly hard to block the person out. I frowned. Maybe I was too weak to sense emotions just yet.

Finally, a small, tentative smile ghosted on Dan's face. "I'd like to try."

"Good, me too." I would have hugged him if Kat hadn't started dragging him away.

"Time to go," she said. "I think that's Kane's car coming up the drive."

"But what about Meri?" Dan asked.

"Jade's too weak for that right now. Go." She gave him a push out into the hallway. "We'll talk about it later."

She shut the door behind him and came back over to the bed, smiling as if nothing had happened.

"Talk about what?" I asked.

She started to tell me not to worry, but stopped when I fixed her with an intense stare. "He wants to bring Meri in so we can find out if either of you are still in danger."

"I see. Well, I can't say that task is high on my bucket list at the moment."

"Exactly. We'll worry about that later. Right now I'm headed downstairs to let Bea know you're awake again. She'll want to check you out." Kat waved as she disappeared.

I let out a long breath and closed my eyes, wishing with all my heart I was at Kane's house. I opened my eyes and stared down at his ring. Right then, I made the decision to move in with him. Immediately. I wasn't willing to wait until after we were married. He'd asked once before, but I'd been reluctant to give up my own space. Not anymore. I just wanted him to take me home. To our home.

Over the next few days, Bea, Gwen, my mom, and Kat took turns keeping a watchful eye on me. It would've been annoying if I hadn't been so happy to just be alive. I'd finally gotten over balking at Bea's herbal pills. Damn, sometimes I even asked for them. They were little miracles in a capsule.

"No," Bea said after I'd asked for some extras to keep on hand. "You're becoming an addict."

"No, I'm not." I sat up cross-legged in the bed. "I just want to make sure I stay on schedule."

"I find that hard to believe since I caught you sneaking downstairs for one last night."

"I was thirsty!" I cried in mock offense, but started laughing. She was right. I loved the little energy burst they gave me. It was better than a jolt of coffee.

"Next time—" she pointed to the bathroom across the hall, "—get some water."

"There isn't going to be a next time. Kane's taking me home today."

She paused in the doorway. "Don't think I haven't already gone over the regimen with him."

I nodded, knowing full well she wasn't kidding. Bea had played the part of Nurse Ratchet while she was in charge of my health. I'd been on a strict diet, combined with short walks down the hall to get my strength back, and she'd kept all my friends away except Kat and Kane. Between Mom and Gwen hovering, she said my dance card was already full.

A small stab of apprehension ran through me at the thought of leaving. I was safe here. No rogue demons or angels could get to me. If I lived another hundred years, I'd be satisfied to never see any of them again. Except for Lailah. She'd grown on me.

After Bea left, I rose and took a shower. The glorious hot water worked wonders on my bed-worn muscles. Sure, I'd taken short walks, but a week in bed was too long…at least, it was when it didn't involve a gorgeous, naked man doing unspeakable things to you.

I grinned. Kane had started to enter my dreams again. After what we'd done in the dreamwalk the few nights before, I couldn't wait to get him out of his clothes and horizontal somewhere. Preferably not a bed.

I packed in record time, which wasn't saying much, considering all I had was pajamas, one pair of jeans, and a T-shirt Mom had brought me the night before. Lugging the small suitcase down the stairs proved to be much more difficult. By the time I got to the bottom step, I was sweating and winded.

"Way to overdo it," Bea said wryly.

"I have to build up my stamina somehow," I gasped out.

"You probably should've waited." She nodded toward the window, where I spotted people milling around outside.

I dropped the suitcase and went to investigate.

Kane, Mom, Gwen, Lailah, Dan…and Meri. I froze. "Why is she here?"

Bea came to stand next to me. Gently, she rested her hand on my shoulder. "It's time to test your soul."

I didn't want to. I wanted to go home to Kane's house and forget anything ever happened. "But I'm not one-hundred percent."

"That is why today is perfect. You'll know right away." She tugged my arm. "Come outside. If anything goes wonky, I'll stop it. I've got a spell or two already set."

Reluctantly, I let her drag me out the door. Meri stood at the far end of the deck, separating herself from the rest of the group.

Each one of them took turns giving me a hug—except Meri. She stayed where she was. But that wasn't what unsettled me. Every one of them had touched me, and I hadn't sensed any emotion.

Something wasn't right. I'd never gone a day in my life without being privy to someone's emotions.

Inside Bea's house, I'd come to the conclusion that she'd put a ward on my room to silence my visitor's emotions. But here I was, outside, in a circle of the people most open to me, and I couldn't feel anything. Not from Kane, Kat, or even Gwen. Frowning, I tried to send out my awareness and found I couldn't grasp on to anything. I concentrated harder, scrunching my face up in the process.

Kane put his finger on my brow, smoothing it out. "What's wrong?"

"I can't feel anything," I whispered. "I mean, no emotions. My empath ability is broken." A sense of loss seized me. Just like when I'd given up my coven leadership to Lucien. Except this was a thousand times worse. I'd always had the ability to feel those around me. My sixth sense had literally vanished.

He draped an arm around me. "You're probably just still healing. Don't worry, I'm sure it'll come back."

"I don't think so," Meri said from behind us, and I jumped higher than a cat in a frying pan.

"Geez, Meri. Give us a warning next time," I said.

"You didn't know she was there?" Kane asked, confusion written all over his face.

"No. I told you. I can't feel anyone."

Kane must have finally gotten used to that little quirk. The ability to sense emotions means I'm usually hyper-aware of the people around me.

"I can," Meri said.

I spun to look her in the eye. "You're an empath."

"I am now...or so it seems." Her tone implied she wasn't happy about the new development.

"Holy cripes!" Kat said, grabbing Dan's arm. "Did you know that?"

He nodded. "Yeah, we think she got it from Jade."

Holy cripes was right. Somehow my ability had transferred to Meri during the soul exchange. Jesus, could I still use magic? Panic seized my brain, and I frantically searched for my magical spark. The power jolted in my chest, sending a ripple of current through my limbs. I let out a long relieved sigh. At least that wasn't broken.

"Oh my God," Kat said in a hushed tone, coming to the same conclusion I had. "Do you think it's permanent?"

Meri shrugged. "I hope not. Being exposed to everyone's emotional state isn't my idea of a great time."

I couldn't disagree with her. The gift was a burden, and my week had been blissfully quiet. Still, I didn't feel like myself without my unique ability. What else had she gotten from me? I could still do magic, but could she? "Does this mean you're a witch now that you have part of my soul?"

Meri shook her head. "No. When you almost destroyed me and sent me back to hell, you actually only destroyed the demon part of me. I don't know what I was then. But once I ended up with part of your soul, I morphed back into an angel. The council reinstated me just this morning."

I stared at her, trying to comprehend what she just said. I'd destroyed the demon part of her. Bea had told me killing demons was impossible. But is that what I'd done? No. Impossible. By some stroke of luck, Meri had lived. Though who knows what would have happened to her if she hadn't gotten a piece of my soul? I shook my head trying to clear my thoughts. I didn't want to think about it just then.

"Let's go," Bea said and motioned for Meri and me to follow her.

I hesitated as it became clear she was headed for her yard. Exactly where I'd taken down Meri, destroying her demon side. Meri held back, as if she might bolt.

"Follow me, ladies. Everything is quite safe, I assure you," Bea ordered.

Both of us took our places beside her.

"Now what?" I asked.

"We wait," she said.

"For what?" I kicked an ant off my shoe, wondering what happened to Bea's bug-be-gone spell. Ants in Louisiana bite.

"To see how your souls react." Bea held a hand out to each of us.

We stood together for what seemed like forever, though it was probably more like five minutes. Eventually, she dropped our hands and declared, "You have nothing to worry about. Your souls are content where they are."

She took off before I could ask what she meant.

"She means neither part is longing for the other. They're adapting," Meri said.

I stared at her, wondering what it meant that she now owned part of my soul. I didn't feel different, just battered. Would weird complications arise later? Like unfortunate psychic connections? "Did you just read my mind?"

"No. Your confusion." She shrugged. "Sorry, I can't help it."

The situation was so absurd, I almost laughed. All those years I'd hated my ability. Hated that I was different. And now I was certain I'd miss it. I'd been an empath since...well, forever. "Don't worry," I assured her. "If anyone understands, it's me."

We talked for a few more minutes and then suddenly Meri wrapped her arms around me and squeezed for dear life.

Half-laughing, half-choking, I finally got out, "What's that for?"

"Giving me my life and at the same time holding on to yours." She released me and took a step back. "If they'd given me your soul and you died, I wouldn't have been able to live with myself. It wasn't right what they did."

I nodded in agreement. "You're right, it wasn't. For what it's worth, I'm glad you're getting a second shot."

She shook her head. "After the things I did, I don't deserve it."

"Hey! What happened to you wasn't your fault." I took a step closer. "Do you hear me? Not. Your. Fault. "

She met my gaze with tears in her eyes.

I lowered my voice. "Just take this second chance and use it wisely. Okay?"

One tear rolled down her cheek. "I'll do my best."

This time I caught her in a hug. It was weird and awkward, but also necessary. When we broke apart, she took a few steps back, nodded an unspoken promise, and took off across the grounds.

I wondered if I'd see her again. With my luck? Yeah. Probably sooner rather than later.

After two days of lying around Kane's house, most of the time spent naked, Kane kept going on about taking a drive. "I have something I want you to see."

"Okay, okay. I just thought we weren't going to get dressed today."

He kissed my bare shoulder. "We'll only be out for a couple of hours. Then we can come back here and discard as many garments as you like."

He wouldn't tell me where we were going, not even once we were in the car. In fact, he'd made the suggestion he should blindfold me. I put the kibosh on that right quick. No way was I getting car sick for whatever harebrained scheme he had going on.

Besides, once we crossed the Mississippi river and headed down Highway 90, I had no idea where we were anyway. I'd only been south of New Orleans once and that had been to pick up the airboats.

After about twenty miles, he exited the freeway and turned onto a state highway. Five minutes later we entered the quaintest little town I'd ever seen. Wood-sided cottages lined the residential streets. Main Street looked like something out of a movie set, and people waved from the sidewalks as we drove by.

"Kane? Do these people know you?"

He smiled mysteriously. "You'll see."

No amount of badgering pried any information out of him, so I sat back and enjoyed the southern charm. Soon enough, we came up on a historical plantation home. A giant oak tree claimed the front lawn, complete with a mass of Spanish moss.

"It looks just like a painting," I said as Kane turned into the driveway.

"You like it?"

"Like it? I love it. It's gorgeous. Are we taking a tour?"

He didn't answer as he pulled the car to a stop. A few seconds later, he hopped out of the driver's seat and opened my door.

"What are you up to?" I asked, narrowing my eyes at him.

His smile turned to a grin.

The door swung open as we climbed the front steps to the massive wraparound deck, and a well put-together southern woman stepped out, holding a clipboard. Her blue silk blouse and black A-line skirt fit flawlessly on her trim body. "Welcome to Summer House. You couldn't have picked a better day for a visit."

I gave her a smile. "I'm looking forward to it."

"This way." She ushered us into the turn of the century home, its foyer bigger than my entire apartment. We moved into the grand great room, where the rich oak stairs curved gracefully to the second floor. I sighed, imagining Scarlett O'Hara running down the steps into Rhett's arms.

"Through here," the guide said, not bothering to give us a history on the place. The house was gorgeous, but the tour sucked.

"Lord help her if there's a comment card to fill out at the end of this thing," I mumbled to Kane.

He suppressed a laugh. We entered what could only be called a parlor, and I gasped. My mom and Gwen and all my friends, Kat, Pyper, Ian, Lucien, Charlie, Lailah, and Bea, sat around a large mahogany table.

"Surprise!" they yelled in unison.

"What's this?" I asked, stunned.

Kane put his arm around me. "It's sort of an engagement brunch."

Warmth spread in my heart and my lips quirked. "A what?"

He shrugged. "You needed to get out and everyone wanted to see you, so instead of a party, we arranged a brunch."

"Complete with wedding planning strategies." Pyper waved a notebook. "Go on, tell her the rest."

Kane grinned sheepishly at me and led me back into the great hall. "What do you think?"

I glanced around. "Of what? The house?"

"Of getting married here."

It was the last thing I'd expected him to say.

"We don't have to have it here," he went on. "It's just this is where my grandparents had their ceremony, and I always thought it must have been something magical to see. I want that for us, but only if you do."

The love shining through his eyes when he said those words was more than enough to make me fall in love all over again. I reached up and kissed him lightly on the lips. "I'd love to."

He pulled me close, kissing me slowly.

We broke apart, and I snuggled into his chest. "I guess that means we need to pick a date. I bet they're booked for months," I said wistfully.

He cleared his throat.

I leaned back and looked up at him. "Don't tell me you already reserved one."

"Not exactly. The house isn't usually available for weddings. Fortunately, I happen to know the owner."

"And this owner would be…?"

He grinned.

"Kane?"

He gathered me close again and whispered in my ear. "You. The house is your wedding present."

"What?" I stepped back, clutching the railing of the stairwell to steady myself. "You bought this place for me?"

His eyes crinkled at the corners with mirth. "No, I already owned it. Mamaw left it to me. You said you always wanted to live in a farmhouse. I thought this might be close enough."

My eyes nearly popped out of my head. "You…I mean… How come you didn't tell me you owned another house?" I waved my hand around. "Look at this place. It's…it's unreal."

A guilty smile turned his lips up. "I did say I had other property."

"Yeah! I thought you meant you had other commercial buildings. Not a freakin' historical treasure."

"You like it then? You'll accept it as a wedding gift?"

I stared at him, wondering if he'd lost his mind. "You can't give this place to me. It's your family house."

"*You're* my family, Jade." He gently pulled me back into his embrace. "The month you were gone? I'm never going through that again. You're stuck with me. Marry me. Live with me here or in the city or in Idaho. I don't care. Everything I have is yours as long as you promise to be my wife."

I stared into those wonderful chocolate-brown eyes and melted all over again. I cleared my throat. "Is the tour guide always here?"

"You mean, Jillian? The house manager?" Kane furrowed his brow in confusion. Clearly he hadn't been expecting the random question.

"Yeah, her."

"No, she only comes when there's an event to coordinate. Why?"

I grinned. "I'm wondering how fast we can ditch everyone and christen the master bedroom. I'd like to test run my role as Mrs. Rouquette."

Kane let out a whoop, picked me up, and spun me around.

I laughed, and he lowered me to my feet, crushing his lips to mine.

When we finally came up for air, Pyper stood off to the side, tapping her foot. "Cool it, horn dogs. We spent a lot of time planning this shindig. Get your sorry asses back to the party so we can celebrate."

I saluted her. "Yes, ma'am."

She spun on her heel and we followed. Right before we joined the others, Kane whispered in my ear. "One hour, tops."

Giggling, I tugged him into the parlor, where the people closest to us waited. The family I never thought I'd have. The family I cherished. And with my second chance on life, I wasn't ever letting go.

About the Author

Deanna is a native Californian, transplanted to the slower paced lifestyle of southeastern Louisiana. When she isn't writing, she is often goofing off with her husband in New Orleans, playing with her two shih tzu dogs, making glass beads, or out hocking her wares at various bead shows across the country. Want the next book in the series? Visit www.DeannaChase. com to sign up for the New Releases email list.